D1233536

Heartland Courtship

Center Point
Large Print

Also by Lyn Cote and available from
Center Point Large Print:

Their Frontier Family

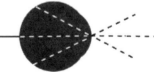

Heartland Courtship

Lyn Cote

CENTER POINT LARGE PRINT
THORNDIKE, MAINE

This Center Point Large Print edition is published
in the year 2014 by arrangement with
Harlequin Books S. A.

The text of this Large Print edition is unabridged.
In other aspects, this book may vary from the original edition.
Printed in the United States of America on permanent paper.
Set in 16-point Times New Roman type.

ISBN: 978-1-62899-221-2

Library of Congress Cataloging-in-Publication Data

Cote, Lyn.
Heartland courtship / Lyn Cote. — Center Point Large Print edition.
pages ; cm.
Summary: "When Quaker Rachel Woolsey nurses a former Civil war
soldier back to health, he agrees to help her achieve her dream of
having her own bakery and a homestead in Pepin, Wisconsin"—
Provided by publisher.
ISBN 978-1-62899-221-2 (library binding : alk. paper)
1. Bakers—Fiction. 2. Quakers—Fiction. 3. Wisconsin—Fiction.
4. Large type books. I. Title.
PS3553.O76378H43 2014
813'.54—dc23

2014020726

For my thoughts are not your thoughts,
neither are your ways my ways, saith the Lord.
For as the heavens are higher than the earth, so
are my ways higher than your ways,
and my thoughts than your thoughts.
—*Isaiah 55:8–9*

Are not two sparrows sold for a farthing?
And one of them shall not fall on the
ground without your Father. But the very
hairs of your head are all numbered.
Fear ye not therefore, ye are of more
value than many sparrows.
—*Matthew 10:29–31*

To my PA and dear friend,
Sara Scholten

Chapter One
꩜

Pepin, Wisconsin
June 2, 1871

In the dazzling sunshine, Rachel Woolsey stood on the deck of the riverboat, gazing at her new home, its wharf and huddle of rustic buildings. After all the lonely miles, she'd accomplished her journey. Relief flooded her when she recognized her cousin Noah standing near the dock, his wife and children at his side.

But she stiffened herself against this warm, weakening rush. She didn't want to dissolve in tears at the sight of family. She would make a life for herself here, fulfill her ambition of independence, start her own business, own a home—no matter what anyone said.

Her empty stomach churning, she smoothed her skirt, calming herself outwardly, and prayed silently for the strength to accomplish all she hoped. *With God's help, I will. Otherwise why did I leave my father's house in Pennsylvania?*

Finally, at the rear, the paddle wheel stilled, dripping and running with water. Porters carried her luggage onto shore where she tipped them and turned to her cousin. When she told him all her unusual—for a woman—plans, would he be a help or hindrance?

Holding his daughter, Noah enveloped her in a one-armed embrace. "Cousin Rachel!"

The intensity in his joyful welcome wrapped itself around her like a warm blanket and went straight to her lonesome heart. "Cousin!" She could say no more without tears.

Then he released her and his pretty blonde wife handed their little son to him and hugged her close. "We're so happy you have come. It's good to have family near."

Rachel sensed a breath of hesitation in Sunny's welcome. And Rachel guessed it must be because she knew of Sunny's unhappy past. How could she let Sunny know she would never, never reveal what she knew? She wouldn't tell anyone here that before marrying Noah, Sunny had borne a child out of wedlock.

"I'm so happy, Cousin Sunny," she said with heartfelt sincerity. "I'm so happy thee and Noah look . . . good together."

And they did. The two children looked happy and well fed. Noah looked healed, content and Sunny touched his arm with obvious affection. Then tears did come.

Maybe this place would be good for her, too. She realized that she did feel welcome, more than in her stepmother's home where she'd been an unpaid servant instead of a beloved daughter. She tried to shake off the bittering thought.

At sounds behind Rachel, Noah looked up and frowned. Speaking past her, he asked sharply, "What are you men doing?"

"The captain say bring this man on shore to the doctor," the black porter said.

Rachel swung around and saw that two porters were carrying an unconscious man, one holding his shoulders and one his ankles. A third porter followed with what looked like a bulging soldier's knapsack.

"We don't have a doctor here," Sunny said, sounding worried.

"Well, then we suppose to leave him anyway," the porter said, appearing abashed. "We got no one to nurse or doctor him and his fare run out two stops south."

Rachel's sense of right balked. "So thee's just going to abandon him?"

The porters looked ashamed, helpless. "That's what the captain order us to do."

Rachel struggled with herself. She couldn't take out her umbrage on these innocent men. She would tell the captain what she thought—

The boat whistle squealed. The porters gently laid down the shabby man and his travel-worn knapsack and then hustled onto the boat, which was already being cast free.

Within moments the boat was far from shore,

heading north, the paddle wheel turning again. Rachel fumed at the departing craft as she dropped to her knees beside the man.

Thin, with a new beard and shaggy chestnut hair, he appeared around Noah's age, in his thirties, and would have been handsome if not so haggard looking. Drawn to help him, Rachel touched his perspiring forehead. Anxiety prodded her. "He's burning up, Noah."

Her cousin knelt on the man's other side. "We can't leave him."

"Of course we can't," Sunny agreed, holding her little girl back from going to her father.

Rachel rose with new purpose. "I'll help thee carry him, Noah." She bent and lifted the man's ankles and Noah quickly grasped his shoulders. They carried him to the wagon and managed to arrange him on a blanket Sunny kept under the wagon seat. Rachel should have had a harder time carrying a man's weight, but he must have lost pounds already, not a good sign.

Some of the shopkeepers and customers had come out to watch and a few helped wedge Rachel's luggage on the other side of the wagon bed along with the man's knapsack. They kept a safe distance from the feverish, unconscious man, evidently fearing contagion.

A man whom Sunny addressed as Mr. Ashford said, "He doesn't look good. Be sure you don't catch this from him."

Rachel understood this sentiment, but didn't let it sway her. Her father hadn't raised a coward.

Noah voiced what she was thinking, "We'll do what we can for him. It's shameful to just drop a man off to die."

"Irresponsible," Ashford agreed, though he backed away. "But not every river man is to be trusted."

Rachel couldn't decide if the man was speaking of the captain who'd abandoned the man or warning them that this man might do them harm—if he lived. Indignation stirred within her.

Noah helped Rachel up onto the wagon bench to sit beside Sunny. Rachel accepted Sunny's sweet little girl to sit on her lap. Noah turned the wagon and headed them home.

Rachel's attention was torn between the beautiful thick forest they drove into and the man moaning softly behind her. As they rolled into and over each rut and bump, she hurt for him. After traveling alone for weeks, she was moved by the man's plight. If she had become sick, would this have happened to her? "What does thee think he might be ill with?" she asked Sunny.

"I don't know. I have some skill in nursing the sick, but he might be . . ." Sunny's voice faltered.

Beyond our help, Rachel finished silently. A pall hung over them and the miles to Noah's homestead crawled by. Rachel mentally went over the medicines she'd brought with her and where they were packed. She questioned Sunny and found that her stock of medicines was meager, too.

Rachel closed her eyes, praying for this stranger, for all traveling strangers. The man's dire situation overlaid her joy at arriving here. Pepin was her new beginning. Would it be this man's ending?

Brennan Merriday groaned and the sound wakened him. He heard footsteps. Someone knelt beside him. A cool hand touched his brow. "I have broth and medicine. Open thy mouth, please." A woman's voice.

His every joint ached, excruciating. His body burned with fever. He couldn't speak, didn't have the strength to shake his head no. A spoon touched his lips. The only act he could manage was letting his mouth fall open. Warm, salty broth moistened his dry throat. Then something bitter. And then more broth. He let it flow into his mouth and swallowed.

He moaned, trying to lift his eyelids. Couldn't. Swallowed. He began to drift again. A face flickered in his mind—Lorena's oval face, beautiful as ever with black ringlets around it, a painful memory that lanced his heart. He groaned again.

The same firm voice summoned him back. "A few more mouthfuls, that's all I ask."

The gentle words fell soft on his ears. He made the effort to swallow again. Again. And then he felt himself slipping away.

Half asleep, Rachel sat in the rocking chair, the fire very low on the hearth, keeping a small pot of chicken broth warm. Every time the stranger surfaced, she spooned as much into him as she could, along with willow bark tea for his fever. She was trying to keep him alive till his fever broke.

Still he looked emaciated and beneath his eyes dark patches showed signs of his decline. Would she succeed? Or would they bury him without a name? The thought lowered her spirits.

She had cared for him around the clock for nearly a week. Weariness had seeped in as deep as her bones, but her overall worry, that they might bury this man never knowing his name, pressed in on her more. Noah had gone through the man's knapsack but had found nothing marked with a name.

Even sick, the stranger beckoned. Something about him drew her—more than merely the handsome face obscured by a wild, newly grown beard and mustache and the ravages of the fever. He looked lost somehow. Would he remain a mystery? Who was he? Why had he boarded the same riverboat as she? Was some woman pacing, worrying about him?

She'd thought she would quickly put her plans for her business into motion. But once again the needs of others took precedence. *Just a little longer. I don't begrudge helping this man, Father.* Her chin lowered and she slipped into that fuzzy world of half sleep.

A loud groan woke her fully. Pushing away the dregs of a dream about home, she sat up straighter and looked down. In the light from the hearth, she saw that the stranger was awake. And this time he opened his eyes. She quickly moved into her routine. She knelt by his pallet and felt his forehead. She pressed her hand there again. Was she imagining that he seemed cooler?

With the top of her wrist, she touched her own forehead and then his. She stared down into his dull eyes. "The fever has finally broken." Cold relief coursed through her.

The man tried to talk, his dry lips stuck together.

She held up a hand. "I'll get the broth." Soon she spooned more into his mouth. This time he didn't fall asleep while she was feeding him. His dark eyes followed her and for the first time she knew he was seeing her. This made her uncomfortable, being so close to a man, a stranger, performing an intimate task for him. Finally, the bowl was empty. "More?"

His head shook yes fractionally.

She quickly fetched more and fed him a second bowl, very aware of her disheveled appearance—

though in his state he wouldn't have noticed even crossed eyes. And their being very much alone, even though Noah and Sunny slept in the next room, affected her oddly, too.

When done drinking, he closed his eyes and drew in a long breath. "How long have I been delirious?" A Southern accent slurred the words.

"Nearly a week."

"Where am I?" His voice sounded rusty, forced. His *I* sounded like *Ah*.

"In the home of my cousin Noah Whitmore in Pepin, Wisconsin."

His face screwed up as if the news were unwelcome. Then it relaxed as if he'd given up some struggle.

He might still die. She must know who he was. She couldn't explain the urgency, but she couldn't deny it. "What is thy name?"

His eyelids fluttered open. He had the thickest dark lashes she'd ever seen on a man. She held back a finger that errantly wanted to stroke their lush upward curve. "I'm Brennan Merriday."

She smiled down at him, relieved.

"What's your name, miss?"

"I am Rachel Woolsey," she said.

"Rachel," he murmured, rolling her name around his tongue. "You're a good woman, Miss Rachel."

Words of praise, so rare, warmed her with satisfaction.

She thought again of a woman, looking for him, a hitch in her breath. "Does thee have family we can contact?"

"No."

The way he said the word saddened her. She'd been without family since her mother died and her father had remarried.

She touched his forehead again, more to connect with him than out of necessity. Was her compassion carrying her off to more than it should?

"Miss Rachel," he repeated. Then he closed his eyes.

She didn't think he had fallen back to sleep. He'd closed his eyes to shut her out. Was it her question that prompted this or was he too weak to talk further? Though his fever had broken, he would need careful nursing before he recovered fully. She sighed long, not letting herself dwell on her own plans, already much delayed.

A man's life was worth more than her business. And this man hadn't chosen to be sick. She pulled the blanket up around his neck and smoothed it. Why had this desire to touch him come?

Finally she pushed herself up onto her feet before she gave in to temptation and did something like touch those thick lashes and embarrassed herself.

She settled back into the rocking chair with her feet on a three-legged stool. She pulled the shawl up onto her shoulders like a blanket and almost fell asleep. One thought lingered—the man did not seem very happy to wake from a fever. That could be due to his weakness. But from his few words, she didn't think so. The lonely recognized the lonely.

Brennan lay on the pallet, still aching, feeling as flat as a blank sheet of foolscap. For the first time, he was aware of what was going on around him. The family who lived in this roomy log cabin had just risen and was getting ready to start its day. He hadn't been this close to such a family for a long time—by choice. Too painful for him.

A tall husband sat at the table, bouncing a little girl on one knee and a baby on the other, saying nursery rhymes and teasing them. The children giggled; the sound made him feel forlorn. A pretty wife in a fresh white apron was tending the fire and making breakfast. Bacon sizzled in a pan, whetting Brennan's once-dormant appetite. How long before he could get away from this homey place that reminded him too much of what he'd lost a decade ago? When he reached Canada, maybe then he could forget. When would he be able to travel again?

The woman who'd nursed him . . . what was her name? His wooly mind groped around, seeking it. Miss Rachel, that was it. She still slept in a rocking chair near him. He could see only the side of her face since her head had fallen against the high back of the chair. Light golden freckles dotted her nose. Straight, light brown hair had slipped from a bun, unfurling around her cheek and nape. From what he could see, she was not blatantly pretty but not homely either. There was something about her, an innocence that frightened him for her.

The smell of bacon insisted on his full attention. He opened his eyes wider and turned his head. His stomach rumbled loudly.

As they heard it, both the husband and wife turned to him. Miss Rachel's eyes popped open. "Thee is awake?"

He nodded, his mouth too dry to speak. *Thee? Quakers to boot?*

"I'll get you a cup of coffee," the wife said.

Miss Rachel stretched gracefully and fully like a cat awakening from a nap and rose from the rocking chair, throwing off a shawl, revealing a trim figure in a plain dark dress. She knelt beside him and tested his forehead. "No fever." She beamed.

He gazed up into the largest gray eyes he'd ever seen. They were serene, making him feel his disreputable appearance. Yet her gaze wouldn't release him. He resisted. *I'm just weak, that's all.*

The husband walked over and looked down. "Thank God. You had us worried."

At the mention of God, Brennan felt the familiar tightening. God's notice was not something he wanted. The wife handed Miss Rachel a steaming mug of what smelled like fresh-brewed coffee. She lifted his head and shoulders. Lilac scent floated in the air.

"I can sit up," he protested, forcing out the words in a burst through cracked lips. Yet when he tried, he found that he could not sit up, his bones as soft as boiled noodles.

"Thy strength will return," Miss Rachel said, nudging his lips with the mug rim.

He opened his mouth to insist that he'd be up before the day was out. But instead he let the strong, hot, creamy coffee flow in. His thirst sprang to life and he drank till the mug was empty. Then he inhaled, exhausted by the act and hating that. Everyone stared down at him, pity in their eyes.

The old bitterness reared. *Enjoyin' the show?* he nearly snarled. His heart beat fast at the inappropriate fury that coursed through him. These innocent people didn't deserve the sharp edge of his rough tongue.

"You'll feel better," the wife said, "when you've been able to eat more and get your strength back."

"How did I end up here?" he asked, the thought suddenly occurring to him. Hadn't he been on a riverboat?

"The captain put you off the same boat I arrived on," Miss Rachel replied, sounding indignant.

Brennan couldn't summon up any outrage. What

had the captain owed him? But now he owed these good people, the kind who usually avoided him. The debt rankled.

"You're from the South?" the husband asked.

There it came again. Most Northerners commented about his Southern drawl. Brennan caught his tongue just before his usual biting answer came out. "Yes." He clenched his teeth.

The husband nodded. "We're not still fighting the war here. I'm Noah Whitmore. This is my wife, Sunny, and our children, Dawn and Adam. And Rachel is my first cousin."

Brennan tried to fix the names to the faces and drew in air. "My brain is mush," he admitted, giving up the struggle.

Noah chuckled. "We'll get you back on your feet. Never fear."

The immense, unasked-for debt that he owed this couple and this Miss Rachel rolled over Brennan. Words seemed paltry, but they must be spoken. "You have my thanks."

"We were glad to help," the wife, Sunny, said. "We all need help sometime."

Her last phrase should have eased him but his reaction was the opposite. Her last phrase raised his all-too-easy-to-rile hackles, increasing his discomfort. How could he ever pay what he owed these people? And he'd be forced to linger here to do that. Canada was still a long ways away. This stung like bitter gall.

●●●

Three days had inched past since Brennan had surfaced from the fever that had almost killed him. Noah had bathed him. And humming to herself, Miss Rachel had washed, pressed and ironed his clothing. The way she hummed when she worked, as if she was enjoying herself, made him 'specially fractious. Each day he lay at ease under their roof added another notch to his debt.

From his pallet now, he saw the sun barely lighting the window, and today he'd planned to get up and walk or know the reason why. He made himself roll onto his knees and then, bracing his hands against the wall, he pushed up onto his feet.

For a moment the world whirled around. He bent his head and waited out the vertigo. Then he sat in the chair and pulled on his battered boots. His heart pounded and that scared him. Had this fever affected his heart? Visions of old men sitting on steps in the shade shook him, moved him.

He straightened up and waited out a momentary wooziness. He shuffled toward the door and opened it. The family's dog lay just outside. Brennan held a finger up to his mouth and the dog didn't bark, gave just a little yip of greeting. Brennan stepped outside and began shuffling slowly down the track toward the trail that he knew must lead to town. The dog walked beside him companionably.

Brennan tried not to think, just to put one foot in

front of the other. A notion of walking to the road played through his mind. But each step announced clearly that this would not be possible.

About twenty feet down the track, his legs began to wobble. He turned, suddenly wishing he'd never tried this stunt.

"Brennan Merriday!" The petite spinster was running toward him, a long housecoat nearly tangling around her ankles.

He tried to stand straight, but his spine began to soften.

She reached him just as he began to crumple and caught him, her arm over his chest, her hand under his arm. "Oof!"

Slowly she also crumpled. They fell together onto the barely bedewed grass, he facedown, she faceup. She was breathing hard from running.

"Brennan Merriday," the little Quaker scolded, "what was thee thinking?"

"Why do you always use both my names?" he snapped, breathing hard too and saying the first thing that came to mind that didn't smack of rudeness.

"That is the Quaker way, our plain speech. Titles such as mister and sir are used to give distinction, and all are equal before God."

She lay beside him, her arm lodged under his chest, much too close to suit him.

"God and Quakers may think that but hardly anybody else does," he panted. He rolled away to stand but halted when he'd gained his knees. He had to get his breath before trying to stand to his feet, get away from this soft, sweet-smelling woman.

The Quaker sprang up with—he grumbled silently—a disgusting show of energy. "I'll help thee."

"I prefer to get up by my lonesome, thank you," he retorted, his temper at his own weakness leaking out. He glanced at her from the corner of his eye.

Her hair had come loose from a single braid and flared around her shoulders. Her skin glowed like a ripe peach in the dawn light. He took a deep breath and tried to turn his thoughts from her womanliness.

"Why did thee do this without discussing it first, Brennan Merriday?"

"I reckon," he drawled, "I overestimated my strength, Miss Rachel."

"I don't think thee understands just how ill . . ." She pursed her lips. "A little patience is what is needed now. I had planned to help thee take a short walk today. It is exactly what is needed."

"Well, I saved you the trouble and took my own walk." He couldn't stop the ridiculous words.

She gave him a look that mimicked ones his sour aunt Martha had used often when he was little.

"I'm not a child," he muttered.

A moment of silence. Miss Rachel pressed her lips together, staring at him. Then she glanced away. "I know that," she murmured.

Slowly he made it onto one foot and then he rose, woozy but standing.

She waited nearby, both arms outstretched as if to catch him. "Should I call Noah to help?"

"I can do it myself. Just let me take my time."

The family dog stayed nearby, watching as if trying to figure out what they were doing.

"You can go on in," he said, waving one hand.

She studied him. "Very well, but since thee has so much energy, thee can help me today. I am going to try a new recipe and I need the walnuts I bought in Saint Louis shelled and chopped."

"I'll look forward to it, Miss Rachel," he said with a sardonic twist and bow of his head.

She walked away and he had to close his eyes in order not to watch her womanly sway. Even a shapeless housecoat couldn't completely hide her feminine curves. Why hadn't some man in Pennsylvania married her? She wasn't ugly or anything. And why was he, Brennan Merriday, drifter, thinking such thoughts?

He was the last one to speak about getting married. His wife had betrayed him, but perhaps from her point of view he'd betrayed her. Either way, Lorena was dead and he had no business wondering why someone was or wasn't married.

24

• • •

After breakfast, Noah went outside to work on some wood project. Brennan watched him leave, wishing he had the strength to do man's work. The pretty wife and children were off to visit friends and that left him alone with the spinster.

Miss Rachel began setting out bowls, eggs, flour, sugar and such. "I am baking rolled walnut yeast logs today. I recalled that it's one of Noah's favorites and I want to thank him for his kindness to me."

Her remark caught Brennan's attention. So she felt beholden to the Whitmores, too? And then he recalled that she had said she'd arrived on the same riverboat as he had. "What'd you come here for? To find a husband?"

If looks could slap, his face would have been stinging.

"No, I am not looking for a husband. I could have had one back in Pennsylvania. That is, if I didn't mind being a workhorse, raising six stepchildren under the age of twelve." Her tone was uncharacteristically biting.

She reddened. "I didn't resent the children, honestly, but if I'd felt any love for their father . . . or sensed that he might ever . . ." Her jaw tensed. "I like to do business but marriage should be a matter of the heart, not something akin to a business contract. Doesn't thee agree?"

A matter of the heart. His jaw clenched and his

unruly mind brought up Lorena's face. Miss Rachel wanted to be loved, not just needed. And he'd found out that his beloved one could let him down, turn her back and walk away.

Wrenching his mind back to the present, he held up both hands. "I get it. I ain't looking for a wife."

"That suits me." She lifted her chin. "I've come to set up in business here."

He couldn't mask his shock. "You plan to have your own business?"

"I intend to open a bakery and sweet shop. And Pepin is just the kind of town that can support one."

"Are you out of your mind?" he blurted. "A bakery in this little half-horse town?"

"No," she said, dismissing his opinion. "I am not out of my mind. Pepin's a river town. Boats stop daily, dropping off and picking up passengers and goods. I will sell my confections to the river boatmen and passengers. Candies and baked goods. I've rarely met a man without a sweet tooth."

He glanced directly at her for the first time. "You good at makin' candy and such?"

He glimpsed a flash of pleased pride in her eyes. "People have said I have a gift for creating sweet things."

"Well, when am I gonna taste some?" he asked with a sly glance.

He'd made her smile. "Well, if you start shelling these walnuts, that would be today."

She set a cloth bag of nuts, a small hammer and a slender, pointed nutpick in front of him. "Take thy time. I must mix the dough and it must rise once before I'll need to roll it out, then spread the filling of honey, cinnamon and crushed walnuts and roll it back up to rise again."

He usually spent his days sweeping out liveries or saloons or lifting and carrying at docks. It had been a very long time since he'd sat in a kitchen with a woman while she baked. There was something cozy about it. Then memories of shelling pecans for his aunt Martha came back to him. He shook out a few walnuts from the bag and stared at them.

Many minutes passed as Miss Rachel measured and mixed.

"I've been thinking about a proposition for you, Brennan Merriday." She took a deep breath and plunged on, "I also intend to stake a claim for myself here."

The few words shocked Brennan again. He'd never conceived of a woman doing something like this. "A single woman homesteadin'? Is that allowed?"

"It is. I am determined to have my own place."

Unheard of. "You couldn't do it. You wouldn't have the strength to prove up, to do all the work."

Proving up meant fulfilling the government

27

requirements of building and clearing the land within the five year time limit. She went on, "That is where my proposition comes in. I was wondering if I could hire thee to help me out for a few weeks." She wouldn't meet his eyes, concentrating on her mixing and measuring.

He gaped at her. Work for a woman?

"Around here, men only work for others upon need or when their own chores are done," she explained what he could already guess. "And this is the growing season. Men are plowing and planting . . ." Her voice faded away.

Work for a woman, he repeated silently. When he'd been without funds in the past, he'd done chores for women in payment for meals. But *work* for one like a hired hand? The idea sent prickles through him. He swallowed down the mortification.

"So?" she prompted.

"Even if I accepted this employment, I can't build a cabin all by myself, not even with Noah's help," he pointed out.

"Noah says there is an abandoned homestead near town." Her voice had brightened. "There is already a cabin. So that would mean just fixing it up. But I'll also need someone to dig me a garden and so on." She looked him in the eye, her expression beseeching. "Is thee interested in such employment?"

Brennan's mind struggled to take this in. A

28

woman stake a claim? A woman run her own business? Preposterous. And him work for a woman? An outlandish idea. Men didn't do that. He could hear the kind of comments he'd get from other men about working for this spinster.

And Miss Rachel was just the kind of woman—respectable and straightlaced—he generally steered clear of. And he never stayed in one place long and this suggestion would interfere with that—mightily. Canada was calling him.

But then he recalled his debt to her and picking up the little hammer, he whacked the nearest walnut so hard it cannonaded off the table and hit the wall.

Miss Rachel's finely arched eyebrows rose toward her hairline. She walked over and picked up the walnut. "Try it again, Brennan Merriday. If thee doesn't wish to work for a woman, I will understand." She turned her head away.

He could tell from the mifftiness of her tone that he'd insulted her. He hadn't meant to. But Miss Rachel was going against the flow and probably knew what was in store for her, probably knew what people would say to him for working for her.

Why would she do this? He looked down at the returned walnut. He remembered Aunt Martha, his father's unmarried sister, who'd lived with them. He'd just accepted that unmarried women spent their days looking after other women's children and washing other people's clothes. Had that made his aunt so crusty? Had she hidden blighted dreams of her own?

He couldn't actually work for a woman, could he? He looked up. Did he have a choice? He owed this Quakeress his life. "I can't take the job formal-like, Miss Rachel. But I will help you get set up."

"Thank thee, Brennan Merriday. I'd shake thy hand but . . ." She nodded to her hands, already kneading the large bowl of dough. Her face was rosy from the oven and from their talk no doubt. He wondered why this woman kept catching him by surprise, causing him to want to shield her. She was not like any other woman he'd ever met.

He expertly tapped another walnut and it opened in two clean-cut halves. He felt a glimmer of satisfaction and began digging out the nuts, breathing in the scent of yeast and walnut oil.

He'd help this woman get started and then he could leave, his conscience clear. He'd start north to Canada again—Canada, where no one had fought in the war and held no grudge nor memory. Where he might finally forget.

Chapter Two

A week later, Rachel climbed up on the bench of the wagon with Brennan's help. He had insisted that if he was accompanying her, he would do the driving. She'd given in. Men hated being thought weak and this man had been forced to swallow that for over a fortnight now.

Finally she'd be able to get started doing what she'd come to do, create her new life. A fear niggled at her. What if someone had gotten the jump on her and already claimed the property? Well, she'd deal with it if she had to, not before.

Another worry pinched her. The homestead might need a lot of work, more than Noah and Brennan could do. "Did Noah tell thee where to find the abandoned homestead?" she asked, keyed up.

"Yes, Miss Rachel, you know Noah explained where it was. What you're asking me is, do I remember how to drive there."

She grinned at him, ignoring the barely disguised aggravation in his tone. "Thee must be feeling better if thee can joke."

He looked disgruntled at her levity but said nothing, just slapped the reins and started the horses moving. They rode in silence for the first mile. Against her own will, she studied his profile, a strong one.

Freshly shaven and with his face no longer drawn with fever, he was an exceptionally handsome man. She brushed a fly away from her face. She turned her gaze forward. Handsome men never looked at her. Why should she look at this one?

Brennan spoke to the horses as he slowed them over a deep rut. His Southern accent made her wonder once more. The horrible war had ended slavery, yet tensions between the North and South had not eased one bit. And after four years of war, the South was devastated. What had brought this Southerner north?

She watched his jaw work. She wondered what he was getting up the nerve to say to her. She hoped he wasn't about to repeat the usual words of discouragement.

"Are you sure you're ready to set up a place all by yourself?" he asked finally.

Rachel did not sigh as loudly as she felt like doing. Her stepmother's voice played in her mind. *An unmarried woman doesn't live alone. Or run a business on her own. It's unnatural. What will people say?*

"Brennan Merriday," Rachel said, "if thee only knew how many times that has been asked of me. I am quite certain that I can homestead on my own land." Her tone was wry, trying to pass his concern off lightly—even though it chafed her. She had become accustomed to being an oddity —a woman who didn't marry and who wanted to do things no woman should want.

"Why do you say thee and thy and your cousin doesn't?"

This question took her by surprise. "I don't really know except there isn't a Quaker meeting here."

"I take it that Noah's the preacher hereabout, but not a Quaker."

She barely listened to his words, still surveying him. His body still needed feeding, but he had broad shoulders and long limbs. Most of all, the sense of his deep inner pain drew her even though she knew he didn't want that. She turned her wayward eyes forward again. "Yes, he seems to have reconnected with God."

"Don't it bother you that he's not a Quaker no more?"

"We were both raised Quaker but I don't consider other Christians to be less than we are. Each Christian has a right to go his own path to God."

"And what about those who don't want to have nothin' to do with any church?"

She heard the edge in the man's voice and wondered how to reply. She decided frankness should be continued. "When he enlisted in the

Union Army, Noah was put out of meeting."

The man beside her said nothing but she felt that he absorbed this like a blow to himself. She recalled praying for God to keep her cousin safe and reading the lists of the wounded and fallen after every battle, hoping not to see his name listed. The horrible war had made a dreadful impact on all their lives. Still did.

She brushed away another fly as if sweeping away the sadness of the war, sweeping away her desire to hold him close and soothe him as she would a wounded bird.

Brennan remained silent. His hands were large and showed that he had worked hard all his life.

Just as she had. "I know that people will think me odd when I stake a homestead," she said briskly, bypassing his digression. "But I intend to make my own way. I've worked for others and saved money enough to start out on my own."

Any money a woman earned belonged to her husband or father. Still, in the face of her stepmother's disapproval, her father had decided that Rachel should keep what she earned. No doubt he thought she might never marry. His wife would inherit everything and leave Rachel with nothing. This had been her father's one demonstration of concern for her. How was it that when she'd lost her mother, she'd also in effect lost her father?

Except for Brennan murmuring to the team, silence again greeted her comment. Finally he admitted, "I see you got your mind made up."

They rode in silence then. The homestead Noah had told her about lay north of town within a mile and had been abandoned just before deep winter the previous year. Rachel gazed at the thick forest and listened to the birdsong, trying to identify the different calls.

Her mother had taught her bird lore. She heard a bobwhite and then a robin and smiled. A pair of eagles swooped and soared overhead. She realized she already loved this place, the wildness of it, the newness.

Another mile or so and Brennan drove through town and then turned the horses onto a faint track and into an overgrown clearing. A small log cabin and a shed sat in the middle of it. Stumps poked out of tall grass, dried from weeks without rain. Only deer had grazed here earlier this spring. The sight of the almost cozy clearing wound warmly around her heart. Would this be her home?

Brennan halted the team with a word and set the brake.

She started to climb down.

"Miss Rachel," he ordered, "ya'll will wait till I get there to help you down. I may be riffraff but I know enough to do that."

She froze. "Thee is not riffraff."

He made no reply but helped her down without meeting her eyes. Again, she longed to touch him, offer comfort, but could not.

So this man had also been weighed by society and found wanting. She recalled all the times people had baldly pointed out her lack of beauty or wondered why she wasn't married yet—as if either was any of their business. And of course, she couldn't answer back without being as rude as they.

Lifting her skirts a few inches, she waded through the tall, dry grass, which flattened under her feet. Noah had been praying for rain. The cabin's door was shut tight. A good sign. She stepped back and bumped into Brennan, nearly losing her balance. He steadied her. She was shocked at the rampant and unusual sensations that flooded her. She pulled away. "My thanks."

He reached around her and tried to push open the door. It stuck. With his shoulder, he had to force it. Looking down, he said, "Mud washed up against the door and under it and grass grew on it."

She stepped into the dim interior and let her eyes adjust. Brennan entered and waited behind her. Finally she could see a hearth on the back wall, cobwebs high up in the corners and a broken chair lying on its side. Otherwise only dust covered the floor. "It just needs cleaning."

"Look up."

She obeyed. "What am I looking for?"

"I see stains from a few roof leaks."

She turned to him. "Is that hard to make right?"

"No, I just need to bring a ladder to get up there and see where the shingles have blown loose or cracked."

She considered this. "Thee can do that?"

"Sure." He looked disgruntled at her question.

"Let's look at the shed then."

They did. Just an empty building but in good order. *Excellent.* Mentally she began listing the new structures she'd need. She noted how Brennan looked around as if tallying something, too. Finally she asked, "What's thy opinion? Will this be a good homestead for me to claim?"

"Well, it's fortunate to already have a cabin and shed on it."

She pointed to a mound between the cabin and the shed. "Could that be a well covered over?"

"Might be." He strode over to it and stooped down. "You're right. They were good enough to cover the well and mud got washed onto the boards and then grass sprouted." He rose. "Do you know why the family left the claim?"

"Sunny said the wife died."

The bleak reply silenced them for a moment.

"Life is so fragile," she murmured. Then she took herself in hand. "But we are alive and I need a home."

"I do, too."

She took this to mean that he'd decided to accept her position, but couldn't bring himself to say so. And he would know he couldn't live anywhere on the property of a single woman.

Tactfully she said, "I'm glad making this livable will not take long. It's important I get my business up soon because the prime season for making a reputation for my sweets up and down the river is summer, when the boat traffic will be at its peak. This far north the Mississippi freezes, according to Noah."

"You make good sense," he allowed grudgingly.

She moved to look directly into his eyes. After a mental calculation she said, "I could afford to pay you two dollars a week. That would include meals."

"I won't take anythin' for my work, but I'll need to pay for a room." He left it open that he'd need her to cover that.

"Where will you live?" she asked finally.

"I thought I'd ask in town who has room for me."

She offered him her hand. "It's a deal then. Let's go to town and stake this claim."

"Yes, Miss Rachel." His words were polite but she caught just the slight edge of irony under them. What had made this man so mocking of himself and others? She would just take him as he was. Until he moved on.

And she ignored the sensitive currents that raced up her arm when he gripped her hand and shook it as if she were another man. Were foolish school-girl feelings going to pop up now when she least needed them? And when to show them would embarrass both her and this complex man?

Brennan halted the team outside the narrow storefront. In the window, a small white placard read simply Government Office and beneath that a smaller placard—Agent Present. He went around and helped Miss Rachel down. She looked sturdier than she felt as he assisted her. She was such a little bit of a woman—with such big ideas.

He seriously doubted she would be allowed to register for a homestead. The idea was crazy. Still, he asked, "Do you want me to come in with you?"

She looked up at him with a determined expression, her large gray eyes flashing and direct. "No, I can handle this myself."

He listened for any sign she might want him to accompany her. But he caught only a shade of tartness in her tone. He accepted her decision. He didn't like people hovering over him either. "Then I'll be going to find me a room."

"Very well. If I am not here when you need me, look for me at the General Store." Without waiting for his reply, she marched to the door and went inside. He wondered idly why she never wore any lace or pretty geegaws. And she skimmed her hair back so severely. Didn't she want to look pretty?

He stood a moment, staring after her. Northern women were different all right and up to now, Miss Rachel stood out as the most different he'd met. Lorena's biddable face flickered in his mind, stinging as it always did. He walked resolutely away from the starchy Yankee and his own taunting memories.

He paused, scanning the lone dusty street for a likely place to ask for a room. This little dot on the shore of the Mississippi hadn't progressed to having a boardinghouse yet.

Whom could he ask? Then he noticed the saloon at the end of the street, the kind of place where he always found an easy welcome—as long as he had money in his pocket.

No doubt it would irritate Miss Rachel if he went in there. So he strode toward it, reveling in the ability to walk down a street healthy once again. He pushed through swinging doors into the saloon, almost empty in the late morning. A pudgy older man leaned back behind the bar.

"Mornin'," Brennan greeted him.

"What can I do for you?" the man replied genially.

Brennan approached the bar. "I'm new in town, need a room. You know any place that'd be good for me to ask at?"

They exchanged names and shook hands.

"You're from the South?" Sam, the barkeep, commented.

"Yeah." Though bristling, Brennan swallowed a snide reply.

After eyeing him for a few moments, Sam

rubbed his chin. "Most shopkeepers have family above their place or build a cabin behind their business. Got a blacksmith-farrier in town. Single. Think he's got a loft empty. Can't think of anybody else that has room."

"Don't have many businesses in this bump in the road," Brennan drawled, leaning against the bar, suddenly glad to have someone more like him to talk to. The Whitmores were good folk, but he had to watch his errant tongue around them.

Sam smirked. "You got that right."

A look of understanding passed between them. Brennan drew in a deep breath. "Thanks for your advice about the room."

"Glad to help. Drop in some evening and we'll have a tongue wag."

After nodding, Brennan headed outside. Miss Rachel probably hadn't finished in the government office yet. So under the hot sun, he ambled toward the log-constructed blacksmith shop. The clang of metal on metal announced a smithy hard at work. Would the blacksmith be anti-Southerner, too?

He entered the shady interior and fierce heat rushed into his face. A broad-shouldered man in a leather apron pounded an oblong of iron, shaping it into some long-handled tool, sparks flying. Finally, after plunging the tool into a barrel of water, the sweating blacksmith stepped back from his forge. Over the sizzling of the molten iron meeting cold water, he asked, "What can I do for you, stranger?"

Brennan moved forward and offered his hand. "Name's Merriday. Ah'm lookin' to rent a room."

Pulling off leather gloves, the blacksmith gripped his hand briefly. Brennan felt the power of the man in that grip.

"You sound like you're from the South," the man observed.

"I am." Brennan said no more, though smoldering.

"Comstock's my name. Levi Comstock," the tall man said. "How long you staying here?"

"A few months maybe." These few words cost him. He never spent a month in any place anymore. The disorienting flashes of memory and restlessness always hit him after a few weeks. He hoped in Canada he could finally settle down. *But I owe Miss Rachel.* "You got room for me?"

The blacksmith studied Brennan.

Brennan didn't like it and pressed his lips together to keep back a nervy comment that itched to be said.

The man finally nodded toward a ladder. "I built me a lean-to to sleep in for the summer. Get the breeze off the river. Not using my loft now. It'll be hot up there. I've been meaning to cut out two small windows for some air. Maybe you could do that."

"How much do you want a week?"

"Four bits?" Comstock asked.

"That's all?"

The man's blackened face split into a grin. "You ain't seen the loft yet. No bed. Just a dusty floor."

"And two windows when we cut them." Brennan knew he'd just taken a liking to this practical man and dampened down the lift it sparked in him. He'd be here only as long as Miss Rachel needed him. Then he'd move north and get settled before winter. The two men shook hands.

"When you moving in?"

Brennan considered this. "Soon. Maybe tomorrow."

"See you then." The smith turned back to his forge.

Brennan stepped outside and gazed around at the nearly vacant main street and sighed. What would he do in this little berg for a few weeks? And how was Miss Rachel faring with the land agent? He headed toward the office. Maybe Miss Rachel needed some backup by now.

Just inside the door of the government office, Rachel paused to gird herself for battle, quelling her dislike of contention. She knew she faced one of the biggest battles of her life, here and now.

The small, middle-aged man in a nondescript suit behind a small desk rose politely. "Miss?"

She smiled her sweetest smile and went swiftly forward. "Good day, sir. I am Miss Rachel Woolsey." She never used sir. Quakers didn't use titles. But she couldn't afford to be Quaker today. After she told him what she'd come for, she was going to brand herself odd enough as it was. Their hands clasped briefly.

"Please take a seat and tell me what I can do for you, Miss Woolsey."

She sat primly on the chair he had set for her and braced herself. "I'm here to stake a claim."

Shock widened the man's pinched face. "I beg your pardon."

"I am here to stake a claim," she repeated, stubborn determination rearing up inside.

"Your husband is ill?" he asked after a pause.

Hadn't she introduced herself as Miss? "No, I am unmarried."

"Then you can't stake a homestead claim." Each of his words stabbed at her. "It isn't done."

She'd expected this reaction and she had come prepared. "Excuse me, please, but it can be done." She tried to keep triumph from her smile. "And quite legally. My father consulted our state representative to the U.S. Congress before I left Pennsylvania." She pulled out the creased envelope. "Here is the letter."

The man did not reach for the envelope. "I know the law, miss. But a single woman homesteading, while legal, is ridiculous. You will never prove up your claim. Why put yourself through that?" His last sentence oozed condescension.

Her irritation simmered. So many sharp replies frothed on her tongue, but she swallowed them. "I have already hired a workman and the claim I want is the one that the Ryersons left last winter. May I please begin the paperwork?" She gazed at him, giving the impression that she would sit here all day if need be. And she would.

He glared at her.

Seconds, minutes passed.

She cleared her throat and pinned the man with her gaze. "Is there a problem?"

"I think it's shameful that your father would let you leave home and homestead on your own. What will people think of you—a single woman without a male protector? Have you thought of that?"

Rachel shook off this measly objection. "Sir, I cannot think that anyone here would take me for a woman of easy virtue. And—" she didn't let him interject the retort that must be reddening his face "—my cousin Noah Whitmore is here to watch over me."

"You're Noah Whitmore's cousin?"

"Our mothers were sisters."

He stared at her again, chewing the inside of his cheek—no doubt trying to come up with another objection.

She kept her steady gaze on him. The door

behind her opened. Glancing over her shoulder, she glimpsed Brennan enter. She lifted one eyebrow.

"Miss Rachel, aren't you about done here?" he asked, hat in hand, but the willingness to dispute with the agent plain on his face.

"I still need to fill out the claim form," she replied evenly and then turned to face the government official who should be earning his money by doing his job and not wasting her time.

With a glance at Mr. Merriday, the man whipped out a form and jumped to his feet. "I need to walk a bit."

She didn't reply. Outside sea gulls squawked; the sound mimicked her reaction to this officious little man.

After he exited with a huff in each step, she moved to his side of the desk and, using his pen and ink, neatly and precisely filled out the form. All the things she wished she could say to the agent streamed through her mind. She wore skirts—why did that make her incompetent, inferior?

She knew all the various restrictions society placed on women and knew that many quoted scripture as their justification. But she never knew why submitting to a husband or not speaking in the church had anything to do with regard to a woman without one. And the Quakers didn't believe in either anyway.

Soon she finished filling out the form and read it over carefully to make sure she hadn't omitted anything. When satisfied, she rose.

"Miss Rachel, why don't you go on to the store and I'll find that government agent and give him your claim?"

She paused to study Brennan's face. Then she understood him. Oh, she hadn't thought of that. Papers could go astray so easily. Though this goaded her, she said nothing, merely handed him the paper and walked out the door, thanking him for his help. Brennan might not approve of her intentions but he wasn't treating her like a female who couldn't know her own mind. A definite point in his favor. And no doubt why he'd begun popping into her mind at odd moments. She must be wary of that. He would be gone soon. She tried to ignore the shaft of startling loneliness this brought her.

Brennan accepted the paper, accepted that once again he was going against the grain by backing the unpopular horse, his curse it seemed. He let the lady go, determined to get her what she wanted. As little as Brennan approved of Miss Rachel's filing for her homestead, he wasn't going to let some scrawny government weasel gyp this fine lady. Not on his watch.

Outside the office, he scanned the street for the man. When he didn't see him, he headed for

47

the saloon. Maybe the barkeep would know where the agent stayed when in town.

He stepped inside and found the man he was looking for, pouring out the affront he'd just suffered in his office. "I don't know what this country is coming to. Giving black men the vote and now a woman thinks she can stake a claim like a man. Next they'll want the vote, too! A woman homesteading—I ask you!"

"I know it's not the usual," Brennan drawled. "But it's a free country. For women, too." He didn't like meddlesome little squirts like this man who liked to throw around their half ounce of power.

The land agent glared at him. "Who are you?"

Brennan eyed the man with distaste. Suddenly he felt proud to say, "I'm the one who's workin' for the lady."

"Then you're as crazy as she is," the agent declared.

Sam moved back and leaned against the wall behind the bar as if enjoying a show.

"I been called worse than crazy." Leaning against the bar, Brennan began enjoying this rumpus. He didn't cotton to the fact that he had to stay in this little town. So why did this man think he could have everything his way?

The agent turned away from him, venting his spleen by muttering to himself.

"I brought Miss Rachel's paper." Brennan said

the words with a barely concealed challenge in his voice. "I want to make sure it gets into the mail today and marked in your records nice and legal." Brennan had never staked a claim or done anything else with any government except enlist in the army. But he figured the agent should keep a record of the transaction and send one to Washington. That sounded right to him.

The man swung around, glaring at him. "Nobody tells me how to do my job. Least of all some Johnny Reb."

Sam's amused gaze swiveled back and forth from one to the other.

Brennan did not respond to the derogatory Yankee nickname for Confederate soldiers. "I'm not tellin' you how to do your job. Just . . . helpin' you do it. After you." Emphasizing the final two words, Brennan swept one hand, gesturing toward the door. Brennan itched to grab the man's collar and drag him out.

The man glared at him.

So Brennan waited him out—not changing anything in his expression or stance, barely blinking.

The land agent finally caved in, growled something under his breath about stinking Southerners, and stalked past Brennan out the door.

Hiding a grin, Brennan nodded politely to the barkeep and followed the man to his office.

Lounging against the doorjamb, he said nothing as the man sat at his desk, filled out a ledger. Brennan moved to look over his shoulder.

The agent then slapped Miss Rachel's application into a mailing pouch. "There! Are you satisfied?" the man snapped.

"Anything else need doin'?" Brennan asked in a mild tone.

"No!"

"Then after you write me out one of those receipts—" Brennan gestured toward a pad of receipts on the desk "—I'll just help you by taking this mailbag to Ashford's store. I seen the notice in the window that he's the postmaster hereabout."

The agent resembled a volcano about to blow, but he merely chewed viciously the inside of his cheek. Then he dashed off the receipt, ripped it from the pad and shoved the mail pouch at Brennan.

"I'll bid you good day then," Brennan said drolly and strolled outside.

A stream of epithets followed him, including "Confederate cur."

He ignored them and crossed the street, his boots sending up puffs of dust with each step. The drought filled his nose with dust, too. His destination in sight, he moved forward. He'd been inside Ashford's store only once before on a trip to town with Noah. But he nodded politely at Ashford's hesitant greeting and handed him the leather pouch, which read Official U.S. Documents. "I brought this over for the land agent. Do you think the mail will go out today?"

Ashford, middle-aged with thinning hair, consulted a notice on the wall. "Yes, if the *Delta Queen* arrives on schedule." The storekeeper cocked an eyebrow at Brennan. "It's odd that the agent let you bring this over."

"Oh, I just told him I was on my way here. Now you watch over the mail pouches, don't you? You don't let *anybody* mess with the letters, right?" Brennan asked.

"I certainly do not let anybody interfere with the mail. I took an oath." Ashford starched up.

"Excellent. Glad to hear it." Brennan turned to Miss Rachel. "Here is your receipt for the land transaction."

"Thank thee, Mr. Merriday." She accepted the paper and slid it into her pocket, then dazzled Brennan with a smile that cast her as, well, pretty.

At this realization, Brennan stepped backward. Whoa, he had no business thinking that. Why had he thought her plain? Was it the way she hid behind that plain Quaker bonnet?

"I just staked my claim, Mr. Ashford," Miss Rachel explained, "on the Ryersons' abandoned claim."

Ashford goggled at her. "Indeed?" he finally said.

"Yes, Miss Rachel's makin' her own way in the world." Brennan regained his aplomb. "An independent woman." Brennan relished setting another pillar of society on edge.

"And Mr. Merriday will help me as my hired hand," Miss Rachel agreed. "Mr. Ashford, I will be back next week to pick up the flour, sugar and other items I've ordered. And please let it be known that I want to buy a cow and chickens from anyone who has any to spare. I'll pay what's fair."

"Yes, Miss, but I still think you should have ordered much less flour to begin with," the storekeeper said.

"I appreciate thy concern," she replied, but this didn't show in her tone. "Mr. Merriday, I think our town business is done now."

He was back to himself. So he did find the lady pretty—what did that have to do with the likes of him? "Yes, Miss Rachel," Brennan said, grinning with sass as he followed her to the door, opened it for her and let her step outside. He glanced over his shoulder to catch Ashford frowning. And mocked the man with a grin.

Back on the wagon bench beside Miss Rachel, Brennan slapped the reins and piloted the team toward home. A rare feeling of satisfaction suffused him. And he was beginning to like Miss Rachel. That was all. "You called me Mr. Merriday," he teased. "Thrice."

"Yes, I thought if I called thee by thy first

name as Quakers do, the storekeeper might misunderstand our relationship. I think it will be best if I use Mr. Merriday so everyone understands. . . ." Her voice faltered.

"I take your meaning, *Miss* Rachel." He couldn't stop his grin from widening. Working for Miss Rachel would certainly bring zest into his life for a time.

From the corner of his eye, he gazed at her profile. She sat so prim and proper, her back straight and her gloved hands folded in her lap. What would she do if he turned and kissed her? A startling, disturbing thought.

Then she glanced at him out of the corner of her eye. "My thanks, Mr. Merriday, for thy support today."

"Just part of my job, miss," he said, taking control of his unruly mind. He owed this lady a debt, that was all.

And then the two of them rode in outward silence toward the Whitmore claim. But one sentence ran through Brennan's mind—*What have I gotten myself into this time?*

Chapter Three

On the dusty drive home, Rachel felt unsettled again. She tried not to think of those first few days on the journey here when nothing had seemed right and she hadn't been able to eat. And sitting beside this handsome man who'd stood up for her added more confusion.

"How soon could I move into my cabin?" she asked, forcing herself to stop musing.

"Just need a day or two to get it cleaned out and fix the roof."

"I will do the cleaning so thee can concentrate on the fixing." She had succeeded in staking her homestead claim. She should be experiencing relief but she wasn't. Her stomach churned. *What's wrong with me?*

The ride home passed much more quickly than the ride to the homestead and then to town. The hot sun beat down on Rachel's shoulders and bonnet. But she found herself more aware of Mr. Merriday with every mile. She hadn't expected him to abet her in town. Also she'd seen in Mr. Ashford's expression that having the Southerner work for her would be frowned on. *Well, so be it.*

When Noah's cabin came into view, Rachel's

heart started jumping oddly. She stiffened her self-control and tried to remain unmoved as Brennan helped her down from the wagon with his usual courtesy, which was not usual to her.

Noah hailed them from outside his woodshop. With their little boy in her arms, Sunny opened the door and greeted her warmly.

Rachel burst into tears.

Everyone rushed forward as if she'd fallen, which shamed her. She turned away, trying to hide her face.

Sunny came to her and grasped her elbow. "Come. I'll make you some tea."

When Rachel looked up, the two men had disappeared with little Dawn and only she and Sunny went to the bench outside the cabin. Rachel sat while Sunny went inside. The toddler in his dress rolled in the grass, playing with his toes. Tears dripping down her face, Rachel watched him, envying his innocence.

Soon Sunny handed her a cup of tea and sat beside her. "Was the land agent very rude?" Sunny asked conversationally.

"Of course he was." Wiping her eyes with her hankie, Rachel tried to keep bitterness from her tone, but failed. "Why are men so . . . ?" Words failed her.

Sunny made a sound of agreement. "They certainly can be."

Rachel sipped the sweet, tangy tea. "Life would

be easier if I just went along with what's expected of me," she finally admitted.

More tea. "Yes, but would that be easier on you?"

"No!" Rachel's reply flew from her lips.

"Then you will just have to thicken your skin."

Rachel sighed. "I thought I had."

"It's just this starting out part. Everyone here will get to know you, begin to see that you're a good person. You'll become part of the town and then they'll resent anybody who disparages you."

Rachel turned to Sunny. "Really?"

"Yes, that's how it happened with us."

"Really?"

Sunny beamed at her. "Noah's the preacher now."

For some reason, Rachel couldn't swallow a chuckle. Then the two of them were laughing out loud.

In a while, no doubt drawn by the sounds of mirth, the men approached, looking as if the women's behavior mystified them. And that only caused Rachel and Sunny to shake with more laughter.

The next day Brennan climbed the ladder onto the roof of Rachel's cabin, no clouds masking the hot sun. He crawled across the rough surface till he reached the spot where he thought the leak was.

Three wooden shakes or shingles had blown loose.

His lady boss was humming below, sweeping out her cabin. And soon Noah would arrive to start work on the large oven Miss Rachel needed for her business. The question over whether to add a kitchen to the cabin had been debated completely. Finally a summer kitchen connected by a covered walkway to the cabin had been deemed best.

Thinking of Noah, Brennan found himself filled with potent envy. Noah Whitmore had it all—a place of his own, a pretty wife and two great kids.

Reminiscence of a time when he'd thought Noah's kind of life would always be his life goaded him. Lorena's slender arms slipped around his neck and her soft voice—

Then the worst happened—one of his infrequent spells hit him. The past flooded him. Waves of darkness engulfed him. That awful day before the war? Or all the awful days of war after it rolled into one? He was surrounded. Fists pounding him, the stench of stale sweat, curses bombarded him. He tried to keep his eyes open, tried to keep in touch with his surroundings—which way was up and which was down. He lost.

He felt himself sliding, the rough shingles hitting his spine as he slid. He wrenched his eyes open and at the last minute jammed his heels into another space where shingles had been blown away. His hands scrabbled for something to cling to. He stopped and then he lay back, gasping for air.

"Is thee all right?" Miss Rachel called up.

Brennan couldn't answer. The world still tilted and swayed around him. Then he heard Miss Rachel climbing up the ladder.

He had to stop her, couldn't let her see him like this. Brennan wanted to send her away with a flea in her ear, anything to prevent her from asking what the matter was. Upon the rare occasion when he had one of these spells, he just left town.

But I can't leave this town. And Noah saved my life as much as the little spinster. Brennan waited for the inevitable questions.

But Miss Rachel asked none.

Brennan finally could sit up. His slide had taken him within a foot of the ladder and there stood Miss Rachel near his boots. Still she didn't speak. Brennan's heartbeat and breathing slowed to normal. He didn't know what to say. Better to let her think he just slid. "Sorry to give you a scare, Miss Rachel."

She tilted her head like one of the robins nesting in the tree nearby. She reached out her hand to him.

And surprising himself, he took it.

"Please be careful, Brennan Merriday. I wouldn't want to see thee laid low again."

He tried to ignore the softness of the hand in

58

his. Tried to ignore the fact that the sun glinted off the threads of gold in her hair and that her expression drew him like bees to honey. In any other woman, he would have interpreted her comment as selfish, as indicating that she wanted him to keep well and in working condition. But did this woman have a selfish bone in her body?

The moment was broken when they heard Noah's whistling.

Their hands pulled apart. She blushed and he looked away.

"Morning, Rachel. Brennan, I was thinking," Noah called out as he approached them, "it makes more sense for us to work together. I think we'll get more done. Why don't I hand you the shakes we cut? You can be nailing new ones in place and I'll go over the roof, checking every shake to make sure none are loose. I don't think Ryerson did a very good job on his roof. Then you can help me with the oven."

"Sounds good to me," Brennan said, forcing out the words.

Miss Rachel slowly disappeared from view as she climbed back down the ladder. Brennan felt the loss of her and hardened himself. What had they been thinking? Holding hands in broad daylight?

About two weeks later Rachel tried to calm her fluttering nerves. Tonight she'd stay alone in her cabin for the first time. As the shadows darkened, Noah's family, who had helped her move in today with her new table and chairs and bed Noah had made her, was leaving. Sunny had helped her prepare the first meal in her new home. The day had been busy and happy. A nearby farmer had delivered her young cow, chickens and a rooster. Now she would have cream and eggs for her baking. But Brennan's distant behavior had pruned her enjoyment of the occasion.

Noah's wagon had just turned the bend out of sight when Brennan ambled over to help her carry the last of the chairs inside.

"Thee didn't join in much today," she said.

"Didn't feel sociable."

She sensed that he was about to lay out the last chores he would be doing for her and then announce he'd be leaving. His restlessness over the past few days had not gone unnoticed. She didn't like the gloom that realization opened inside her. Yet she'd wanted to be on her own and now she would be.

Three strangers appeared on the track to her cabin. This was an odd occurrence. "Hello, may I help thee?" Rachel called out, though as they came closer she recognized that the three looked disreputable.

"We're looking for the lousy Confederate you got here!" one declared, slurring his words from drink, no doubt.

"Yeah, we don't want any scurvy dogs like that hanging around," another added belligerently.

To her dismay, Brennan picked up a tree limb lying on the ground and moved to confront the men.

"The war is over," Rachel said, trying to stem the confrontation.

Brennan ignored her. "There is a lady present here. From your voices, I'd say you men have been imbibing today. Too liberally."

The men glowered at her. Even in their inebriated state, Brennan saw, they realized that fighting with a proper lady present would be roundly condemned.

Rachel stepped forward, hoping her presence would send the strangers away.

Instead, a fist shot past her.

Brennan dodged it easily. Then he slammed his fist into his attacker's nose. Blood spurted.

Rachel cried out. Brennan pushed her out of the fray. She stumbled and fell to the grass.

The other stranger rushed Brennan. He dealt with him. The third one turned and bolted. The two who had been bested followed suit, cursing as they ran.

Rachel put her hands to her ears, shocked to silence. "Oh!"

Just as they disappeared from view, the first one, his hand pressed over his bleeding nose, shouted, "This isn't over!"

"Yes, it is," Brennan muttered, rubbing his knuckles.

Rachel began to weep, trembling.

Brennan gripped her hands and pulled her up and into his arms. "There, there," he said, holding her against him. "You're safe now. I wouldn't let anyone hurt you."

The temptation proved too great to resist. She let herself lean against him, feeling the strength of him supporting her. She tried to stop her tears. "I'm sorry to be so weak."

"I'm sorry you had to witness such behavior." As he said this, his lips actually touched her ear. "You're not weak."

The last of the weeping swept through her like a wind gust and left her gasping against him. "I've never been near violence before."

"Then you're a lucky woman." He patted her back clumsily.

She wiped her face with her fingertips and looked up into Brennan's face. His expression of concern moved her and she reached up and stroked his cheek.

What am I doing?

Rachel straightened and stepped back. She must break contact before he did. An unwelcome thought lowered her mood more. Tonight would be her first night sleeping alone in her own house. She'd never spent a night alone in her life. And these violent men had come tonight.

"Maybe I should sleep in the shed tonight," Brennan said, his gaze going to the trail to town.

The idea had appeal. But she would be here alone every night, perhaps for the rest of her life.

In the clearing, Rachel and Brennan faced each other. "Thee doesn't think I am really in danger of them coming here again tonight?"

Brennan bumped the toe of his boot into a tussock of wild, dry grass. "No, not because the three show any sense, but they're probably all passed out from drink by now."

Rachel stared at the ground, listening to the frogs in the nearby creek.

"I'll bar my door," she said with a lift of her chin, which belied her inner trembling.

"Maybe you'd be better off if I didn't hang around any longer."

"Brennan Merriday, in case thee has not noticed by now, I am not a woman who gives way to pressure from others. I have hired thee and I expect thee will show up for breakfast tomorrow and continue the work that still needs doing here."

He looked up.

And suddenly she was very aware of how alone they were here just outside her door. Funny sensations jiggled in her stomach. "You were very brave," she murmured.

He started digging at the tussock of grass again with the toe of his boot.

Her mind flashed back to her schoolgirl days. She'd watched boys do this when they talked to girls they liked but didn't want to show it. Did he like her that way?

She turned abruptly. "I bid thee good night."

"Okay, Miss Rachel, I'll head to my place then. See you in the mornin'."

She didn't trust herself to reply. The desire to hold him here and the residual fear had worsened and she was afraid her voice would give her away. She entered, shut the door and lifted the bar into place. Few cabins had such. But Noah had insisted on this and now she understood why.

Once inside, she scanned the inside of her new home. Sunny had helped her wash the dishes so there was nothing to do. Noah had made her a rocking chair as a gift. She sat in it now and tried not to feel her lonely state. She picked up the socks she'd started to knit for Brennan as a going away thank-you. The thought hit her as unwelcome.

For just a second, she imagined Brennan Merriday sitting on a chair across from her, whittling the way he always did. She was knitting and the two of them enjoyed that companionable quiet that happily married couples sometimes shared.

Where did that come from?

She shook off this foolishness, put down her knitting and lifted her small portable desk. She began working again on a recipe she'd thought of, something with chocolate and nuts no man could resist. Except Brennan Merriday in one of his touchy moods.

She would have to be very careful around him—he was too handsome for his own good—and hers—and he was staying to help her. She thought of his courtesies. Brennan Merriday treated her like an attractive woman, not a spinster. This alone must be working on her, drawing her to him.

But he carried some deep wound and would be leaving very soon. Even if he was momentarily attracted to her, nothing would come of it. Nothing ever had. And she'd accepted being alone, hadn't she?

Brennan marched to town, boiling for a fight. Cold reason halted him a few yards from the saloon. Only a fool barged into to a three-to-one fight. He planned his strategy and sidled to a side window. What he saw flummoxed him.

He entered the saloon and Sam was alone, wiping down the bar. "What's wrong? Customers find out you were watering the whiskey?"

Sam gave him the eye. "That's an unfounded accusation. It might have been better if I had tonight. Some people just don't know when to stop."

Brennan leaned against the bar. "What happened?"

"Had to kick out a bunch earlier. They drank too much too fast and wanted to pick a fight with anybody who came near."

"I know the type." He described the three and Sam nodded. Brennan continued, "Someone must have told them that a Southerner lived around here. And they wanted to run me out of town. They actually started a fight in front of the lady I work for."

The barkeep rubbed his face with his big hands. "That's not right, fighting in front of a decent woman. Had to show my rifle to get rid of them. Most locals left. Tame crowd lives around here. The troublemakers are probably on the boat that brought them by now."

Brennan chewed on this. "Okay. Thanks." He offered his hand to the man.

"When you coming in just for that tongue wag?"

"Soon." Brennan left with a wave, not satisfied. What if after he left town, rowdies came looking for him and bothered Miss Rachel? He felt her again in his arms, so petite and slight. A fierce protectiveness reared inside him. He couldn't leave her unprotected. How could he make sure no one would bother her?

The next morning, Rachel hadn't experienced such quaking since the morning she'd left her father's home in Pennsylvania. Under the clear, late-June sky, she drew in a deep breath and let

Mr. Merriday help her down from the two-wheeled pony cart she'd borrowed from Noah's neighbors. The blue sky did not sport even one cloud. When would the rain come?

Brennan's strong, steady hand contrasted with her shakiness. After he'd held her close last night, now she had trouble looking him in the eye. She felt herself blush and turned her face away.

She'd filled several large trays with baked goods and Brennan had set them in the back of the cart. Today she would launch Rachel's Sweets, what she'd come here to do, what her future hinged upon.

"I still think you should call it *Miss* Rachel's Sweets," Brennan grumbled.

She realized then that she still held his strong, calloused hand, not for aid but for comfort. This jolted her. Was she going to start having foolish ideas? No.

Scolding herself for this lapse, she quickly smoothed her skirts. "But Miss might imply to some that I cannot cook since no man married me." She repeated her objection with an attempt at humor. Why was she so nervous? No one was going to arrest her for selling sweets.

"The name of your business needs some swank. That's all I'm sayin'."

She had to admit that having this man with her bolstered her and she didn't like that, couldn't let herself depend on him. Brennan Merriday had made it clear he was staying just so long and then heading north.

She turned from him. "Well, I'm a Quaker and we don't go for 'swank.' And my baked goods don't need that to sell. Just a lot of creamy butter and sweet sugar." She walked briskly toward the rear of the cart.

There her products lay on tin trays, covered with spotless, crisply starched white dishcloths. Yesterday Brennan had rigged up a sling that would support the tray and then go around her neck to help her carry it.

Now as he arranged the sling on her, his nearness flooded her senses. She could smell the soap she'd given him. He'd also shaved this morning and his clean chin beckoned her to stroke it. She jerked herself back into her right mind.

Then she wished he wouldn't frown so. His negativity prompted her stomach to flip up and down. And she noticed he'd worn a hole in one elbow of his blue shirt. She'd need to mend that before it dissected the sleeve completely. It was a wifely thought that she resisted. He was her hired hand, not her responsibility.

When he finished, she smiled bravely to boost her resolve and strode toward a boat that had just docked. She had sold her baked goods before, but never to strangers and all by herself. Brennan had come only because he was paid to, not because he was part of her venture. *But I've always been by myself. And I'll likely always be so.* She shook her head as if sending the thought away. *I like being alone.*

"Are you sure you want to do this?" Brennan asked from behind her.

"Quite sure," she said, denying that what she really wanted to do was run home, denying that she'd like him to come along for support. Speaking to strangers always tested her.

She lifted her mouth into a firmer smile. She marched toward the dock, repeating silently, *I will not run from my future. My plan will succeed.*

She expected Mr. Merriday to stay and watch her. However, when she glanced over her shoulder, she saw that he'd walked away from the wagon and was heading toward the saloon. This nearly halted her in her tracks. What? Did the man drink? And in daylight?

The fact that she had reached the pier, her goal, shut down this line of thought. She reinforced her thinning smile. "Good day!" she called out to the men standing or working on the boat, tied to the pier. "I'm Miss Rachel." She had intended to say her full name but Brennan's voice had somehow seeped into her mind. "I have baked goods for sale."

She had expected smiles. People always smiled when she offered them her treats. The men merely looked wary.

Finally one man asked, "What kind of baked goods?"

"I have apple fastnachts and sugar cookies." Fastnachts, yeast doughnuts filled with fruit jam or creamy custard and sprinkled with sugar, were popular in Pennsylvania.

"Got any bear claws?" one man asked.

"No, I don't."

The faint hope in many faces looking toward her fell. And so did her own hope. Then a thought bobbed up in her mind. She walked past the workmen on the pier and stepped onto the moored boat. "May I speak to the captain, please?"

Soon Rachel smiled up into the captain's face. "I'm offering a sample of my baked goods."

The tall, trim man with dark sideburns and harsh features did not look friendly. But then he glanced down. "Fastnachts?" His voice echoed with surprise.

"Yes, with apple jam and cinnamon. Please help thyself." And he did. And with his first bite, a powerful smile transformed his unwelcoming expression. "Just like my grandma used to make. You must be from Pennsylvania."

She nodded, her heart calming. "Yes, I'm homesteading here and plan to sell baked goods and sweets to the river trade. I'm Miss Rachel Woolsey."

"Pleased to meet you, miss. Do you have more

of these? I know they won't keep for more than a day, but I'd love to have one with my coffee later."

"I fried three dozen this morning." Then she turned to the crew hovering nearby. Her spirits were rising like dough on a warm, humid day. "I'd like each of thee to have a sample, too. Please." She motioned toward them.

The men lined up and cleaned off her tray in seconds. One black porter gushed, "Best I eat since I was in New Orleans and had beignets, miss. And I thank you."

"Beignets?" Rachel echoed. "Are they similar?"

"Yes, miss, but with powdered sugar."

"Was it the same dough?"

"I'm no cook, miss." The man shook his head and then grinned. "But you certainly are!"

The other men agreed heartily. And her spirit soared.

"Miss Rachel, thank you for letting us sample your wares. I'd like to buy another two dozen for me and my crew," the captain announced.

Rachel thrilled with pleasure. "Wonderful. Thee is my first customer."

"But not your last," the captain said, smiling down at her.

Elated, she scurried back to her cart and Brennan met her there. "We need to bag up two dozen for this boat." She busied herself wrapping each doughnut in waxed paper and filled two paper sacks. She delivered them to the captain.

He bowed. "Thank you, miss. You brought me sweet memories I had long forgotten."

"My pleasure, captain. Please, I'd appreciate thy letting others know I'll be here with fresh baked goods daily. I also plan on making fudge and other candy."

A happy murmur from the crew greeted this.

Grinning and promising to see her the next time they docked in Pepin, the captain bowed again and then called cheerfully to his crew to get busy or they wouldn't get another doughnut.

Buoyant with her success, Rachel walked back to the cart. Brennan lounged against it.

"We goin' home now? That's the only boat here today," he asked.

She sensed now he was worried about something. What? "Let's fill up the tray with the remaining goods." Rachel glanced up the street. "And please help me with the strap again."

He did so, arranging it around her neck once more. Their nearness once again distracted her, stirred odd sensations. She brushed aside their brief embrace the night before.

"What are you up to, Miss Rachel?"

"I need to make the mouths of my neighbors water, too." She grinned at him. She'd learned today that while generosity should be its own reward, it also made good business sense.

Soon she entered Ashford's store, jingling the bell. Brennan followed her in as if curious. Near the chairs by the cold stove sat only an older man in a wheelchair. He nodded to her politely. Had she met him?

Rachel nodded to him in case she had, then turned. "Good day, Mr. Ashford," she greeted brightly.

The storekeeper looked dubious. "How may I help you, Miss Woolsey?"

"I am here to offer samples of my baked goods." She stopped right across the counter from him.

He looked at her and then at the tray. He reached for one just as his wife walked down the stairs into the store. His hand halted in midair.

"Miss Woolsey," Mrs. Ashford said disapprovingly, "I saw you just now talking to men on that boat."

"Yes, I am starting my business. Today I'm giving away samples of my baked goods."

Mrs. Ashford studied the tray of cookies and doughnuts. "I wonder that your cousin will abet you in this. You will find yourself in the company of all sorts of vulgar men." Then the woman glanced pointedly past her and frowned deeply at Mr. Merriday.

Rachel guessed that she was suggesting Mr. Merriday was one of these low men. That goaded Rachel. She bit her lower lip to keep back a quick defense of the man. She must not insult so prominent a wife and perhaps start gossip.

And after a moment's reflection, Rachel realized

that Mrs. Ashford was the kind of woman who wanted to be consulted, to be the arbiter of others' conduct. She'd met her ilk before.

This too grated on Rachel's nerves. But nothing would be gained by telling the woman to mind her own business. "No doubt thee is right," Rachel said demurely. "But even vulgar men will not insult a woman offering sweets."

Brennan chuckled softly.

Discreetly enjoying his humor, she masked this with her most endearing smile. "Please, Mrs. Ashford, taste one of my wares and tell me thy opinion. I hear that thy baked goods are notable." She did not like to be less than genuine, but the old dictum, that one attracted more flies with honey than vinegar, held true even in Wisconsin.

Mrs. Ashford picked up a fastnacht and tore it in two, the fragrance of apple and cinnamon filling permeated the air. The storekeeper's wife handed half to her husband. They both chewed thought-fully as if weighing and measuring with each chew. They looked at each other and then her.

"Very tasty," the woman said, dusting the sugar from her fingers. Her husband nodded in agreement, almost grinning. "But most women here do their own baking," Mrs. Ashford pointed out discouragingly.

"That's why I'm courting the river trade," Rachel assented. "And single men hereabout. And occasionally a woman might want to purchase something for a special occasion like a wedding."

Mrs. Ashford listened seriously as if she were a senator engaging in a debate in Congress. "True."

"Then I'll be going on. Good day—"

"I'd like a sample too, miss," the older man by the cold stove piped up.

Rachel turned and offered him her tray. He scooped up one sugar cookie and chewed it with ceremony. After swallowing his first bite, the older man announced, "I'm Old Saul, Miss Rachel. I heard from Noah you would be arriving this month. Much obliged for the cookie. I foresee success in your endeavor."

His puckish style of speaking made Rachel chuckle. It was as if he had enjoyed her parrying Mrs. Ashford, too. "My thanks, Old Saul. Nice to meet thee." She walked outside, feeling another lift in her spirits. She could do this. She walked toward the blacksmith shop, ready to offer another free sample.

Mr. Merriday walked a step behind her. She felt his brooding presence hanging over her spurt of victory. Why did people always have to make rude comments to him? Or stare at him with unfriendly expressions? The war had been over for better than six years. Wasn't it time to let the old animosity go? And once again, the unwise attraction that drew her to him surged within.

He helped her restore the tray to the rear of the cart and then helped her up onto the seat. She had never been shown these politenesses before. Her father of course performed them for her step-mother, but Rachel was left to help her smaller stepbrothers and sisters. That must be why it touched her so every time he did this for her.

But I mustn't become accustomed to his courtesies. I will be on my own soon enough. Too soon.

Brennan rolled over, half asleep, in the dark loft. Something had wakened him. What? Fire? The grass was tinder-dry and that had been a worry for the past few days. He listened, alert, to the sounds in the warm, humid summer night. More times than he wanted to recall, his acute hearing had saved his life. Then he heard the faintest tinkle of breaking glass.

Probably high spirits at the saloon. He rolled over. Still, sleep didn't come. Why would there be a fight at the saloon? That usually happened only when several riverboats moored at the same time for a night.

He rolled away from his pallet. Since he couldn't stand up in the low attic loft, he crawled to the open window draped with cheesecloth to keep out the mosquitoes. From his high vantage point, he scanned the street. The half-moon radiated little light.

Just as he was about to go back to lie on his pallet, he glimpsed movement down on the street.

Three men were creeping around the stores. One had a large, full sack thrown over one shoulder. A man didn't have to have much imagination to come to a quick conclusion.

Thieves.

The three men were slinking toward the front of Ashford's. Better to access the store on the side away from where the storekeeper slept.

The uppity face of the owner's wife came to Brennan's mind. Her expression a few days ago—as she'd weighed and measured him and pronounced him wanting—had been burned into him. If she'd had the power, she would have caused him to vanish from her prissy sight that day. It rankled. Yet that he cared what she thought of him rankled more.

He watched as the shadowy men paused as if waiting for something.

Their plan unfolded in his mind. These river "rats" were using the saloon's loud voices to mask the sounds of the thievery. He let out a breath. These little river towns were without any presence of the law and were easy pickings for thieves.

The thought suddenly rolled like thunder in his mind. He didn't want this little bump on the river to become a target for unlawful types. Not with Miss Rachel living just outside town. The memory of the ruffians who'd come to her place to find him goaded him. The thought of the innocent Miss Rachel being accosted sent icy shivers through him. *Never.* He had to make sure the reputation of this town stayed strong—for her sake.

He crawled over to his knapsack, retrieved his two Colt 45s and checked to be sure both were loaded and ready. He scooted to the ladder and slipped down to the blacksmith shop. He paused, thinking of who could provide him backup. He crept to the lean-to and roused the blacksmith. Seeing Brennan's index finger to his lips, Levi swallowed a waking exclamation.

Brennan leaned close to the man's ear. "Thieves." He motioned toward the rifle hung on the wall and then for the blacksmith to get up.

Soon, the two men stood side by side in the lean-to. Brennan outlined a plan and the smith nodded. They crept along in the shadows and took their places—Brennan across from the front of the General Store, closest to the river, and the smith slipped along another store behind Ashford's. The familiar sensations of preparing for battle prickled through Brennan, keenly heightening his aware-ness of every sound and sight.

Laughter echoed from the saloon and then one of the thieves raised his hand to break the glass next to Ashford's door.

"Hold!" Brennan roared, hidden in the shadows.

The three men started and glanced around frantically.

"Hold!" Brennan repeated.

The three scampered toward the rear as if to hide themselves.

Brennan let loose a warning shot over their heads. The smith let his rifle roar from the rear. The three men stopped, not knowing which way to run. Two had drawn pistols.

"Drop that bag and empty your pockets!" Brennan ordered.

The three started to run toward the river. One shot toward Brennan, but the bullet went wide. *Idiots!*

Brennan shot into the dirt in front of them, halting them in the middle of the street. "Drop your guns and that bag, then empty your pockets! Do it! Or this time I'll shoot one of you!"

The man with the bag put it down and raised his hands. The other two put their pistols on the ground, yanked out their pockets and raised their hands, too.

"All your pockets!" Brennan commanded.

The bagman pulled out his pockets.

"Run!" Brennan bellowed.

The three obeyed, racing toward the river.

Just then Ashford ran out the front door, dressed hastily and holding a rifle. "What's happening?"

Before Brennan could reply, more men armed with rifles bounded into the street. Brennan wondered if they had any sense. It was crazy to show themselves so plainly before they knew who was shooting whom. Some, he noted, did cling to the shadows, probably veterans like him.

Not wanting to be the center of attention or suffer being thanked, he slipped away, back to the blacksmith shop and up to his loft. Still his heart pounded with the excitement. He listened to the buzz of voices below. Levi explained, loud enough for him to hear, what had happened.

The town men shouted and ran toward the river. Brennan looked out his riverside window and saw a rude boat sliding out into the current. The town men shouted and shot toward the craft, their bullets sizzling as they hit the water. But the night had only half-moon light and soon the craft became invisible, lost in the dark.

Brennan lay down on his blanket, his heart still racing. The thieves had gotten away, which was best. What would the town have done with them if they'd been caught? Pepin didn't have a jail and somebody might have gotten hurt trying to corral them. Better they escaped. They wouldn't come back anytime soon. But what about others like them?

This staying in one place was costing him. He lay listening to the men talking, and hoped no one would disturb him. He hadn't done this for any of them. He'd done it for Miss Rachel, but if he said that, they would think something was going on between them. Better to lay low.

How long would they have to hash over this minor dustup? People here didn't cotton to him.

And he generally didn't cotton to people so they were even. That suited him. But what else could he do to keep Miss Rachel safe after he left town?

Just after dawn the next morning, Brennan freshened up down at the river as usual, glad to wash away last night's sweat. He then set out toward Miss Rachel's place, his stomach rumbling for the breakfast she'd provide. The heat was already climbing high and not a hint of a cloud showed on the horizon.

As he passed Ashford's store, the proprietor burst out and ran toward him. Brennan halted. What did the man want?

Mr. Ashford panted. "I just came out to thank you." The man's face looked tired from lack of sleep. "For last night. All the storekeepers are grateful. The smithy told us you woke him up and were the one who ran off the thieves."

Brennan hadn't expected appreciation. And didn't want their gratitude. He looked at the man, giving nothing of himself away. "Didn't do it for your thanks."

"We owe you."

Brennan shrugged. "Don't mention it," he said with finality and tucked in an edge that promised unpleasantness if the man went on thanking him.

The man's wife came running out of the store and offered him a folded new shirt and trousers. "Just a token of our thanks."

Brennan didn't take the clothing. "Thank you, ma'am, but I'm expected at Miss Rachel's for breakfast." He hurried on.

Brennan spent the morning building a chicken coop strong and high enough to outfox any fox or other varmint. To start with, he'd logged the needed wood and dug postholes. This afternoon he'd set posts.

With a rumbling stomach and sharp anticipation of another tasty meal, at noon he sat down at Miss Rachel's table. When she carried in the steaming crock from the outdoor kitchen, he noted she did not look happy. What was the bee in her Quaker bonnet?

"Mr. Merriday, why didn't thee tell me what happened last night?" She made it sound like a scold.

He bristled. Why did she sound mad? After all, he'd done it for her. "Because I didn't think it was worth mentionin'. That's why," he replied, eyeing the bowls of stew she was dishing up.

She set the crock on the table and sat down.

He waited quietly for her to finish silently blessing the meal as she always did. When the amen came, he picked up his fork and dug into her stew. The woman could cook as well as she could bake.

"The Ashfords told me all about it. And about thy graceless behavior this morning." She motioned toward the chair by the cold hearth. The dratted new clothing the storekeeper's wife had offered him sat there, evidently drying after being washed. This aggravated him but he kept eating.

"We have something in common," she said, also beginning to eat. "We are different from everyone else here. I'm the pitiful and eccentric Quaker spinster."

Brennan suddenly felt ashamed of thinking of her with this less than flattering term. But he hadn't meant it in a bad way. And Miss Rachel was unusual, who could argue that?

"And Mr. Merriday is thought of as a shiftless wanderer. And ex-Confederate," she finished.

He chewed, trying to focus on the rich taste of the wild onions in the stew. After all, she wasn't saying anything he didn't already know.

"Last night thy quick action saved the town from thievery. They wish to show their thanks. Why refuse it?"

Annoyed suddenly, he barked, "Because I don't care what they think of me!"

She gazed up at him, unperturbed. "Everyone, even we, put labels on people. No doubt thee thinks Mr. Ashford is a prosy storekeeper and his wife, a know-it-all busybody."

Her apt descriptions of the two hit his funny bone. His heat turned to laughter. Chuckling, he picked up his fork once more.

"But we all have worth to God."

His grip on the fork tightened. Easy for Miss Rachel to say. She hadn't seen what he'd seen in the war. And what he'd seen he sensed was the root of his spells and nightmares, the horror of bloodshed and needless loss of life.

"Thankfully God doesn't judge by our outward appearance but looks into our hearts." Before he could respond, she reached over and tugged his cuff, ripping half the sleeve loose.

He drew in a sharp breath.

"Thankfully I think Mrs. Ashford guessed the size correctly," Miss Rachel continued in an even tone, "but I'll have to hem the trousers of course."

He gawked at her in disbelief. "You tore my shirt."

"It didn't take much," she said in a matter-of-fact tone. "I think the polite thing to do on the way home after supper is to stop and thank Mrs. Ashford." Then she sent him one of her managing, very determined, gray-eyes-flashing looks.

He didn't respond, but returned to eating in silence, trying to hold his temper. Soft-spoken Lorena would never have ripped his shirt to make a point.

Then he recalled Miss Rachel's description of herself as a pathetic spinster. He didn't think that about her now, but he struggled again with guilt over originally disparaging Miss Rachel—just like everybody else. The memory of holding her in his arms . . . He had to stop thinking about that.

He was leaving for Canada as soon as he'd done everything to get Miss Rachel set up here.

He didn't care what other people thought of him. But Miss Rachel thought more of him than the others did. That was dangerous. He'd let down everyone in his life. Would he let down Miss Rachel, too?

Chapter Four

Brennan did not want to do this, did not want to go to the Ashfords', hat in hand, and thank them for the unwanted, unasked-for new clothes. Wearing his new clothes now, he didn't even feel like himself. Earlier, after the new clothing had dried, Miss Rachel had hemmed his pants and pressed everything up nice. The new clothes felt stiff and thick, not thin and shaped to him like his old clothes. Made him feel strange. As strange as pausing here, looking to go somewhere he was not welcome.

He stood, looking at the store. The closed sign sat in the window, granting him a reprieve. He turned to head to the blacksmith shop to jaw with the smithy.

"Mr. Merriday!" a woman's voice called from above. "Did you need anything?"

Irritation ground inside him. Mrs. Ashford with her windows overlooking Main Street didn't miss a thing. He looked up, pinning a smile on his face. "Yes, ma'am, I came to thank you."

"Come to the rear and we'll let you in," she ordered.

He wanted to decline but Miss Rachel didn't want him to be rude to this busybo . . . this good woman. So he walked around to the rear and Mr. Ashford let him in. "I just came to thank you—"

"Ned, ask Mr. Merriday to come up!" Mrs. Ashford called down.

Ned dutifully motioned to Brennan to precede him up the stairs.

Brennan gritted his teeth and climbed to the living quarters. As he topped the stairs, he snatched his hat off and schooled his face into a smile. "Evenin', ma'am."

"Mr. Merriday, so glad to see you accepted our gift of thanks." The storekeeper's wife sat in the dining area that took up half the large, open room overlooking the river. There were several people around the long table, two he'd never seen in town.

"Cousin, this is Brennan Merriday, a workman in our village," Mrs. Ashford said. "He saved our store from thievery last night. Mr. Merriday, my cousin, Mrs. Almeria Brown, and her grand-daughter Miss Posey Brown. They arrived today by boat."

Brennan glanced at the plump older woman who lifted an eyeglass on a string to study him like a bug on a pin. He bowed his head to her, his neck stiff. "Ma'am." And then to the younger lady who looked about seventeen, too slender but pretty in a common way with brown hair and eyes. "Miss."

"Are you homesteading hereabouts?" the older woman asked, piercing him with her gaze, her eye magnified by the glass. Some of her iron-gray hair had slipped from its bun.

"No, ma'am, just working to help set up Miss Rachel, the preacher's cousin, on her homestead."

Two other young people, one a young girl and one a young blond man, also sat at the table, looking at him. "This is our daughter Amanda and her friend Gunther Lang," the storekeeper said.

Brennan nodded, feeling beyond awkward. These were not the kind of people he associated with. He knew where he belonged—down the street at the saloon.

"You did very good last night," the young man said with the trace of a foreign accent.

"Yes," the young girl agreed, "you were so brave."

"I didn't do much. They weren't too dangerous, just sneak thieves."

"Please sit down, Merriday," Ashford invited, coming up behind him. "I'm sure Miss Rachel has fed you, but would you take a cup of coffee with us?"

From the shopkeeper's tone, Brennan knew these people were experiencing the same disorientation. They weren't comfortable with his sort in their dining room. And the old biddy with the eyeglass on a string was staring bullets at him. "No, thanks. You're right, Miss Rachel fed me to the brim. I just wanted to say thanks. This morning I wasn't ready to accept anything." *Anything from you people.*

"We wanted you to know that we appreciated your quick action," Ashford said.

Brennan nodded, his head bobbing like a toy. "Just did what anybody would."

"I think you did more," the young man said.

Brennan nodded once more. "I'll bid you good evening then." He waved Ashford back into his seat and tried not to jog down the stairs.

Unwillingly he overheard the old woman say, "What kind of man works for some woman when he could stake his own claim? Must be shiftless."

Insulted yet irritated that a stranger's opinion could get to him, he let himself out and breathed with relief. And headed straight for the saloon.

He walked through the doors and let out a big breath. The saloon didn't have a piano player and the atmosphere was more drowsy than raucous, but nobody here would make him wonder if his shoes were shined bright enough.

He headed straight for the long bar and ordered an ale.

Sam poured his drink and then leaned his pudgy elbows on the bar. "So you're the man of the day now?"

Brennan snorted. "Right. Me?"

"From what I hear, you rousted them robbers efficient-like."

"They were just a few paltry sneak thieves. No big effort needed."

A man came up and clapped Brennan on the back. "The town hero!"

Brennan recoiled. "I didn't do nothing special, okay?"

"Ah, does not the laurel rest easy upon thy brow?" the man asked grandiloquently.

Brennan picked up his glass and tried to ignore the man. "Thought we'd finally have that tongue wag, Sam."

But it was not to be. More men crowded around, asking Brennan for the whole story. He bridled.

Sam leaned forward and muttered, "Play along. They don't get much excitement in this bump on the river. Tell them the story and they'll leave you alone."

So Brennan did, forcing himself to tell the story in full to prevent questions. He had a rapt audience. These people really didn't get much excitement. "So that's how it happened," he concluded.

Brennan suffered through a few more minutes of felicitations and gratitude and then, finally interpreting his silence as a desire to be left in peace, the men moved away, discussing the occurrence among themselves. Brennan refused all offers to buy him a real drink. He just wanted a refreshing mug of ale, nothing strong. Strong drink brought him nightmares and he didn't want that.

Brennan swallowed deeply of his drink, his mouth dry.

One man, middle-aged, better dressed and polished looking, stayed near him. "This place needs a sheriff. You might think about running in the fall election."

"Won't be here then," Brennan said.

"A pity." The stranger tipped his hat and walked out.

Sam swabbed the bar and then looked up from under his bushy eyebrows at Brennan. "You know who that is?"

"No." *And I don't care either.*

"That man sits in the state legislature. He's traveling around, drumming up support for the November election."

Brennan shrugged and repeated, "I won't be here then."

"Why not?" Sam asked. "You got a good reputation here now. Why leave?"

Even the barkeep had an opinion? Brennan stifled the urge to yell his frustration. "I'm just staying long enough to help Miss Rachel get set up and then I'm leavin'." He downed his drink and stalked outside.

In the hot evening, he marched to the blacksmith shop, looking for a place to get shut of all this attention. Once there, instead of resting, he paced up and down along the riverbank. Everything within him wanted to pack up his knapsack and catch the first boat north. But he couldn't.

His mind racing, he recalled sitting at Miss Rachel's table, watching her serve up another tasty meal, something she seemed to do as easily as breathing. Her biscuits were the lightest, the best he'd ever eaten. And her soft cheeks had been flushed pretty pink from making them for him. The thought of stroking one froze him in place.

He growled at the bullfrogs bellowing along shore, trying to attract females of their own kind. He wasn't trying to have anythin' to do with females. He had nothing to give any woman, not a home or a heart.

Miss Rachel was upsetting him by making him think about her that way. Why did she have to be such a good cook? And so honest and open? She was always so good-hearted, not a mean bone in her.

She made him think of settling down here, not Canada—far from all the war did to him, to everyone. Canada would let him forget all that, start over fresh.

He tried to focus on how she'd torn off his sleeve. *Managing woman.* His unhappy thoughts twisted around into a rat's nest. But one thought stood out clear. He owed Miss Rachel and he wouldn't leave her, couldn't leave her still needing help.

Two weeks later, nearing the beginning of August, Brennan fidgeted in the bright summer sun near Miss Rachel, who stood at the dock watching her brand spanking new stove be carried off the boat. She glowed with evident satisfaction over her major purchase while he shifted from one foot to the other. He wished he were waiting to get on this boat and go.

Irritating Ashford stood nearby, saying he wanted to make sure that the purchase matched all that the firm had advertised. *What a fuss about a stove.*

Brennan stayed near the lady, but felt miles and miles away already. Tomorrow he'd dig her future garden plot. Then he would be gone on the next riverboat that docked here. Restlessness consumed him. At times the itch to leave became physical, as if he wanted to jump out of his skin. But how to tell Miss Rachel? Something about her kept him confused, unsettled, making it hard to leave, and this was the first time in memory this had happened. *But I'm goin'.*

The boatmen pushed the stove, supported on a

wooden skid, off the boat onto the pier. Noah had come to help Brennan and held his team unhitched from the wagon.

Though the boatmen moved as slow as molasses on a very cold January day, Brennan held himself in check. *Move it along, why don't you?*

"Miss Rachel Woolsey?" a boatman asked, looking down at an invoice.

"Yes."

Brennan noted she could barely speak, she was so happy.

"Sign here, please."

"Miss Woolsey must examine the stove first," Mr. Ashford said, holding up a hand.

The boatman looked chagrined but motioned for another two men to crowbar off the sides of the wooden box.

Brennan held his tongue between his teeth. He'd been ready to say that. Of course Ashford would butt in. And take his time about it, too.

Rachel examined each side, looking for any imperfection. "It looks fine."

"Open and close the doors. Check to see if the latches fit tight," Mr. Ashford suggested.

She did so and then signed the invoice. The boatman had the men nail the crate back together.

Brennan noted her convoluted signature revealed her excitement. *All over a stove.* Miss Rachel, pink with pleasure, made a pretty picture. He looked away.

"My cousin Noah and Mr. Merriday will attach the horses to the skid. Isn't that right, Noah?" Miss Rachel asked.

Brennan held tight to the ragged fringe of his temper. Couldn't they just get this going?

"Rachel's place is just a half mile up the road," Noah said, gesturing toward the other end of town. "I'll bring the skid right back to you."

"Sure. Fine." The boatman handed Rachel her copy of the invoice and then turned away.

Finally. Now they could get this home and in place and then he could begin to lay out the garden. And if all went right, he'd be off tomorrow. Somewhere inside him, deep down, a voice whispered, *Stay. Why leave?*

Stonewalling the thought, Brennan helped Noah secure the team to the skid. The horses began to drag the heavy iron stove up the road. The progress was excruciatingly slow, with a lot of creaking. Brennan's nerves tangled into knots, but he kept from showing it. Miss Rachel had become a trap for him. He'd escaped other orchestrated marriage traps. But Miss Rachel had set no trap for him— that made it harder. He knew he was making no sense.

Finally they reached Miss Rachel's cabin door.

Noah and Brennan had already prepared a row of short logs of similar size, stripped of branches and bark, to use to roll the stove inside. The hard part would be getting it up over the threshold.

They contrived a little ramp for this. Now the two of them painstakingly shifted the stove in its crate off the boat's skid and onto the logs and steadied it.

"I need to take the skid back first. Wait for me. I'll be quick." Noah turned the team around and headed back to town at a run.

Miss Rachel came near Brennan or rather her new stove. She stroked it the way another woman might have stroked a fur coat. Her nearness made his stomach twist. Her soft cheek tantalized him, beckoning him to press his lips . . .

Unable to brook further delay and needing to distance himself, Brennan started to roll the stove ponderously away from this woman. The stove picked up momentum—off balance because only one man had started it.

"Brennan Merriday, please wait for Noah. Thee might hurt—"

Unsettled, the stove began to tip and rock on the logs, rolling forward. Brennan tried to dodge the out-of-control iron beast, but—

Rachel cried out.

Stifling a curse, Brennan gasped with pain. His arm had become pinned between the cockeyed stove and the doorjamb of her cabin. Backed up against the log wall and half sitting, he struggled to keep outwardly calm but inside he was kicking himself down the road. And fighting to keep on top of the pain, ride it out, keep it in.

She hurried forward, voicing her upset. She moved as if to try to shift the stove, half on the logs, half off.

"Don't!" he thundered. "It might come off completely and crush me."

She stared down at him, wringing her hands. "Going for Noah won't help. He will not delay in returning."

Brennan couldn't meet her eyes so he focused on her chin. If he hadn't given in to his own haste, this wouldn't have happened. He waited for the lady to point this out.

Instead her mouth moved as if she were chewing tough meat. Finally, she said, "Thee has been behaving like a fly caught in flypaper. What drives thee, Brennan Merriday, to chafe so?"

The pain goading him, he almost bit off her head, but now *his* mouth chewed on that imaginary tough meat. He had no answer for her. Why did he get so restless?

But now all his concentration was tied up in not showing how much he suffered. He could not shift the unwieldy weight of the stove pressing on his wrist and upended forearm. Had he broken his arm? Inwardly he called himself every name he could think of, venting the pain.

Rachel stood over Brennan, folding her hands, murmuring a prayer for help.

The minutes spent waiting, bearing the brunt of the iron stove on his hand and wrist, depleted

Brennan like hours spent working in the sun.

Within minutes Noah, accompanied by the young man Brennan had met at the Ashfords', entered the clearing.

"The stove rolled!" Rachel called out the obvious. But she didn't add the fact that Brennan had caused this by his haste. Brennan nearly gagged on the fact that it was all his own fault. That admission and the pain were nauseating him. But still Miss Rachel protected him.

Noah and Gunther hurried to Brennan. Without wasting any time asking questions, the men surveyed the situation and with quick commands, they hefted the stove back squarely onto the logs, releasing Brennan.

At the sudden deliverance, Brennan could not suppress a long moan. The two men rolled the stove inside.

Rachel dropped to her knees beside Brennan.

At first he resisted Rachel's efforts, holding his painful arm close to his chest, shielding it with his other arm. Finally he let her support his injured arm. He sent her an anguished look, their eyes at a level.

"How bad does his arm look?" Noah asked in his unruffled voice, standing over them.

Rachel gently probed the arm from the shoulder downward. When she prodded Brennan's wrist, he sucked in air sharply, not only from the pain but from her touch.

"Bend the wrist, please," Rachel instructed.

Brennan tucked his lower lip under his front teeth and bent his wrist, stifling a groan. Sweat popped up on his forehead but he did as she asked, knowing a broken wrist wouldn't bend.

"Rotate it?" she pressed.

Again Brennan suppressed any show of pain and obeyed, watching his wrist move.

"Well, that's a relief," Rachel pronounced.

"Easy for you to say," Brennan gasped. Her prodding and instructions had aggravated the pain of the injury. Her soft shoulder was so near his cheek. He imagined resting his head there. He closed his eyes, willing away the image, the temptation.

"It's a relief that the bone isn't broken," Rachel said with force. "The wrist is sprained, I think."

"Take a week to ten days to heal," Noah added.

"It's good I'm right-handed," Brennan said through gritted teeth. He looked to the young man. "Glad you came along to help Noah." Though Noah wouldn't talk, this lad probably would. Everybody in town would soon hear about his foolishness.

"I am Gunther Lang," the young man introduced himself to Rachel. Then he glanced down at Brennan. "Sorry you are hurt."

"I think soaking the wrist in cold water may help," Miss Rachel said, rising. "I'll get a basin.

Brennan, come sit inside." She nodded toward the door.

"I must go," the young man said and hurried away.

Noah reached for Brennan's good hand. "I'll help you up and then I'll hook up the stove."

Looking away, Brennan accepted the hand, managed to get to his feet and followed Noah inside where he sank into the rocker by the cold hearth. The pain was weakening him.

Rachel entered with a basin of water from the well and set it on her small sewing table. She reached to lift his hand in.

"I can move my hand," he said gracelessly. He folded up his sleeve and lowered the hand into the cool water. His gaze met hers over the basin. The concern he saw there chastened him.

"Very well." Rachel turned away. "Noah, is there anything I can do to help thee?"

Brennan toughed it out, the cold water making his bones ache more.

"Yes." Noah and she worked together, connecting the stovepipe sections and sliding it through the hole Brennan had cut for it this morning. Noah accepted Rachel's thanks, commiserated briefly with Brennan and headed home with his wagon and team.

Rachel retrieved her jar of arnica, pulled the bench over and sat down near him. She opened the jar and began tenderly rubbing the ointment into his wrist.

Even her gentle touch caused him pain and he didn't like her having to care for him again. Her nearness worked its way through him—even in his pain. Her tender touch awakened something within that he didn't want to acknowledge. He lowered his eyes, not wanting to let her know her effect on him. Finally she brought out a large white dishcloth and folded it into a triangle.

"I don't need a sling," he objected irritably, knowing that he sounded like a boy.

She just stared at him, waiting.

"Oh, all right," he finally conceded and rose, cradling his arm.

Their faces a hairbreadth apart, Miss Rachel efficiently looped the sling around his arm and tied it behind his neck.

The scent of the lilac soap she always used filled his head and again he yearned to lean his head on her soft shoulder.

Obviously unaware, Miss Rachel adjusted the sling. "I know why thee couldn't wait for Noah." Her tone did not scold, merely informed. "Why are thee so fretful and champing at the bit to leave?"

Brennan wouldn't meet her gaze.

"Rest. I'll make some willow bark tea for the pain." She went to her new stove.

He sat down, watching her from under his

lashes. Was she unscathed from contact with him? Her cheeks glowed pink—from touching him, from imagining his touch?

He turned his mind from this foolishness. How could something like this sprain take so much out of him? He closed his eyes and leaned back against the rocker. His wrist throbbed. He'd been so close to leaving, and now this. In his mind, old Aunt Martha's voice hectored him. *Worthless, thoughtless boy.* He couldn't argue with her.

And why *was* he so fretful and champing at the bit to leave? For the first time in a long time, he had a place to stay, a job, good food, new clothes . . . But he didn't belong here. He needed a new start far from . . . everything, especially this woman who continued to surprise him, to pull him to stay.

The next morning, Miss Rachel hummed to herself as she scattered chicken feed. Brennan sat in the shade against a maple, resting his arm in his sling, trying to think of some chore he could do with one hand. His wrist was swollen and painful. He'd felt guilty over eating breakfast at Miss Rachel's table when he couldn't work.

From the corner of his eye, he noted the young woman who looked to be seventeen or so, the one he'd met at the Ashfords' that evening when he'd gone to thank them. She was edging closer to them through the trees, as cautious as a doe. Fine, just what they needed—company. And what did she want?

"Good morning," Miss Rachel called out in a cheery voice that grated against his temper.

The young woman entered the clearing. Her clothing looked as if it had been refurbished to look new, but was in fact an old dress. And her manner was cautious. "Good morning. I'm Posey Brown. I was taking a walk and I saw your clearing—"

The distinctive call of a robin interrupted their conversation. The Quaker lady looked up and then imitated the birdcall. The robin hopped farther down the branch, moving in the breeze toward Miss Rachel, and sounded its call again. Miss Rachel replied, going to get the full water bucket. She then filled up a large wooden bowl attached to a stump. The bird flew down, perched on the side of the bowl and began drinking.

Brennan watched and listened, reluctantly fascinated by the interaction of the bird and the lady. Finally the bird sang its thanks and then flew and hopped back to the crook of the oak tree to its nest.

"That was like you were actually talking to each other." Posey's words radiated with wonder.

He'd almost said the same words aloud. And suddenly he was more aware than before of his sour mood. He hoisted himself up onto his feet.

"You put out water for the birds?" the girl asked as if this were the first birdbath she'd seen.

"It's been so very dry and several birds have nested nearby. I do it so they don't have far to go."

"Cousin Ned says if we don't get rain, one spark could burn the whole town," the girl said in a voice that spoke of living in the South.

Brennan thought Ned Ashford was right.

Miss Rachel turned to the girl and smiled. "My mother taught me birdsong. She spoke to birds. And they seemed almost to understand her."

The way Miss Rachel said these words he knew that her mother had died and what was more, that she had been a beloved mother. His own ma had died young. He didn't want to feel the connection to Miss Rachel this brought.

"How old were you when she died?" Brennan asked gruffly in spite of himself.

"I was nearly thirteen." Miss Rachel turned back to scattering chicken feed.

Posey edged closer. "My mother died during the war. That's when Grandmother came to live with me," Posey paused. "And Pa died in the war. He was in the Kentucky Militia."

At this Brennan looked at her sharply.

Rachel motioned for the young girl to come forward. Rachel held open the bag of chicken feed, encouraging Posey to help her.

Though sorry for the young woman and uneasy

that she hailed from Kentucky, Brennan moved away from the tree, his unabated restlessness goading him.

"It's just my grandmother and me now," Posey said, scattering the feed.

"I'm glad thee has her."

"Yes," Posey said, not looking up and not sounding happy.

Sensing the girl had come to tell Miss Rachel her sad story, like females did, Brennan turned and started toward town. He had to get away from this homey scene, from hearing how the war had torn this girl's world into shreds. He found that unfortunately he couldn't walk fast without jarring his wrist.

"I'm finishing cinnamon rolls this morning, Posey. Perhaps you'd like to help me get them ready to take into town. A boat is expected today."

"I heard how you sell baked goods. You must be good at that."

"I do my poor best," Rachel admitted.

Brennan walked carefully across the uneven ground through the wild grass, trying to get away.

Miss Rachel made the best sweets he'd ever eaten and that's all the credit she'd own up to. Yes, Miss Rachel was too nice. Didn't she know such goodness only invited trouble? This was a nasty world and it destroyed niceness.

The two females turned toward the cabin.

Though he'd begun to walk away, some curiosity prompted Brennan to ask, "Your father remarried, Miss Rachel?"

"Yes" was all she said.

And that told him more about this lady and why she'd come West than she'd probably ever put into words.

His wrist was aching so he couldn't be of help to this good woman. What could he do with one hand? "I'm heading to town!" he called out. Maybe he could have that quiet tongue wag with Sam the barkeep at last and think of something else. Maybe that would take the edge off his keen craving to leave.

He had to get away from this woman who made him remember things like family and belonging, things he'd long kept sleeping in the back of his mind. Miss Rachel was waking him up to . . . to feeling, caring. *I've got to get away—soon.*

Chapter Five

On the next morning, yet another steamy summer day, Brennan did not show up for breakfast. Rachel stood at her door, looking for him. Concern needled her.

Had he left town?

Or had he been hurt worse than she thought?
Or since he couldn't work, was he lying in bed, moping?

The idea of going into town and finding him to put a flea in his ear tempted her. But she turned from it and went inside. If the man didn't want his breakfast, so be it.

She cracked an egg in the skillet, listened to its lonely sizzle and then toasted a single slice of bread for her breakfast. She sat down to eat alone. Well, she wanted to be on her own and now she was.

Recalling Brennan's edginess over the past week didn't diminish her uneasiness. This morning he might have just up and left town. Men like him did that: drifters drifted.

But she'd become accustomed to his laconic wit. And in his company, she never felt judged and found wanting. She now recognized that this feeling was something she'd lived with daily since her father remarried. She stared at the solid walls of her snug cabin, her own home, grateful for it yet feeling so isolated, set apart.

She snapped off this self-pitying train of thought and began her day. Soon she loaded her dishcloth-covered trays of just-out-of-the-oven, fragrant cinnamon rolls onto the narrow shelves of the two-wheeled pushcart Noah and Brennan had built for her. Mr. Merriday didn't like her meeting boats without him. But she had to start doing that. If he weren't gone already, Brennan Merriday would be soon.

At this thought a weight settled over her lungs. She shoved against it but it refused to budge. The feeling would pass, she told herself. Perhaps it would be better if Brennan had left. Then she could face her solitary life starting today and make peace with it.

A boat's whistle prompted her to hurry along so she wouldn't miss one that might just be stopping to pick up the mail.

Soon she rolled the cart into town. She forced herself to smile despite the stubborn weight that was making it hard to breathe. She was rolling her cart past Ashford's store when she saw Posey hurry out from it.

"Hello, Miss Rachel!" she greeted her.

Rachel smiled but didn't stop. Posey joined her and kept in step at her side.

Out of the corner of her eye, Rachel noted Brennan Merriday coming out of the blacksmith shop. So he hadn't left town. The weight she'd carried vanished. *That is not good. I must not depend on him.*

He was hurrying as if to catch up with her.

She picked up her pace, letting him know she wasn't waiting around for him.

"Posey Brown!" a strong, shrill female voice called out across the main street.

Posey halted. Now it appeared that the girl

might have been escaping from the store. Posey turned. "Yes, Grandmother?"

"I was not done with our conversation. Please come here."

Posey did not look happy but she obeyed.

Rachel continued on, reaching the boat dock. Brennan trailed her. Somehow she sensed him scowling behind her back.

She smiled with professional cheer. "Good morning!" she called to the boatmen. "I have cinnamon rolls and sponge candy for sale today!"

Boatmen, who'd evidently heard of her business, swarmed onto the dock and surrounded her.

A wiry man with a young boy around ten pushed past the men, coming toward Rachel on land. She was handing out rolls in wax paper as fast as she could and men were dropping coins into a small bucket at her feet.

As the wiry man passed, she noted the stormy look on his face as if he was spoiling for a fight and the shuttered expression on the boy beside him. And how he hung back. The man reached behind and yanked him forward. *So unkind.* But Rachel was keeping up with business.

"Brennan Merriday!" the wiry man bellowed. "So you are here in this little backwater town!"

Everyone within hearing distance went silent. Rachel's hand faltered. The man's bellow had clearly been a challenge. The boatmen still snatched pastries from her hands and dropped in their coins, but they did it with haste and then crowded onto the shore as if they didn't want to miss the show . . . or fight.

And this man had called out Brennan's name. Who was he? She glanced over her shoulder but stayed where she was.

When the cook from the boat arrived with a tray and scooped up the rest of her fare, she was sold out. Her pulse jumping, she accepted his payment, offered her thanks and turned around, trundling her empty cart through the crowd at the dock.

In the center of the town's street, Brennan and the stranger and boy stood, confronting each other. The two men glared as if about to battle. Would there be fisticuffs?

Rachel parked her cart and unable to stop herself, moved closer.

"What're ya'll doing here, Jean Pierre?" Brennan asked, his voice low with an edge of menace.

Aware that Brennan would not appreciate any interference from her, Rachel halted, keeping her distance, but remained watchful.

"I never thought I'd be forced to set eyes on your worthless face again," Jean Pierre sneered with obvious relish. "But it's time you took responsibility for your get."

The man's last word, a vulgar term for *child,* sent a spike of ice through Rachel. Brennan's "get"? The shock forced a gasp from her. "Oh."

Brennan looked confused. "What are ya'll saying?"

"I'm saying this is your son, Lorena's child, Jacque."

Brennan appeared speechless.

"Your own kin and Lorena's were glad to be rid of a coward like you," Jean Pierre continued. "Then I read about you in the Saint Louis paper." He pulled a folded newspaper from his back pocket. He slapped it into Brennan's hand. "Guess you aren't the coward we all thought you were."

Brennan looked at the paper, but still reacted only with mute shock.

"Everybody in both our families in Mississippi and across in Louisiana is dead or scattered. I'm headin' West. I was going to drop your boy off at an orphanage run by some Quaker woman near Saint Louis when I seen this paper and read about you running off the thieves here. So here's your son. You take care of him." With that, Jean Pierre turned on his heel and stalked back to the riverboat.

Rachel tried to take this all in, but had trouble grasping what had just taken place. *Brennan—a son?*

Brennan didn't move or speak, just stood staring after the man heading toward the boat.

Then the boy took action. He turned and ran after the stranger. "Don't leave me here, cousin! Take me with you!"

At this, Brennan woke up. He chased the boy and grasped him by the shoulder, halting his flight. "Jean Pierre! Are you tellin' me that Lorena had my son and never told me?"

"Why would she tell you? She was well shut of you. Boy, stay with your father. He's all you got!"

The boy jerked away from Brennan and ran after his cousin. "Don't leave me!"

Jean Pierre ignored his calls and boarded along with the boatmen. A river porter, carrying the mailbag, hurried back toward the dock. When he reached the deck, the whistle sounded, the few boatmen left on land scurried on deck, and the riverboat began pulling away.

"Come back!" the boy at river's edge shouted, a rending hysteria in his voice.

The riverboat swept into the current and steamed away.

Tears sprang to the boy's eyes and he swiped at them with his tattered sleeve.

The sight wrenched Rachel's heart. She instinctively drew nearer Brennan and his son. *His son.* Was this Brennan's son? The idea of his having a child startled her, shook her—in a way she hadn't expected. She resisted it and didn't have time to examine the wave of emotion now.

Brennan stood a few paces behind the boy, obviously still in the grip of his own bewilderment.

His lips quivering, the boy appeared about to burst into sobs. Rachel knew that would crush his spirit. Men and boys didn't cry. She glanced once more at Brennan's frozen expression and decided she must act. *Father, help me. I must do something but I don't know what.*

"Hello," she said, coming close to the boy, trying to behave as normally as she could. "I'm Miss Rachel Woolsey. I am thy father's . . . Mr. Merriday's employer."

With dirt-smeared cheeks, the boy looked into her eyes without much comprehension.

His naked anguish hit her like a broadside. She offered him her hand. "Welcome to Pepin. We are a small town but we have a school and a general store," she babbled, very aware that everyone in town was listening to her every syllable. She looked to Brennan once more.

"Mr. Merriday hurt his wrist recently and has been resting in town." She prayed again for guidance. She saw that she could do nothing but try to proceed as if nothing unusual had happened. "I need a few things at the store before we head back to my homestead."

She looked at the boy and his basic needs were too plain. He needed clothing, food and a bath. The first was a good place to start. "Mr. Merriday, I think I should stop and purchase some fabric for new clothes for your . . . for Jacque." The last words were more an order than information.

Brennan stared at her as if she were speaking Chinese.

She sent him a silent message with her expression, telling him to command himself. Now. She resisted the impulse to draw near and touch his good arm.

"That's right, boy. Go with Miss Rachel," he said and turned away.

Rachel watched him head for the saloon and sighed deeply but quietly. *Not the best choice, Brennan Merriday.*

Touching the boy's thin, boney shoulder, she urged him to follow her into the store. There she tried to behave as if suddenly having a boy with her was an everyday occurrence. All three of the Ashfords, as well as Posey and her grandmother, stood behind the counter, gawking impolitely. This stiffened her instinct to protect the child.

"Mr. Ashford, I need some cloth to make this boy a new shirt and pants." Mr. Ashford helped her choose suitable dark fabric and Mrs. Ashford helped her figure out how much she would need for the new garments.

Then Rachel ordered more flour and sugar as she had planned. On the way out, she noted the boy looking at the candy display. "Don't worry, Jacque. I have sponge candy at home. Needs somebody to eat it."

She handed him the brown paper wrapped package of fabric and walked him to her cart.

She motioned for him to put the package on the empty, cloth-covered trays. "Will thee push the cart? Home isn't far."

As they passed the saloon, the urge to march inside and collar Brennan Merriday nearly turned her from her path. Instead, she faced forward and guided Jacque toward home. Some food, some gentle conversation, some candy— that was all she could provide for this child. She hoped it would be enough to help. *Mr. Merriday, is this your son?*

Brennan stood at the bar, staring at Sam, unable to talk.

"What is it, Merriday?" Sam asked with concern. "You look like you seen a ghost."

Brennan's mind felt like scrambled eggs. He braced his good palm against the bar, trying to get hold of himself. He'd sought this place to hide while he dealt with this turn of events. The expression on Miss Rachel's face when she heard Jean Pierre . . . He shook his head as if that would shake it loose.

"Is that kid really yours?" Levi in his leather apron asked the words before he even cleared the doorway.

"What kid?" Sam asked. "What did I miss?"

Brennan stared at the blacksmith he'd come to like and shook his head as if coming up from underwater. Was this boy his? "Gotta go."

He started up the road toward Miss Rachel's at full steam but faltered, his mind dragging him back in time. Something like the Gulf surf roared in his ears. His senses reeled. As from far away he glimpsed familiar faces, then the blows began falling on him, forcing him to fight . . .

He shouted aloud, "No!"

The present sounds returned to normal, birds in the trees, squirrels chattering. The roaring in his ears receded. He bent and braced his good hand on his knee, panting for air. The urge to turn and run and keep running rolled over him. He stood his ground.

Could it be possible? Had Lorena borne him a son before she died? When he'd gone back to Mississippi after the war, why hadn't anybody told him? He recalled the bitter words and the sneering faces he'd encountered while trying to find out if his wife still lived and if she needed anything. They'd told him Lorena had died and they had literally run him out of town at gunpoint.

And now he must face this child who—if he was really his son—probably hated him, too. And what did Miss Rachel think about him and this boy?

Wondering when Mr. Merriday would appear, Rachel halted Jacque at her door, seizing upon everyday needs to show her concern. Brennan must face this problem, but would he?

"Jacque, please wash thy hands before entering."

She gestured toward the outdoor washbasin with its bar of yellow soap and linen towel on the peg.

"Why?"

"Because I promised thee sponge candy and one must eat only with clean hands."

The boy began to wash his hands that appeared to have several layers of dirt on them.

When he reached for the towel before he'd worked his way through all the layers, she shook her head. "Keep washing till they are completely clean."

He glared at her but obeyed, his stomach growling. Finally clean skin appeared.

Rachel nodded.

He dried his hands and stalked into her cabin.

"Come back and toss the water onto my flowers," she said, standing patiently outside.

He did so, glaring more, his stomach growling more.

Then she motioned him inside. "I think more than just candy would be good for thee. Nibble on this while I fry some eggs." She handed him a cinnamon roll.

He ate it in two bites, standing.

"Sit at the table, please." Then she set her cast-iron skillet back on her stove, stirred up the fire and began cracking eggs. She stopped at four, not wanting to make him sick. The boy looked starved. "Hard or soft?"

"Hard."

She soon set a plate with the four fried eggs and another cinnamon roll in front of him. She added a glass of fresh milk from deep in her root cellar.

Before she finished her silent grace, Jacque began to gobble the food.

She studied his face, trying to discern any resemblance to Mr. Merriday. "Slow down, please. There will be two more meals today and snacks if thee needs them."

"You talk funny."

"Thee do also," she replied, alluding to his thick Southern accent. "Slow down and chew the food. Don't make thyself sick."

"You're not my aunt or anythin'." He sent her an aggrieved look.

Rachel reached over and pulled the plate from him. "I am the one who cooked breakfast. Sitting at my table means obeying the rules of this house. Clean hands to eat with and chew the food."

The boy glared at her, then muttered, "Yes, miss."

She slid the plate back to him.

He began eating again, but marginally slower.

She wanted to ask him questions but decided not to. She needed to talk to Brennan first and find out where this boy had come from.

As if he heard her thoughts, Brennan appeared in her doorway, his hat in hand. "Miss Rachel."

"Has thee eaten breakfast, Mr. Merriday?" she asked, hiding how her heart sped up at the sight of him.

Her question evidently prompted his stomach to growl. "No, miss."

She set another two cinnamon rolls on a plate and poured some coffee that had been keeping warm and then sat down at the table again.

Brennan stepped outside and she could hear him washing his hands. Then he entered, hung his hat and sat down beside Jacque.

"You gotta wash yer hands, too?" Jacque asked, sounding put out.

"That's her rule. You eat at Miss Rachel's table, you wash your hands."

Rachel stifled a grin, but her pulse still beat faster, though she couldn't say why it should. "Jacque, done with breakfast?"

"Yes, ma'am, I mean, Miss Rachel."

"Come here then." She motioned for him to come around to her. "As promised" she offered him a piece of sponge candy, which disappeared instantly. "Now I need to measure thee for thy new clothes." Rising, she began measuring the boy's skinny arms, then scrawny chest, waist and legs with a tape measure from her sewing box. Since she'd be fattening him up—she hoped— she'd make the seam allowances wider than usual to be let out later.

Mr. Merriday's gaze followed her every move. She forced herself not to look back at him. "The clothing should be done by Sunday for church." Suddenly she needed time to sort all this out, figure out how she should feel about this.

She turned to Brennan, who rose. "I know thy wrist is still swollen, but why not take Jacque and mark off my garden? He could begin turning over the sod."

Brennan gazed at her. Miss Rachel had fed the boy and was sewing for him. But now she had informed him it was his turn to deal with the boy. He sucked it up. "Sounds right. Boy, why don't you go out to the lean-to and find the shovel there?"

Jacque looked disgruntled but obeyed, his hands shoved in his pockets.

When they were alone, Brennan looked across the table. Miss Rachel sat again and gestured for him to sit also. He obeyed reluctantly.

"Evidently thee wished to speak to me alone?" she asked coolly.

No, he didn't really want to speak to her alone, not about this. Brennan didn't know what to say so he said the first thing that came to mind. "I didn't mean to burden you more. My wrist is sprained and now the boy . . ."

She gazed across to him. "Is it likely that this boy is thy blood?"

Leave it to Miss Rachel to cut to the marrow. "Could be." He knew he should tell her about Lorena, about what had happened to tear them apart. He couldn't. He had no words to express that dark time.

"It is really none of my business. But a child complicates . . ."

He looked at her, willing her to be silent. *Don't tell me what I already know.*

She tightened her lips. "Very well. I will not press thee now."

He heard the remaining sentence she did not voice—*but we will talk about this, and soon.*

He rose, grabbed his hat from the peg and headed outside, nearly running.

"Come on, Jacque!" he called in the yard, feeling something near hysteria building in his stomach. Why hadn't the past stayed in the past? But it wasn't the child's fault, none of this was. "We'll pace off the garden and start you diggin'."

The two of them began walking to the back of the clearing.

"Isn't it late to be planting?" the boy asked, sounding annoyed. "She should have planted in March."

"She didn't live here in March. She came in June like I did. We're just going to start turning up the soil for next year." Was this silly conversation real?

"This ain't gonna be much of a garden," the boy said, looking at the trees surrounding them. "And everything looks burned up, dry."

"True." Brennan cradled his aching wrist close to his chest, holding in his agitation. "Let's pace out the boundaries and get started."

120

The boy stood, leaning on the shovel handle. "What did you do to your hand?"

"I sprained my wrist." He stared at the boy, his curiosity sparking. "What's your whole name?"

"Jacque Louis Charpentier."

Charpentier had been Lorena's maiden name. "Who was your mother?"

"You heard who my ma was."

"Do you remember her?"

"No."

"When'd she die?"

"During the war."

"So what year were you born?"

The boy gave him a sarcastic look. "Fall of '61, the year the war started."

Brennan stared at him, searching for something of himself in the boy's face.

"Do ya'll want me to dig this or not?" the boy demanded.

"Dig." Brennan experienced a sudden weakness that had more to do with shock over this new revelation than anything else. He moved into the shade of a nearby oak and settled onto the rough, wild grass. That Lorena had taken back her maiden name didn't surprise him. And perhaps he shouldn't be surprised that she'd borne him a son and never tried to let him know.

But if they hadn't wanted the boy when Brennan returned after the war, why wait till now? Had

Jean Pierre brought him someone else's child who didn't remember his mother as a final kick in the gut, a final insult?

What did Miss Rachel think of this? And why did that matter so much to him?

Rachel had smoothed out the heavy cotton fabric for Jacque's new clothing on her table and was calmly fashioning a pattern from brown wrapping paper. Inwardly she roiled, trying to come up with an explanation for what had happened in town. Was Jacque really Brennan's son? Why did she keep asking herself that question?

"Hello the house!" said a feminine voice that sounded familiar as she voiced the usual frontier greeting.

Rachel rose and peered out the open door and saw Posey, the new girl in town, had come again to call. "Oh, hello," she said, trying to hide her lack of welcome.

"A letter came for you today so I told Cousin Ned I'd be happy to bring it." Posey held up the letter as she approached.

The joy of receiving a letter zinged through Rachel. She beamed. "Come in, Posey."

The young woman did so and handed her the letter.

"Please be seated." Rachel didn't apologize, just slit open the letter with a kitchen knife and read it.

July 1871
Dear Daughter,
We were relieved thee reached Cousin Noah's family in Pepin safely. Thy stepmother and I are in good health as are thy sisters. We are going to be blessed again near the end of the year with another child, God willing. Here are notes from thy younger sisters.

Then she read the notes written in childish printing:

Our dog misses thee. The cats looked all over for thee.
Love,
Hannah

I cried for two days when thee left.
Love,
Elizabeth

I MISS THEE AND SO DOES SARA.
LOVE,
MARTHA

Then her father's script resumed.

Your obedient servant,
Jeremiah Woolsey

A pang of homesickness tangled around Rachel's lungs. *I miss thee, too.* "It's from my family. I have four younger stepsisters." And perhaps another on the way. Her father sounded as if he missed her, too.

"A letter from home is always good. What are your sisters' names?"

"They are Hannah, Elizabeth, Martha and baby Sara." Each name pinched her heart. *I do love them, Father. Keep them safe.*

"Those are pretty names."

Wanting to get some distance from this emotional topic, she said, "Posey is a pretty name. Who chose it?"

"When I was born, my pa said I was as pretty as a posey." The young woman grinned shyly.

"Very true." Smiling politely, Rachel folded her letter and slid it into her writing box that sat on a shelf near the window. She suddenly felt tired.

"Where is the new boy?" Posey asked, looking around.

Ah, gossip. Was that Posey's true purpose in coming? "Jacque and Mr. Merriday are out making me a small garden." Rachel began working on the pattern for the pants again.

"Is that for the boy?"

Rachel only nodded, discouraging talk about Jacque.

"If you like, I can make a pattern for the shirt.

At home I often sewed for boys. I took in sewing with my mother."

"How kind." Rachel pushed a sheet of brown paper and another pencil to the girl. "If thee has the time?" *But I won't give thee any information to spread around. I don't have any.*

Posey sighed. "I'm not needed at the store or above it. Four women in one house." She shook her head.

Rachel read more in the tone of the girl's voice than the actual words. Had Posey delivered the letter as a way to get out of the store? Rachel didn't blame her. Mrs. Ashford and the girl's grandmother would be a daunting pair.

Wondering how Brennan was doing behind the house, Rachel opened her roomy sewing box and removed a paper of straight pins. "Is thee going to be visiting the Ashfords for long?"

Posey stared down at the brown paper and began measuring with a tape and drawing the outline of a shirt, glancing at the dimensions Rachel had jotted in one corner. "We aren't visiting. We've come to stay."

"Really?" Rachel tried to keep sympathy out of her tone. She wouldn't want to have to move in with the Ashfords. Rachel borrowed the tape measure and checked the dimensions of the pants. Mr. Merriday's shocked face kept coming to mind. The public scene had stirred up something troubling him. She wished she didn't feel as much concern as she did. *He's leaving.*

"We lived in northern Tennessee but when the war started, we moved to Kentucky." Posey glanced up. "We didn't own slaves, and we were against secession. My father settled us in a boardinghouse and joined the Kentucky Militia. My mother and I made a living sewing and helping the lady who ran the boardinghouse. We were hoping to go back to our home after the war."

"But that didn't happen?" Rachel had heard variations of this story at home and on her way here, her sympathy caught. Had the war spared anybody? Again her mind thought of Mr. Merriday's ravaged expression.

"Father was killed in the war. Afterward, we were afraid to go back to Tennessee. We heard Northern sympathizers were lynched. And Pa fought for the Union so . . ."

"I'm so sorry." And Rachel truly was. The war had brought so much suffering and death. The two out back digging her garden included. She measured a yard and then two by holding the fabric from her nose to her outstretched hand.

"My mother died earlier this year and that ended my father's army pension."

Though grieved by Posey's story, Rachel found her mind laboring over how to help Mr. Merriday. But perhaps this was beyond her power. She sighed and began pinning the paper pattern to the cotton.

"Grandmother decided that we should come north to our cousins and hope that they could help me find a husband. Grandmother said that many men are moving north and west to homestead on free land, make a new start, and would need a wife."

Rachel heard the shame and worry wrapped around each of the girl's words. Heaven knew she had enough to keep her busy with her business and now this unexpected child, but she would try to help Posey discover how to make her way in the world.

Perhaps marriage would be the best solution for Posey, but certainly not marriage solely out of necessity. Rachel had escaped the latter and wouldn't let it happen to this young woman.

"Mr. Merriday's given name is Brennan?" Posey asked, a sudden departure from the topic.

"Yes, Brennan Merriday." Rachel looked at the girl. Did she think to marry Brennan Merriday? She pricked her finger with a straight pin.

"His name is an unusual one. It sounds familiar somehow."

Rachel glanced at the young woman who in turn was busy sketching in marks for buttonholes on the brown wrapping paper. Her mind wandered. If Brennan hadn't sprained his wrist, he would have departed by now. Would Brennan leave and take the boy with him? A totally new feeling rolled through her, a kind of dread mixed with hope.

She didn't want Brennan to leave and now that Jacque had come perhaps he wouldn't.

With a burst of insight, she admitted this to herself. A startling revelation. And she acknowledged that this was more than just about her losing his help. She didn't want to lose Brennan Merriday. *I have feelings for him.* She stood stock-still as waves of shock rolled over her.

Rachel experienced a kind of swirling in her head. Too much had happened and everything had been upended. She gasped, trying to catch her breath. She couldn't. She was breathing too fast.

Suddenly Posey came very close. "Miss Rachel." Then the girl blew into her face. "You're not getting enough air. Miss Rachel!" The girl grabbed Rachel's wrists and pulled her to sit. "Miss Rachel!"

Rachel inhaled deeply and then coughed, shuddered.

Posey patted her on the back. "Are you all right?"

Rachel nodded, far from all right.

She did not want Brennan Merriday out of her life. That much had come clear—disturbing but clear. "I'm fine. Sorry."

"Mama breathed too fast like that when we got word of my father's death," Posey said sadly. "I was afraid you'd faint."

"I never faint." *I've never become attached to a man either.*

Finally Rachel persuaded Posey to go home.

Rachel sat outside on a chair in the shade of one of the tall maples on the edge of her clearing, fretting. She forced herself to go on slipping her fine needle in and out of the stiff cloth, trying not to think of Mr. Merriday, yet straining to hear the sound of his voice from behind the cabin. Would he stay now that the boy had come? She tried to control how her heart lifted at this thought. *I must not let myself hope that.*

Chapter Six

The sun had lowered when she heard Mr. Merriday and the boy join her in the shade. She kept her gaze on her sewing, afraid Brennan might read her feelings for him in her expression. She couldn't imagine the humiliation of caring for a man uninterested in her. Whatever happened, he must never know.

"Jacque, I should have thy new clothing done soon," she said mildly, her heart thrumming in her ears. Mr. Merriday's presence stirred her, waking her somehow. She clung to her self-control.

"Yes, miss," Jacque said in a tone that showed no interest.

Brennan slid his back down the tree.

Her awareness of him slid higher.

"We dug some of the garden—" Brennan started.

"*I* dug some of the garden," Jacque interrupted Brennan.

"Don't correct thy elders," Rachel said out of habit, a scold she'd used on her younger sisters. Tension crackled between the two males. It added to her own. She changed topics, as keeping words flowing provided her some cover. "I received a letter from home today."

"Oh," Brennan said flatly.

His attitude doused her like cold water. She was never one to ignore matters—why should she now? "Jacque," she said, setting down her sewing, "I am going to give thee a towel and soap. Go to the creek and take a bath."

"I'd like a swim," Jacque said, eyeing her.

"The creek is shallow but do thy best." She went inside and came out with the towel and soap. "Don't lose the soap in the creek. And don't forget to wash behind the ears, the back of the neck, and hair."

"I won't." He grabbed the towel and took off running in the direction Brennan had told him.

Brennan had risen when she had. Not meeting his gaze, she returned to her place on her chair and he eased back onto the wild grass and leaned against the tree trunk.

His nearness still affected her, but she bolstered

her resolve. "Is Jacque thy son?" she pressed him again, taking up her needle and thread again, voicing the question perhaps uppermost in both their minds.

Brennan stared forward and did not reply with even a change of expression. The lowering sun glinted on the highlights in his hair. He needed a trim and she nearly reached out to lift the hair hanging over his collar.

"What business is it of yours?" he grumbled.

Instead of biting off his head, she bit off a thread. "I am merely concerned." Not the truth, she admitted to herself. "I am not a gossip." That much was true.

"He could be my son," Brennan allowed grudgingly. "The time works out right."

"I see." That was all he was going to say? Obviously Brennan Merriday didn't want to tell her—now. And did she want him to open up to her? Wouldn't it be better to try to go back to where they had been—if possible?

She made a cold supper for them. Jacque ate his fill and then fell asleep, his damp head buried on his arms at the table. In the stillness broken by the sound of frogs at the nearby creek, Rachel tried not to stare at Mr. Merriday across the table from her. And failed.

Worry lines bisected his forehead and his shoulders looked tense. Again she resisted the impulse to touch his arm, speak comfort to him. She would have to fight these foolish tendencies or he might leave that much sooner just to get away from her. She endured a sharp twinge around her heart.

"I don't know what to think," he said out of the blue.

She didn't pretend to misunderstand him. "Today was a shock. But remember it was a shock to Jacque, as well." She frowned deeply, feeling the hard lines in her face. "That man, that Jean Pierre, will reap a bitter harvest from his unkindness. Such public cruelty."

"He did it to shame me."

"And without a thought for the child." The unkindness sliced Rachel to the heart. She knew Brennan would never abandon a child or treat anyone so thoughtlessly. Under his gruff exterior, Brennan had an innate honor. "This boy has lost much and he's so young."

"I get your meanin'." Brennan rose. "I'll take him to my loft."

Rachel nearly objected. She had room for the boy, but he wasn't hers. The chasm between her feelings for this man and what was appropriate in this situation spread further apart. "I'll loan a pillow and blanket for him."

"Much obliged." Brennan shook the boy's shoulder.

Jacque looked up, blinking.

"Take the pillow from Miss Rachel. We'll head home now."

"Don't you live here?" the boy said, knuckling his eyes.

"No, that wouldn't be proper. I live above the blacksmith shop," Brennan said, accepting the light cotton blanket she offered him.

Rachel watched them walk down the track to town till they vanished from her sight. She wished to help but Brennan plainly had told her to keep her nose out of his business. Until he left town, though, he was her business. How did one stop having feelings for a man? He was a totally unsuitable man yet that didn't make any difference to her heart.

Brennan's nerves still stuttered from the scene earlier that day on Main Street. He led this boy he didn't know, but who might be his only family, through the trees and the deserted town to the silent blacksmith shop. They found Levi sitting on his one chair, looking out over the river.

A refreshing breeze blew over them, dissipating the heat from the forge. But Brennan's stomach felt loaded with lead. What would come next? And for some reason he couldn't stop thinking about Miss Rachel.

Levi sat forward. "Well, hello. I'm Levi Comstock."

Brennan appreciated Levi's uncomplicated

greeting. Both Levi and Miss Rachel could be counted on for kindness. Miss Rachel's face, surrounded by delicate wisps of her light hair, came to mind, drawing him back. He hadn't wanted to leave her, hadn't wanted to take full charge of this child tonight. After fighting in the war and drifting for years, he was completely unprepared to be a father.

Jacque merely nodded to Levi.

"Boy, when a man introduces himself, you say your name and call him sir," Brennan said sternly.

Jacque threw Brennan a scalding look. "I'm Jacque Charpentier, sir."

Levi offered his hand and shook the boy's. "Nice to meet you, Jacque."

Brennan noted Levi raised a quizzical eyebrow, more than Miss Rachel had done. She'd been mighty cool about everything. That stuck in his craw.

"Jacque, I'll show you where we bed down." Brennan walked him inside and waved him up the ladder to the loft. "You'll see my bedroll up there. There's a good breeze so you'll do okay. Be up later."

Jacque raised a shoulder in reply and with his bedding over his other shoulder climbed the ladder. At that moment, Brennan recalled what Miss Rachel had said. *This boy has lost much and he's so young.*

His conscience clipped him hard. "Jacque," Brennan said, making his voice kinder, "everything will work out."

The boy didn't even pause on his way up the ladder.

Brennan didn't blame Jacque for doubting him. *What does he know of me but what's been told him, and none of it good?* Brennan's stomach burned, as he thought about all the lies this boy had probably heard about the man who might be his father. Or had they told him nothing except that Brennan was a coward? Miss Rachel's face kept coming to mind. The good woman she was, she'd been concerned for the boy. Her sweet voice played in his mind.

Outside again, Brennan stooped with his back propped against the rough log wall.

"Charpentier?" Levi asked.

"My wife's maiden name."

Levi looked at him, expecting more.

Brennan stared at the wide river. He could not speak of this now. Again, he wished he could speak frankly to Miss Rachel. She saw human nature clearly, but Jacque wasn't her responsibility.

"You see that new gal in town?" Levi asked finally.

Brennan thought for a moment, his mind a jumble. "You mean Posey?"

"Yeah, she's a pretty little thing."

Brennan looked sideways at the man, relieved to discuss something else. "You lonely?"

"I have been hoping some young ladies would move here, but so far it's only been little girls, couples or single men. If I'd stayed in Illinois, I could have found a wife easy."

Brennan went along, a welcome distraction. "Why didn't you stay in Illinois then?"

Levi frowned. "I wanted to have my own shop. Too many blacksmiths in Illinois."

"And a lot of women." Brennan eased his own mind by teasing the blacksmith.

"But most of them are too hoity-toity to move to the frontier. They want board sidewalks and hat shops."

This forced a laugh from Brennan, a release of tension.

"It's not funny. I want a regular cabin and a wife to snuggle up to in the long winter ahead."

Brennan shrugged. "I wish you luck."

"You don't think your Miss Rachel is interested in getting married, do you?"

Brennan snorted in response; unreasonable irritation sparked within. "Told me she's not getting married," he said, warning the man away.

"Women say that, but do they mean that? She's a great cook and as neat as wax. Pretty, too. She just don't take pains to look it."

This aggravated Brennan. He had no right but it irked him to have another man notice how quietly pretty she was. "You can try, but I doubt she'll come around. She . . . she sounds like some man insulted her by offering marriage . . . for *his* convenience. Had a passel of kids he needed a ma for."

"Ah." The sound conveyed that Levi had no idea what Brennan was talking about and Brennan didn't feel like telling more. Miss Rachel's business was hers alone.

"Women don't like it if you start paying attention to one woman and then switch to another," Levi commented. "You know what I mean?"

Brennan did, but had bigger problems of his own.

"I think I'll start trying to get to know Miss Posey Brown. She's younger and tries to look pretty. That's a sign she's not adverse to marriage." Levi glanced at Brennan. "Wouldn't you say?"

Brennan let out a long breath. Levi was never this talkative. "What've you got to lose?" Brennan asked.

He'd once been so in love and look how it had all turned out. If there hadn't been slavery, abolition, secession, would he and Lorena have done better? The sad truth was in this fiery world, love lasted as long as tissue paper. So letting himself begin to care at all for the Quakeress was more than foolish.

· · ·

When Brennan woke the next morning, he found a thin small body pressed against his right side. He jerked more wide awake, hurt his sprained wrist and cursed under his breath.

Jacque rolled away from him with a stifled yelp of surprise. For a moment the boy looked as if he didn't know where he was.

The panic in his eyes stabbed Brennan; he regretted disturbing the child. "You're in Wisconsin with me, Jacque," he said in a voice he wished sounded more comforting.

The boy lost the panicked look but did not appear very reassured.

"Now, we get up and wash in the river and then go to Miss Rachel's for breakfast."

Jacque nodded. "She cooks good."

"You don't know the half of it yet," he said with deep sincerity. He cradled his aching wrist to himself. After a sleepless night, he felt like a limp piece of rag, and what unexpected unpleasantness might come today?

Soon, the two of them walked through town. Brennan tried not to notice how people, sweeping the steps of their cabins, stopped to gawk. What did he care? What were they to him? He'd be gone before long.

Brennan stumbled on a rock that had rolled onto the path. The false step jiggled his sore wrist. He gritted his teeth. His wrist would heal in its own good time and this matter with the child would have to work its own way out. But how?

After eating a breakfast of scrambled eggs with fried salt pork and buttered toast, Brennan rose to thank Miss Rachel for another good meal.

"How is the wrist?" she replied, already turning to her stove.

He glanced down at his hand. "Still stiff."

She came to him and slid his arm from the sling. Her touch was gentle, nonetheless it rocked him to his core.

"It's mending," he muttered, withdrawing abruptly from her touch. A moment of strained silence passed.

She looked to Jacque. "I'll do the milking again, but I could use this young man to collect the eggs this morning and then scatter chicken feed. Why doesn't thee go rest in the shade, Mr. Merriday? Rest will make the wrist heal quicker."

And then what? he asked silently. This is what happened when a man stayed in one place too long and got comfortable. He pulled back mentally from this cozy woman.

Jacque accepted the basket she handed him and headed out for the chicken coop and yard to look for eggs. Hens could be foolish and lay eggs outside, too.

Brennan put on his hat and followed the boy into the summer day. He sat on the grass under a shade tree, watching the boy gather eggs. The sun was rising and the heat was, too. His eyelids felt heavy and sleep would keep him from thinking thoughts of Miss Rachel he had no right to think.

"Mr. Merriday!" Miss Rachel's voice cut through Brennan's morning nap.

He jolted awake and bumped the back of his head against the rough tree trunk and rubbed it. "Miss?"

"Where is Jacque?"

Blinking at the bright sun beyond the shade, Brennan scanned the clearing. "I musta fell asleep."

"Thee looked exhausted at breakfast. Healing takes energy, too."

And last night I didn't sleep worth a Confederate dollar. He got up quicker than he should have and jiggled his wrist again. He clamped his lips together to keep in an exclamation of pain and refused to look at her. "When did you see him last?"

"He brought in the egg basket full. Then I gave him the feed to scatter for the chickens. I'm about to make lunch so I came out and I've looked all over the clearing and haven't been able to find him."

Brennan stared at her. Was this just kid folly or had the boy run off? In either case, he couldn't think what to do.

Miss Rachel looked skyward. "He might have gone looking for someone to play with."

"I'll go into town and look for him," Brennan said.

She frowned at him and didn't move, just tapped her cheek with one finger.

For some reason this irritated him. "Do ya'll want the boy back or not?"

She looked at him, chin down, almost frowning, that finger still tapping.

He read her look as her repeating his question back at him—did he want the boy? He had a strong urge to yell in frustration.

"Perhaps I'll go into town—" she began.

"I'll go. He's my . . . responsibility." With that Brennan turned and headed down the trail to town. His insides bubbled like a pot of grits. Whether Jacque was his blood or not, he couldn't just let the boy run into trouble.

Rachel watched him go, holding herself back from giving advice or tagging along. Mr. Merriday would have to come to terms with this child himself. Still, as she walked inside to start her next chore, she fretted and couldn't think of anything else but Mr. Merriday and Jacque.

In a few minutes a voice came through the open door. "Miss Rachel?"

Rachel moved to peer outside. The storekeeper's

teenage daughter stood there. "Come in," Rachel said, trying to sound sincerely welcoming.

"I'm Amanda Ashford, Miss Rachel," the girl reminded her.

"Yes, hello, Amanda," Rachel said, hoping the girl would come to the point of her visit. She'd decided to work on her sewing. No use making lunch till Brennan came back with the boy.

"My pa sent me to tell you a boat has come in and people are asking for the sweets lady."

"I didn't hear a whistle."

The girl shrugged. "The boat is stopping long enough for you to come. They are delivering a shipment to my father's store."

Rachel didn't answer with words. She dropped her sewing and turned to the kitchen and began wrapping the fresh-cut caramel squares in wax paper.

"I'll help."

"Wash thy hands first," Rachel said out of habit.

Soon Amanda stood beside her and without asking for instructions, she began to mimic Rachel, rolling the caramel into small squares of wax paper and then twisting the ends.

Soon they filled a basket and headed out the door, striding briskly to town. "I overslept so I don't have any rolls ready," Rachel admitted.

Amanda fiddled with her apron pocket, looking as if she had something to say.

Rachel asked finally, "Is there something I can help thee with, Amanda?"

"I heard about how good your baked goods and candies are."

"Yes," Rachel prompted.

Amanda glanced up. "Would you teach me how to make some?"

Rachel hesitated. Mrs. Ashford might take her daughter coming to Rachel as an insult. "Does thy mother know thee has come to ask me this?"

"No." Amanda looked down at her feet.

So Amanda had the same worry about her mother's reaction. Fortunately, they had reached town and she was able to sidestep the issue. Ahead boatmen unloaded sacks and boxes at the side door of the General Store. Mr. Ashford stood over them with a ledger where he was making notes. And milling in front of the store was what appeared to be a group of passengers.

"This is Miss Rachel!" Amanda called out. "She has fresh caramels for sale!"

The passengers met them in the street in front of the store. "Is your stuff as good as we've heard?" one sour-looking woman asked.

Rachel smiled. "Thee will have to find out. A penny a piece."

A man held out a coin. "A nickel's worth please, miss."

Rachel slipped the coin into her pocket and then handed the man the caramels.

He unwrapped one immediately and popped it into his mouth. He moaned a sound of pleasure. "It's still warm in the center."

At this, everyone was pressing coins on her. Without being asked, Amanda began collecting the money and Rachel doled out the candy. The basket emptied completely within minutes.

The people moved away and she glanced at Amanda. "I thank thee. It is obvious thee is the daughter of a storekeeper."

Amanda blushed with pleasure. In a low voice, she asked, "Will you think about teaching me to bake? I want to be a really good baker."

Rachel thought of how the girl's know-it-all mother would respond to clandestine lessons. But of course, she couldn't say that. "I will give it thought." She smiled her thanks again and then looked around.

Now that the rush was over, her concern over Jacque returned. "I'm looking for Mr. Merriday and Jacque."

"I saw Jacque and Johann go toward the schoolyard."

"Johann?"

"Johann Lang. He's Gunther Lang's nephew."

"Oh." Rachel recognized the family mentioned. "I wonder if Mr. Merriday found Jacque there."

"Did the boy run away?" Amanda asked, sounding shocked and a little interested, reminding Rachel of her mother.

Trying to protect Brennan and Jacque from gossip, Rachel chuckled. "Most likely Jacque did his chores and then decided he deserved some fun." She waved to Amanda and then set off toward the schoolyard. She should have headed home, but couldn't bring herself to turn around. She wanted to see if this simple solution was correct.

Before she reached the edge of town, she heard Jacque's voice. "Let me go!"

"You're going home to apologize to Miss Rachel for runnin' off like that. You finish a chore and then you ask if the lady needs anything more before you run off to find fun." Appearing on the trail south of town, Brennan gripped the boy by the upper arm and was tugging him away from the direction of the schoolyard.

"I don't have to do what you tell me! You're not my pa!"

Rachel froze in place. This was not something she wanted aired on the main street of town.

She hurried forward to the two. "Jacque, we were looking for you! It's time we go home for some lunch." She formed a completely false smile with her lips.

Both males glared at her. Brennan's face was beet-red. Jacque's face defined the term *stormy*.

"Well, come along," she prompted and waved them forward.

The two didn't budge.

She tried to come up with a way to get them moving toward home. People were staring. She glanced down and saw that one caramel had been overlooked even by her. She held it up. "I have a caramel for a boy to eat after lunch," she coaxed.

Jacque's sweet tooth won the day. He hurried forward and Brennan followed. She sighed with relief as she led the two through town feeling a bit like the Pied Piper.

Jacque's words—*I don't have to do what you tell me! You're not my pa!*—echoed in her mind.

I don't have to do what you tell me! You're not my pa! rang in Brennan's mind. Was it the truth or just a retort? He doubted the child even knew the truth.

The three of them sat at Miss Rachel's table, eating a generous lunch of canned beef sandwiches on thick, delicious bread. At first, he didn't even taste what he was eating, but then he realized the sandwich had been made with the best spicy mustard he'd ever tried. Finally this came to the surface of his mind. "Did you make this mustard?"

"Yes, I brought one jar with me. We need to find if there's any wild mustard growing nearby so I can make more. In fact, you and Jacque might go looking for some today. There is a meadow north of town, I've heard."

Was there anything good to eat this woman

couldn't make? He realized again that he respected Miss Rachel Woolsey, not just for her considerable cooking talent but for herself. She was a fine woman.

As she explained to Jacque what a wild mustard plant looked like, he found himself studying her face. Her gray eyes opened wide to the world. He found a small mole by her right ear he hadn't noticed before and a few tiny golden freckles that had popped up on her nose.

"Mr. Merriday, I think we'll all rest a bit till the sun lowers. The heat today is too high for much work. It's not healthy."

"What do I have to do then?" the boy asked, still sounding disgruntled.

"Rest in the shade. That is my plan."

Jacque looked as if he might protest but then he just shrugged. He rose.

"Jacque, you should ask to be excused before you leave the table," Brennan ordered.

Jacque glared at the reminder. "Miss Rachel, will you excuse me?"

"Thee may leave the table and find a tree to rest under." She rose and stacked the few dishes and carried them outside to wash.

Brennan felt bad he wasn't able to carry them for her. He lingered beside her, unable to leave. Somehow being near Miss Rachel made life feel easier. While he felt torn up inside, she possessed a deep peace. It drew him.

She glanced up from the washbasin. "Thee is troubled?" Her voice was a whisper.

He nodded, his tongue like a board.

"I do not think there is any way we can know for certain that this child is thy blood. Thee must make the decision to accept him or not." She said the words plainly, gently, but uncompromisingly.

He wanted to look away from her, knew he should but found he couldn't. He nodded. "I'm going to go sit in the shade."

"I will finish this and do likewise. I thought that Wisconsin would be cooler in the summer than Pennsylvania."

He shrugged. "Feels 'most like home to me." The bitter thoughts of home pushed him away from her. He found the tree he'd patronized lately and settled under it, resting against the trunk. The dried grass crunched under him, reminding him of the rainless summer.

Jacque had chosen a tree near the springhouse and looked to be playing with twigs and pebbles as if fighting a play battle.

Brennan closed his eyes. He didn't want to think but the ideas from the past days swirled in his head. What was he to believe? And what was he to do about it? And how could he stop himself from drawing closer to Miss Rachel? She didn't need him or deserve his troubles.

Chapter Seven

After a late supper Brennan walked Jacque back to town to get the boy to bed. Jacque had washed up in the creek and was already rubbing his eyes and dragging his feet. Brennan's midsection still roiled with confusion and his mind was a tornado of conflicting thoughts. Was Miss Rachel right? Would he just have to accept the child as his? Was there no way to find out the truth about this young'un?

They found the forge empty. With relief Brennan sent Jacque up the ladder with only a wave of his good arm. Then tired but restless, he went outside to gaze at the wide river, hoping for some easing of his turmoil. The Mississippi was his old friend. He'd fished and swam in it as a boy. In the end it had saved his life that awful day in '61.

Forcing out the past and his own confusion, he concentrated on the blue water, now shadowed by the trees on the bank, the eddies swirling near the shore around rocks and driftwood—mesmerizing. A sandbar stretched in a long oval near the middle, and gulls hopped there, eating insects.

Still worry pecked its way in. If it weren't for his wrist and the boy, he'd leave town tonight and head north on foot if he had to. Brennan paced back and forth, telling himself he could not leave, not now, not without a word to Miss Rachel.

The faint sound of a female laugh lifted Brennan from his thoughts. He looked for the source of this interruption and glimpsed Levi and Miss Posey Brown farther up the shore, walking together. At the romantic sight, a sour taste rolled over Brennan's tongue, his agitation leaping higher, sharper.

So Levi was making up to Miss Posey. Brennan watched them; the way they moved, careful not to brush against each other, her head bent coyly. He could almost imagine their conversation, a lot of words with not much said. Just words to be spoken so they could stay together because being near one another was what it was all about.

Miss Rachel came to mind and Brennan thrust her image away, again facing the river, focusing on its steady current. His mounting tension wouldn't be denied. He began to scratch his arm at the edge of his sling. He began pacing again.

Gripping his arm so he wouldn't scratch it anymore, Brennan noted that the couple said their goodbyes at the riverside, not near the store; Levi had not yet reached the point of launching the formal courtship. That would officially start when Levi approached Mr. Ashford and asked permission to court Posey. Bitterness from the past came up, more of the sour taste on Brennan's tongue.

Brennan kept walking, gripping his arm, trying to release the tension goading him.

As Levi neared the forge with a silly grin on his face, Brennan felt one hundred, maybe two hundred years old. No part of him wanted to talk to Levi, a man who didn't realize he was like a burly lamb being led to the slaughter. Brennan swung away to go in.

Levi hailed him.

With a supreme effort, Brennan turned back, trying to ease his edgy mood with a deep breath. "Levi."

Levi grinned, obviously bursting to tell Brennan about walking with Miss Posey.

"I seen you two," Brennan said out of friendship. That surprised Brennan. He hadn't known anyone he considered a friend since the war ended and his militia company had broken up to head home. He halted.

Levi's silly grin broadened. "I saw her walking down the bank and I decided to take a chance and greet her."

Brennan reckoned the girl had probably come out for just that purpose. He knew now that men thought *they* did the courting. *Ha.* "How did it go?" Brennan forced himself to ask.

Levi sank onto his chair. "She's kind of shy and

I'm not much of a talker. But she told me about her home in Tennessee and how sad she was that they couldn't go back. I guess somebody seized their place during the war since they considered her father, who fought for the Union, a traitor to the South."

With a pang Brennan wondered who had taken over his own father's land. Had Jean Pierre told the truth? Was everyone in his and Lorena's families truly dead or scattered? He shoved his good hand through his hair. "That's too bad," Brennan said, manfully keeping up his part of the conversation.

"She sure is pretty and she has a sweet way of speaking."

Brennan thought a nod of the head would suffice for this. Then he felt an easing in his chest. Somehow speaking to this man with an uncomplicated life helped Brennan. He looked at Levi, who was staring at his sling.

"How's the wrist?" Levi asked.

Brennan had been so tangled in his inner worries, he'd forgotten all about the sprain. He moved the wrist. "Better. It's healing."

"Good. Where's the boy?"

"In the loft."

Levi looked at him, his mouth shut holding back something.

"Go ahead and spit it out," Brennan grumbled, afraid to trust the way his stress was leaking out.

He stooped down, pressing his back against the wall, breathing almost normally.

"Maybe I'm talking out of turn," Levi said with reluctance, "but I was thinking. Where the boy was born, would anybody have kept a record of his birth?"

Brennan stopped just short of rebuffing this suggestion—when it occurred to him that Lorena's family had all births and deaths recorded in the local parish church records. He knew the names of the church and the priest. "Why didn't I think of that?" He couldn't hide the rise in his voice.

Levi looked surprised but pleased that his suggestion had found favor. "You think it'll work?"

"I do." The momentary lift evaporated and fatigue from the heat and worry nearly pushed him over onto the ground. "I'm goin' up to bed." *While I can.*

" 'Night."

Brennan started up the ladder and then paused. He heard something—a whimpering sound. Was some small animal caught in a trap nearby? Then he realized it was the boy in the loft, crying. The sound caught him around the chest like a chain. Brennan looked at their situation from the boy's point of view: abandoned by family and stuck with a man he thought a coward. *Poor kid.*

Finding out one way or the other what was really true would help both him and the boy. If he found out the boy was his, he'd deal with that. If the boy wasn't his, he'd make sure the boy got a good home. Maybe with Miss Rachel?

Very, very early the next morning, Rachel stared at Amanda and Posey. The rooster had barely announced dawn. Rachel had just finished dressing and needed to start a batch of ladyfingers, a light little cake for which she'd had a few requests. And she wanted this all done before Mr. Merriday came.

She needed company now like she needed salt in her sugar.

With a fixed, intent gaze, she silently prompted the storekeeper's daughter to state her reason for coming at such an early hour. Emotion rolled inside her as she thought of Brennan and Jacque and what they'd gone through in the past few days. Would Brennan appear this morning or not?

Amanda finally broached the reason for their untimely arrival. "I was thinking we could help you this morning fixing your baked goods."

Posey stepped forward. "Miss Rachel, I come to ask if you'd teach me to bake, too."

Rachel gazed at the two hopeful faces. Though Rachel did not think Mrs. Ashford would like this, she couldn't turn the girls away.

She waved them toward the outside basin. "Always wash hands before baking."

Soon the two girls hurried inside. Each donned an apron she'd brought along.

Rachel glanced at the wall clock her grandfather had given her when she turned sixteen. She must get this batch done before the heat of the day made whipping the egg whites impossible. She showed them how to use a wire whisk and all three began beating egg whites into white glossy peaks.

Brennan and Jacque appeared at the door, earlier than expected, of course.

Immediately Rachel noted the man had something on his mind. She had come to know his moods, a dangerous realization.

If the girls hadn't been here, she'd have tried to find out immediately what concerned him. "I'm sorry, Mr. Merriday. Breakfast will be a little late—"

"Not to worry, Miss Rachel," Brennan replied. "The boy will milk the cow and get busy with chores. Call us when yer ready."

"Please check the outdoor oven and see if it's getting hot."

Brennan nodded and headed toward the back.

The egg whites whipped up pretty well though sweat beaded on the white mounds. "I must move quickly. Just watch." Rachel swiftly folded the egg whites into the dry ingredients and then loaded a pastry cloth and began piping the batter into "fingers" on baking sheets. Soon the batter had been piped onto all six pans. "Please pick up two sheets each and follow me."

The three of them marched out the back door, through the covered walkway to the outdoor oven. There the three of them shoved the sheets inside and Rachel secured the door.

Then the brusque voice of Mrs. Ashford sounded. "Where is Miss Rachel? I'm looking for my daughter and her cousin."

Rachel's stomach suffered a sudden jolt.

"Oh, no," Amanda breathed, sending Miss Rachel an imploring glance. "How did she find out where we went?"

Rachel waved for the girls to follow her and she marched back inside and began clearing away the mess from the table. If Mrs. Ashford wanted to talk to her, she would have to find her.

"Miss Woolsey," Mrs. Ashford said, standing in the doorway, "I'm looking—Oh, there you are, girls. What possessed you to come here before breakfast? I didn't know where you'd gone, but the blacksmith saw you walking this way."

Rachel couldn't come up with anything but the truth. Social prevarication was not her strong point.

"We took a walk," Posey offered.

"And then we realized Miss Woolsey was probably baking—" Amanda continued.

"So we asked if we could help," Posey finished.

"She let us help her whisk egg whites for ladyfingers."

Rachel could see the woman's mind working—Mrs. Ashford eyed the aprons the girls were wearing. They were evidence of planning to come here. And the hour was much too early for a social call, as the girls well knew. Well, this was not Rachel's doing.

"I'll bring some to the store in thanks for their help," Rachel said, hoping the three would leave—now. "I must prepare breakfast and make sure I don't let my ladyfingers burn." With that, she swept the bowls and implements from the table and set them outside in the washbasin for later.

What could Mrs. Ashford do but leave? Amanda and Posey went with her and Rachel sighed in silent relief. Dustup on her doorstep averted. She noticed that on her way through the yard, Posey said something to Brennan and he didn't look pleased. What had the girl said?

Leaving behind speculation, she cut strips of salt pork and laid them in the frying pan. Their fragrance drew in the two males. "Mr. Merriday, will thee watch these? I must go and fetch my ladyfingers before they become too brown." She hurried outside, even surer the man had something on his mind.

She returned, slid the slender little cakes onto cooling racks. Mr. Merriday brought the other trays back in two quick trips. She then finished making breakfast and asked them to be seated.

Brennan's mouth watered as he watched Miss Rachel slide four slices of crisp pork onto his plate and then add three soft fried eggs and two slices of golden toast. The boy got a smaller version for his breakfast. Brennan heard the tiny moan of pleasure the boy made. Brennan knew just how he felt. Miss Rachel had a way of making even simple food more than regular-tasting. Sitting down, Miss Rachel said grace and they began to eat.

As his hunger became satisfied, Brennan went back to ruminating about the request he must broach to this lady today. He'd have to get the boy busy doing something while he talked to her alone.

He didn't want to ask her, but his command of written English was minimal. There had been no town schools anywhere near him in Mississippi. His aunt Martha had taught him his letters and numbers and how to print them and do simple arithmetic—enough for a Mississippi farm boy.

Jacque finished his meal first and at Miss Rachel's silent prompt, wiped his face with his napkin.

"Jacque, you can go outside and start looking for eggs," Brennan instructed.

Miss Rachel raised her eyebrows but said nothing.

"Thank you, Miss Rachel, for the good eats," the boy said.

Brennan felt a tingle of pride at this show of unprompted good manners.

"Thank thee, Jacque."

The boy left, obediently carrying his plate and mug out to the basin.

"So, Mr. Merriday, while thee tells me what is on thy mind, I will take a look at that wrist."

She was a knowing woman all right. But he didn't want her fussing over him. She did anyway.

She sat on the bench beside him. She drew his arm from the sling and held his hand in both of hers.

He tried to ignore the reaction he had to her gentle but sure touch. *It's just because nobody ever touches me,* he told himself. *Especially not a pretty woman with soft hands.*

She probed carefully with both thumbs over and around his wrist, sweet agony. The scent of bacon still hung in the air but he also detected just a breath of some floral scent. Her head bent over his wrist, her soft hair grazed his nose.

"So you done fiddlin' yet?" he asked, goaded.

"The wrist appears to be healing well," she announced. "But thee hasn't told me what is on thy mind."

The time had come. He gathered his gumption. "I need," he began, "to get a letter to the parish priest in my . . . wife's hometown in Louisiana.

The priest would have a record of the boy's birth and parentage." The words had come out in a rush and he burned with embarrassment.

She gazed at him steadily in that way of hers. "I see, and with your wrist compromised it's difficult to write."

Did she believe that or was she offering him a plausible excuse for his not writing the letter? Miss Rachel was thoughtful that way.

"I'd appreciate it," he said, not saying yea or nay about his reason for asking.

"What is the name of the priest, church and town?" she asked briskly. She rose and reached for a pad of paper and pencil she kept on a shelf. She jotted down his answers. "I'll write it today and send it off. This is an excellent idea. The truth shall set us free."

He'd heard that but didn't really agree. He'd told the truth once and had nearly died for it. He stood up, galvanized. "I'm going to look for downed branches and the like with the boy. Good kindling for the winter."

She hopped up too as he'd moved the bench. "Excellent. I must be busy with my ladyfingers."

They rarely stood so close to each other and the air between them appeared to waver, an odd feeling of connection. He tried to move but was captured by the sight of little beads of perspiration on her upper lip, which drew his gaze down to her mouth as pretty as a rosebud, soft pink and . . .

Abruptly, he nodded in assent and headed straight for the door. Outside he pulled on his hat and scanned the yard. The boy was carrying a full basket of eggs toward the cabin. "Let's go. We'll gather some downed wood."

He walked rapidly toward the road and headed north of town, Jacque soon at his heels. Again he wished he'd been able to leave town when he wanted to. Without the boy here, last night he would have bolted for sure. Staying around a special woman like Miss Rachel was giving him foolish ideas.

And now he'd just asked Miss Rachel to contact Lorena's home place. This could stir up the past. Already his stomach wanted to reject his breakfast. He forced down the sensation.

He had to know if the boy was his and the boy needed to know it, too. Another worry niggled. Did Miss Rachel think him completely illiterate? Shame burned his cheeks and he lengthened his strides, hurrying the boy.

A week later Miss Rachel and Jacque stood outside, she washing and he drying the breakfast dishes.

She found herself chewing her bottom lip. This morning, First Day or what most called Sunday, she would as usual attend worship at the schoolhouse and this afternoon go to the church picnic, a social occasion where she could get to know more of her neighbors. She was trying to come up with a way to persuade Jacque and Brennan to come, too. Her earlier invitation had been met with silence. She glanced over her shoulder to where he lounged against a tree in its shade.

Brennan cleared his throat. "Jacque, I decided you're going to church and the picnic with Miss Rachel like she asked. You mind your manners. You'll like it. I remember church picnics. Lots of good food and kids playin' tag."

Jacque didn't reply, merely stared at him, looking confused.

Rachel was just as surprised. She hadn't expected him to allow Jacque to go. "Perhaps thee would like to come, too?" she asked, her heart suddenly speeding up.

"My wrist's healed and I got plans for today," he said, rising. "I'm going to take a walk. Maybe fish a bit." Then he turned and headed up the road away from town.

Unhappy with this response, Rachel handed Jacque the final spoon to dry. She looked down at him. He looked more than usually cheerful and she guessed it was because he wore his new clothing and she'd cut his hair. Worry nipped her. The scene on the main street, when that awful man had so rudely abandoned him, and Jacque's thick Southern accent, would not be ignored.

After Jacque handed her the dried spoon and emptied the dishwater onto her flowers, Rachel and he carried the clean dishware inside and set the stack on the shelf and covered it with a clean cloth.

Rachel rested a hand on Jacque's shoulder. "We will have a good day," she said more to bolster her confidence than his. "I'll get my Bible." Then the two of them walked down the track toward town.

She sighed. "Let me be frank, Jacque. Thee knows how children—and grownups, too, unfortunately—can be to strangers."

Jacque looked up and frowned.

"I remember how children always pick on anyone new or different."

Jacque shrugged. "I can take care of myself."

"Thee intends to fight anybody who is rude?" she asked without rancor.

Jacque repeated the shrug.

"I understand thee might have to . . . defend thyself, *but*—" to emphasize her point, she gripped his shoulder "—don't start the fight." She had been raised to turn the other cheek, but even Quaker boys fought with each other. "Does thee understand me, Jacque?"

He considered this. "I can fight back, but I better not take the first swing?"

"Well stated." The schoolhouse lay on the other side of the village. As they walked through town, Levi came out of his shop and joined them. Rachel nodded in reply to his greeting and noted that

Levi looked as if he'd taken special care with his appearance today. She wondered why. All the while, the fact that Mr. Merriday had not come also prodded her, drawing down her mood. Why had she even hoped he'd come?

At the door of the log schoolhouse community church, Noah waited to greet them. Rachel said, "Jacque, this is my cousin Noah Whitmore. Noah, this is Jacque."

"Hello, sir," Jacque said, but refused to look into Noah's face.

Noah gripped the boy's shoulder. "You are welcome here, Jacque."

This caused the boy to glance up at the man. Then the press of others arriving moved the two of them into the church.

Just inside the door sat Old Saul in his wheelchair. Rachel had met him again in town with Noah, who obviously held the older man in high regard and affection. So she stopped to greet him and introduce Jacque.

The older man took the boy's hand gently. "Jacque, we are happy to have you with us. Just remember God never forgets us even when it feels like He has."

"Yes, sir," Jacque said obediently.

Old Saul smiled and nodded. "You'll understand that when you're older, I pray."

More people wanted to greet Old Saul. Rachel headed straight for her cousin's wife near the front. Jacque sat beside her, craning his neck and swinging his legs.

She noted the attention, some surreptitious and some blatant, that Jacque was receiving. She hoped no one would ruin the day with rudeness. She would make certain to steer clear of certain people, most notably Mrs. Ashford.

Noah went to the front. The service went as usual, hymn singing, prayers for the nation, state and town, and one of Noah's bracing sermons on loving one's neighbor. Rachel hoped it would actually penetrate a few stubborn hearts here. Loving others always brought blessings.

Soon everyone was outside in the blazing summer sun. Sons helped fathers set up tables in the shade of trees and daughters helped mothers set out tablecloths and bowls of food. Families laid down blankets for the children to sit on while the adults sat at the tables.

Rachel enjoyed the festive excitement but Jacque stayed close by her side, which saddened her a little. He should be off making friends, but his situation and history worked against him. Evidently he didn't even trust Johann to be his friend in the presence of others. When Mr. Merriday had ordered Jacque to come with her, had he given this any thought? Probably not.

Then a younger boy with dark hair and eyes approached them. "Hello, Miss Rachel."

She smiled. Everyone had adopted Brennan's

form of address. She liked it. She'd seen this boy before. "Thee is Gunther Lang's nephew?"

"Yes, miss. I'm Johann." He turned to Jacque. "You want to play tag with us, Jacque?"

Jacque looked up at her, asking silent permission.

She nodded with a smile.

Jacque's face lightened. The two boys hurried off together.

Ellen Lang, Johann's new aunt and a former schoolteacher in Pepin, had come behind Johann. She was a tall, elegant woman in a lovely dress of blue cambric and a fashionable hat. "I was happy to see you brought Jacque with you. He needs to start making friends."

"It was kind of Johann to invite him."

"Johann understands being the new boy in town." Then Noah called everyone to quiet for grace. A few solemn moments, then a loud Amen and the buzz of happy voices, young and old.

Rachel smiled. Memories of childhood meetinghouse gatherings came back to her with a pang of homesickness. Then she noted how Levi had managed to get himself seated at the table where Posey Brown sat with her imposing grandmother and the Ashfords. *Brave man.*

Rachel found herself at the next table, sitting with Noah, Sunny and their children and other neighbors, Martin and Ophelia Steward and Nan and Gordy Osbourne. Rachel contented herself with listening to the chatter though her eyes kept straying to the edges of the clearing, hoping to see Mr. Merriday appear.

From the corner of her eye, she also kept track of Levi's shy pursuit of Posey and of Jacque's behavior. He had been invited to sit with Johann at another table. She had never seen the boy happier than when he'd run over to ask her permission to sit with the Langs. *God bless Johann.*

Posey kept looking over at Jacque, and Rachel wondered why.

After everyone had eaten their fill, they rose and began putting food away in the shade or in the springhouse. Posey passed by Rachel. "Mr. Merriday didn't come?"

Rachel merely shrugged, wondering why the girl asked.

"That day we helped you whip up ladyfingers, I asked him if he ever was in Kentucky. He said he doubted we'd met before. But his name just sounds so familiar. I wish I could place it."

Rachel didn't know what to say and then Mrs. Ashford called Posey.

The quiet, friendly afternoon passed pleasantly. Rachel sat on a blanket near Sunny, whose two children were napping in the shade. Rachel noticed that Levi and Posey were nowhere to be seen. The young woman's grandmother Almeria sat dozing against a tree and Mrs. Ashford was talking to another woman. Rachel told Sunny to lie down and nap, too. She'd watch the babies.

Rachel relaxed against the tree behind her, watching the sun and shadows play over the dry grass of the schoolyard, hearing the clink of the horseshoes and the voices of children playing as quietly as they could manage since it was the Sabbath.

Breathing in the heavy August air, she wished Mr. Merriday had come and was here tossing horseshoes with the other men. She now knew that something bad must have happened to separate him from his wife, but what? Why had Jean Pierre called him a coward?

Then a strident woman's voice snapped Rachel completely alert again. "You should show more sense."

Rachel, along with almost everyone else, turned to see a sad-looking Posey being reluctantly led by the hand back to the clearing.

Red-faced, Levi followed a few paces behind.

"But Grandmother—" Posey started.

"Do not bother to argue. I will not change my mind."

Posey sent Levi an agonized glance over her shoulder. Her grandmother kept pulling Posey through the gathering toward town. Levi turned away into the trees, evidently aware of how everyone was staring.

Rachel was embarrassed for Levi and the girl

and as she glanced around she saw she wasn't the only one. Rachel's gaze met Sunny's.

Sunny shook her head, frowning. "Levi is well liked in town and Almeria is a newcomer," she whispered. "Why make such a ruckus in front of everyone? This will not be appreciated."

Rachel sighed in agreement.

And then she heard raised voices. She glimpsed the corner of the schoolhouse where Jacque was taking a swing at a bigger boy. She leaped up and ran toward the boys.

When she reached them, she halted. The two boys were fully engaged. Swinging punches. Yelling. At the sight of her, the other children, except for Johann, scattered. Noah hurried to catch up with her.

Before she could even speak, Noah grabbed Jacque by the collar, dragging him away from the fight.

Another man yanked the bigger boy away, saying that the child should have known better than to pick a fight on Sunday in front of the whole town.

Rachel thought the man had missed the point.

"It is not Jacque's fault," Johann insisted. "Clayton always starts fights. He called Jacque's father a . . . a name."

"That was very wrong," Noah cut in, "but fighting never solves anything."

Jacque looked up resentfully.

"That takes time to learn," Noah said. "And some never do. Jacque, why don't you wash your hands and face at the pump?"

"Come on," Johann encouraged Jacque. "I'll go with you."

Jacque allowed Johann to lead him toward the pump at the other end of the school building. Clayton and his father stalked away in the opposite direction.

Rachel looked to her cousin. "Thank thee, Noah." She didn't know what else to say.

Noah touched her arm. "Sunny and I pray faithfully for you, Mr. Merriday and Jacque."

For some reason, this comment brought moisture to her eyes. She pressed her hand over his and then turned, noticing Mr. Merriday at the edge of the clearing.

Rachel nearly called out his name, but stopped herself. She didn't want to bring attention to him. They'd both had enough of that. How could she smooth matters for Jacque after the fight? She couldn't of course. But she could prompt them to leave.

She lifted a hand and motioned toward the basket she'd brought, still resting beside Sunny in the shade. He obviously saw her silent request and moved to get it, sliding through the others also gathering up their goods. A few stopped to look at him; a few shook their heads in silent judgment, raising her hackles.

Jacque returned to her side, looking down-hearted. A bruise under his left eye was just beginning to show. "Johann has to go home now."

"Perhaps when his family comes to town, he will be able to drop in for a visit."

Jacque hid his reaction to this, but pointedly did not look toward his father . . . toward Mr. Merriday, even when he joined them walking home.

Rachel naturally wanted to ask Jacque what the other boy had called his father, but she did not give in to curiosity. Still, she did not miss the glares Jacque was sending Mr. Merriday. Whatever Brennan Merriday had done to cut himself off from his family was still bearing bitter fruit. The strife between the two had not abated in the least.

And why had Brennan come at the end of the picnic? "I didn't expect to see you till supper," she murmured.

"Fishin' was a bust." Then he glanced toward the saloon, but like everything else, it was closed on Sundays. She couldn't believe plain boredom brought him to the schoolyard.

Rachel drew in a deep breath as she walked between two unhappy males. She ached to help both of them, but how? And was it her place? Within her power?

Chapter Eight

Back at Levi's that evening, Brennan sent the boy up to bed. Thoroughly disgruntled from a lonely and tedious and empty day, he was filled with thoughts of Miss Rachel, thoughts he shouldn't be having.

Grumpily he sank down beside Levi outside to watch the river flow by and the setting red sun dip into the blue water. Gulls swooped and screeched, tightening Brennan's nerves. The grass under Brennan had been seared by the sun. A green line of watered grass edged the river. Levi sat in a chair propped back against the wall. The silence was not their usual companionable one.

Finally Brennan hazarded a glance at his friend, whose glum face shouted a dark mood. Once again his regard for this big man prompted his sympathy. "You don't look very happy," he said quietly.

Levi humphed in a disgruntled way.

"How was the picnic?" Brennan didn't want to pry but he couldn't leave it for some reason.

"That grandmother of hers caught us . . . talking by a tree."

Many responses popped into Brennan's mind,

172

but he chose his words with care. "What's wrong with a man talking to a girl?"

"I don't know. The way she acted you'd a-thought I was a convicted felon or something. We were *just talking*. Posey . . . Miss Brown has a way of making conversation easy."

The blacksmith had it bad all right. Old hurt and resentment gathered in Brennan's throat, but he refused to voice it. "She seems like a sweet young gal. But you got to look at the big picture. Maybe you're better off without her. I mean, if you married Miss Brown, the old tartar might come live with you."

Levi thumped his chair forward, full on the ground.

Brennan looked up, startled.

"If the old tartar doesn't even want me talking to her, how am I going to get to court her, much less marry her?"

With that Levi left him, stalking down the riverbank.

Brennan sighed, happy that he wasn't interested in courting. Then Miss Rachel's face came to mind yet again. She'd looked worried on the way home today and hadn't said much at supper. Usually nothing much rattled her. He recalled her singing with that robin not long ago. She was too good for this town. Irritation gathered in his middle. Who had upset Miss Rachel? And what could he do about it?

• • •

At the cock's crow, Rachel woke the next morning not her usual cheerful self. She hadn't slept soundly as usual. And upon waking, she instantly began to worry about Jacque and what had been said to hurt him yesterday.

And on top of this, today already felt as if it would be a scorcher. Still she had a business to run. She quickly dressed and started a fire in her outdoor oven—grateful it was away from her dwelling. Then she mixed up a double batch of cinnamon muffin batter. Soon she was filling muffin tins.

"Good morning, Miss Rachel."

Rachel turned to find Posey at her open door yet again, looking unhappy. "Good morning," Rachel said curtly and discouragingly. "I don't have time to talk. I'm about to put these muffin tins into the oven."

"Can I help?" Posey asked, looking ready to cry.

"No, I'm sorry." Rachel softened her voice, but she couldn't help this young girl and was not about to interfere. "I'm trying to get these into the oven before Mr. Merriday and Jacque arrive for their breakfast. Pardon me."

She turned and carried two muffin tins outside. When she reached the oven, she turned to find that Posey had carried out two tins also. Irritation pinched her. *Please go home, Posey.* "My thanks," Rachel said in a tight tone.

The girl slid the tins into the oven. Waves of heat flooded against their faces. Then Posey trailed her back inside, wiping her eyes with a lace hanky.

Rachel swallowed her pity for the girl. Butting into other people's affairs was not her chosen course.

"Will you be making candy later?" Posey asked. The girl sounded . . . lachrymose, a word Rachel had heard but never used. Then she recalled when Posey's grandmother had caused a scene yesterday. *Poor girl.*

Rachel drew in a deep breath, reminding herself she had no business prying into what wasn't her affair. "No, I think it's going to be much too hot today to make anything more." She glanced at the wall clock so she would time the muffins correctly and nearly shooed the girl from her kitchen. "I must start breakfast."

The girl nodded, looking disappointed, down-hearted.

It tugged at Rachel's heart and she relented. "I may be making candy early tomorrow morning," Rachel said, unable to help herself. "Perhaps you could come then?"

Posey burst into tears. "You saw what happened yesterday at the picnic, Miss Rachel."

Yes, she had. She'd tried not to comment, get involved. She now failed. "I noted Mr. Comstock's interest in you," she said.

"Mr. Comstock is so . . ." Posey began and then tears overcame her again. She shook with their power.

Rachel patted Posey's arm. She didn't want to become enmeshed in this girl's difficulties, but she was a stranger here, too. That was probably why the girl had sought out Rachel as a confidant. "What is the problem, Posey?"

"Grandmother says she won't let me marry a man without land. She says a blacksmith's widow is left with a forge and some tools. What good does that do her? If a farmer dies, at least he leaves his wife with land, something that lasts, something of value."

Rachel moved a step closer. She understood instantly why the grandmother would take that stand. Their family had been dispossessed and forced to depend on other family. She didn't know what to say, so she merely murmured some comforting sounds.

Posey continued crying.

Through the open door, Rachel was relieved to see Mr. Merriday and Jacque coming toward her cabin. Or at least she was till she saw their grim expressions. *Oh, dear.*

Posey left then, sniffling. And though Rachel tried to resist it, the girl's mood had affected her. As did the scowls on the two males who would be eating breakfast at her table.

Halfway through breakfast, Rachel finally lost

patience. "Isn't my breakfast well prepared? Why so glum this morning?"

Both males looked up from their plates and frowned at her.

In that instant she did catch a likeness between them, the way their brows wrinkled when troubled. Could that be a family trait or just coincidence?

"Jacque, I'm sorry our pleasant Sunday afternoon ended in a fight," she said. "I don't think my cousin scolded thee too harshly."

Jacque slammed down his fork. "That's not what's wrong."

Rachel pulled back in the face of such a hostile answer.

"Keep a civil tongue in your head, boy," Brennan insisted.

"I told you—you ain't my father, but people think you are. They think you fought for the Confederate army. That's why that kid called you a stinkin' Reb. But I know the truth. You're a coward. You didn't fight for the Cause, for the South." With that, the boy leaped from his place and bolted outside.

Mr. Merriday rose, looking ghastly white.

"Perhaps," Rachel said uncertainly, "it would be best to let him cool off."

Brennan sank back down. Several minutes passed before he could speak.

She didn't know what to say so she said nothing.

"How long do you think that letter will take to get to Louisiana?" he asked.

"As little as a week, as long as a month. One never knows."

"And we don't know how long it will take to get an answer." Merriday lifted his mug of coffee. "I wanted to be in Canada before the end of summer."

"Canada?" Somehow the country sounded farther away to Rachel than it really was.

Draining his cup, Mr. Merriday rose. "Yes, I'm sick of the war. And nobody here can forget it." Though he spoke quietly, each word vibrated with deep emotion. "I want to go where nobody fought in it and nobody cares about it."

"But thee fought in it and thee cares about it."

He glared at her. "What's that supposed to mean?"

"Thee can leave America and the war, but can thee take them out of thyself? Both had a part in who thee has become."

"But nobody would keep bringin' the war up to me."

Rachel tried to think of how to explain what she meant to him but couldn't bring up the words. She changed her approach. "If Jacque is thy son, he is a gift, not a penance. And thee is Brennan Merriday, and a good man, a worthy man."

"To you, maybe. Not to anybody else—least of all, this boy. And you don't know what happened between my wife and me . . ." He bowed his head.

Well, that stopped her. She didn't know and he didn't look like he was going to tell her.

He stood. "You're a good woman, Miss Rachel. But you can't make this world all nice and sweet like one of your cakes. It doesn't work that way. I'll go to Canada. It can't be any worse than here."

"That day when thee fixed my roof," she began hesitantly, but this needed to be addressed, "something happened, something inside thee . . ."

"I don't want to talk about it." And he left.

She sighed, lifting her coffee mug to her lips. So that's where he planned to go. The only problem with his plan was that he carried the war with him. Anybody could see that. And if the child proved to be his blood, he'd be taking with him a child scarred by the war to Canada, too.

She sipped her coffee though it had gone cold. Running away from problems never solved them. Perhaps someone might say she ran away from her problems in Pennsylvania, too. But they'd be wrong.

Brennan tried to focus on the day's chores. He was milking the cow when he heard the sound of a boat whistle. Not usual this early in the morning, but he finished milking and helped Miss Rachel load her trays of cinnamon muffins and rolled her cart into town.

Jacque shadowed them, but stayed out of reach.

The boy's words from breakfast mocked Brennan. His son, or this boy, hated him because he was a coward who hadn't fought for the Cause. If he only knew the truth . . . But no one here knew the truth and he would never speak it. It was nobody's business.

Dockside, Miss Rachel quickly sold out. Counting the coins from her bucket, she smiled. "I'll have to make some candy in case another boat comes through. I never want to disappoint customers. Product excellence and consistent supply are necessary to success," she recited as if reading from a book.

He grumbled and steered the empty cart for home.

The young gal Posey came running out of the store. "Mr. Merriday! Mr. Merriday!" she called out, waving a letter.

Instead of slowing so Posey could catch up with them, he picked up his pace. There was nothing she had to say he wanted to hear.

"Be polite," Rachel hissed into his ear. She tugged on his arm, insisting wordlessly that he stop.

He paused, grumbling into her ear, "What now?"

"I knew I'd heard your name before, Mr. Merriday!" Posey exclaimed for all the world to hear.

Brennan steamed as he watched people coming

out of stores, stopping to listen to the fool girl. Did she have to choose the main street of town to blab her mouth off? He began to push the cart, hurrying away from her.

"I recalled this morning on the way home that I had read your name in my father's letters while he was in the Union Army. And I found it!" She waved the sheet of stationery again. "You knew my father! You were in the Kentucky Militia with him and fought for the Union! Mr. Merriday, you're not a Confederate at all!"

Brennan did not imagine the upset this pronouncement released. But his inner outcry overwhelmed the noise and sudden commotion around him. He had eyes for only one person—the boy. He glimpsed him through the people who gathered around. The boy looked stunned and then bolted. Apparently he'd known only that Brennan hadn't fought for the South—not that he'd fought for the North.

No! Brennan dropped the cart handles and raced after him, ignoring the people who tried to speak to him. This town was just bad news all around. He'd never been recognized as more than a drifter, a Southerner. He'd kept the truth hidden. Too much to explain. Too much to expose.

He tried to catch the boy but Jacque was fleet of foot and soon disappeared into the trees. Brennan's heart pumped blood and he ran full out. "Jacque! Wait!" And then thinking of the vast forest around them, he shouted, "Jacque, stop! You'll get lost!"

Rachel stood frozen beside the abandoned cart, watching Mr. Merriday and Jacque vanish from sight.

"Why did they run away?" Posey asked, sounding dumbfounded. "This is good news, isn't it?"

Released from her shock, Rachel turned to face the young innocent. "Matters about the war that tore our nation in two are never easy." She picked up the push handles of the cart and started in the direction Mr. Merriday and the boy had run. "Thee of all people should know that."

Posey kept up with her. "But I wanted to read him the letter. Father said—"

Heat went through Rachel in waves as she thought of Mr. Merriday's shock at having his private affairs shouted on Main Street. Rachel lifted a shoulder. "I think thee should stop now. Mr. Merriday is a very private man and just days ago, his son . . . Jacque was abandoned here in a very public scene. Thee should have gone to him privately." People hearing her words began to drift away as if caught eavesdropping.

Posey blushed. "I'm sorry . . . I didn't think . . ." She stopped keeping pace with Rachel. "It's just everybody thinks he was a Confederate, looks down on him and . . ."

Rachel shook her head and kept walking. The news that Mr. Merriday had not fought for the South surprised her and didn't surprise her.

Something awful had happened to him in his home place, something that had torn him from his family and turned them against him. Posey's revelation could explain what that had been. Had Mr. Merriday been cast out because he didn't believe in secession?

But this eye-opener would make matters even more difficult between the man and his son. Jacque had berated him for being a coward and not fighting for the South. What did he think of his father fighting for the enemy, the North? That was no mystery. His reaction had been clear and swift.

Brennan raced after the boy, frantic. He must explain what had happened, how he'd come to fight for the North. The dark head disappeared into the mass of trees north of town.

Brennan ran on, branches slapping him in the face, grazing his hands. The boy disappeared from sight. Children could get lost in the thick forest and never be found—alive. He ran, though his mind tried to tell him to stop and listen—think.

He stumbled over a tree root and fell hard, flat on his chest. Hitting more tree roots knocked the air from his lungs. For a moment he was breathless. The strength flew out of him and he was weak again. "Jacque!" he tried to cry out over and over. "Jacque!" Then he fell silent, gasping for air and hurting with each gasp.

Finally he listened and heard nothing except his own breathing. Failure closed in around him like an impenetrable smoke, choking him. Would he ever have the chance to explain? And now he knew he wanted this child to be his. Then he heard her voice, not shouting, just saying his name.

"Mr. Merriday," Miss Rachel summoned him. "Mr. Merriday."

At first he didn't reply. Then he dragged himself to his feet. "Here," he said, suddenly feeling a sharp jab as he said the word. He pressed a hand to a rib, a tender spot he hadn't pinpointed before.

Miss Rachel stepped out from the surrounding trees. "Did thee catch him?"

Do you see him? he snapped silently. Brennan hung his head, hiding his frustration, and rubbed his side.

"Did thee fall?" she asked in so calm a voice.

Her question irritated him. "Of course *I fell.*" The outburst cost him another, sharper, deeper jab of pain.

"Thee must have hurt thyself." She approached him and put out her hands to touch his chest.

He grabbed her hands to stop her. Then the need to be near this woman swept away all sense. He folded her in his arms and held her close. Bending his head, he buried his face in the crook of her neck, reveling in the sweet scent of lilac. In this unpredictable and hard and dreadful world, this woman stood in stark contrast—steady and soft and kind. He couldn't push himself away; he held her.

"Brennan," she whispered at last.

The sound of his given name in her gentle voice jerked him back to propriety. He released her and stepped back. "I beg pardon." He couldn't meet her eyes.

"Thee has just experienced an upsetting . . . incident. Posey should have shown more . . . discretion. But the milk is spilled and it can't be hidden."

Her now matter-of-fact voice contrasted with her soft voice as it had said his given name. Night and day. He felt like kicking himself. He might have misled this fine lady into thinking he had feelings for her. He didn't have feelings for her, for anyone. "I'm sorry," he mumbled, ignoring a whisper asking why he'd just held her in his arms—if he didn't have affection for her.

"Thee was distressed," she said briskly. "Now let's get back to the road."

"What about the boy?" he asked, not moving.

"Blundering about in the woods will not bring him home," she said in a reasonable tone.

The reasonable tone rasped his tender nerves. The child was his responsibility, not hers. "He could get lost—"

"He is able to climb a tree and when he does, he will see the smoke from a chimney and find his way back. He will come home when he gets hungry enough."

How could she be so calm? The urge to shake her nearly overcame him. Instead he followed her out of the woods to the road to her cabin. The two of them walked home, not speaking. He let her push the cart because his side was paining him. Frustration smoldered within. He'd just got the use of his wrist back and now this?

She rolled the cart near the cabin and then waved him inside. "Please sit at the table."

He did so with ill grace. He wanted to yell at someone, Posey Brown for instance, but he couldn't yell at Miss Rachel.

She gently moved away the hand he had pressed to his side and then even more gently pressed the area. When she hit the right spot, he gasped.

Then she straightened and stared at him, barely taller than he was sitting down. "I think thee has cracked or sprained a rib."

He groaned deeply and then regretted it. Shallow breathing was the less painful course.

"Take off thy shirt," she said, turning toward her linen trunk.

"What?" Again he regretted speaking sharply.

"My father fell once and I will do for thee what my stepmother did for him." She brought out a length of muslin, a wide bandage it appeared. "I

186

will bind thy chest firmly. Please remove the shirt."

Brennan couldn't meet her gaze, but obeyed her reluctantly. It felt improper for him to be shirtless here alone with her.

Rachel most certainly did not want Mr. Merriday to sit in her cabin shirtless. She still reeled from the sensations and emotions his embrace had released inside her. "Raise thy arms level so I can bind this around."

She tried to tightly wrap his chest without touching or looking at him. An impossible task. An unnerving task. He had a fine chest and shoulders, so smooth to the touch. Her eyes followed the line dividing his tanned neck and untanned skin of his chest and upper arms. She chastised herself for noticing. Why had he drawn her into his arms?

No doubt it had been a moment of anguish and he merely had needed the comfort of another human being. A deflating thought. She finished binding his chest tightly. She tied the bandage neatly and securely. "That should help thee breathe with less discomfort."

He nodded and lowered his arm and drew on his shirt quickly, as if embarrassed and pained. He stared down at the table. "You really think he'll come back by himself?"

"Yes, but not until he's exhausted himself and is

hungry and thirsty. He will not be happy and will probably be rude to us."

He looked up at her then, just a slight tilting of his chin. "He thought I was a coward. They all did when I wouldn't enlist in the local militia. My wife left me over it and they . . . I left town."

His explanation did not feel complete. She could imagine the commotion, the fury his refusal may have caused. Secession had stirred the whole nation to a fever pitch. "Thee didn't believe in secession?"

"Or slavery. I was against slavery."

This startled her. Most Southerners who fought for the North had been against secession, not against slavery. Indeed Mr. Lincoln had not advanced emancipation till well into the conflict in order to keep the border states, the states that still held slaves but fought for the Union. Men like Posey Brown's father.

Rachel looked at Brennan Merriday with new eyes. And she couldn't stop herself. She leaned over and kissed his forehead. "Bless thee," she whispered. Shocked at herself, she pulled back and bustled over to the chest to return the length of wide bandage she hadn't used, chastising herself with every step.

"I don't think he'll come back," Mr. Merriday said.

"We will see if I'm right. I hope I am." *Please, Father, let me be right. Bring Jacque home soon.*

Chapter Nine

Second by second, the endless day passed. A day of watching, waiting to see a thin boy with black hair walk into her clearing. But Rachel and Brennan waited in vain. Now Rachel watched the sun's rays glimmer through the trees. The last of her energy faded with the day.

"It's late. Thee must go," Rachel said at last, not wanting to send him away but knowing she must. She didn't want to think of the gossip that would come if townspeople didn't see him return to the blacksmith shop before dark.

She struggled with herself. She wanted to fold him in her arms and comfort him.

Brennan stared at her. "I shoulda kept going on after him."

She shook her head. She even imagined kissing Brennan's face and smoothing back his hair . . . She stopped her unruly mind there. *Such thoughts.* "Thee lost sight of him. Stumbling around in the forest could injure thy rib more and probably not find Jacque anyway."

He exhaled with visible pain and left without a further word.

She watched him go, his head down, his step

slow. Her feelings for him were increasing, causing her to think about him when she should not. And she knew she stood in danger of being deeply hurt when he left town. But that didn't seem to matter to her heart.

Brennan tried to come up for air from the gloom smothering him, but could not. Now he realized that the boy meant something to him. He couldn't think why. Jacque might not even be his son, his blood. *But he's from home. He's my responsibility. And he's been treated bad and I can help make that up to him—if he'll let me.*

Again he felt Rachel in his arms. He'd forgotten how soft a woman felt. Grimly he shut down his mind. He'd been foolish beyond measure to reach for her when he had no intention of staying and was unworthy of her. He'd behaved like a cad.

When Brennan reached town, he was glad to see the street deserted. The saloon was quiet but held no attraction for him. He didn't want to talk to anybody. He slipped into the blacksmith shop, hoping Levi wouldn't hear him.

But Levi had evidently been watching for him. The big man stood in the doorway, his back to the river.

Brennan halted, staring at him, suddenly breathing faster.

"The boy didn't come back?" Levi asked.

"No." Brennan hid the deep heart spasm this caused him. He pressed a hand to his side as if that was where he hurt.

"Come through and sit out riverside," Levi invited. "I heard about you serving for the Union, but I won't talk you to death."

Relief rolled over Brennan. Levi had sense. Brennan realized then that while he didn't want to talk, he didn't want to be alone either. Imagining the boy alone in the coming darkness clawed at him. *I should have told him myself, told him all what happened. He deserves the truth.*

Levi waved Brennan outside into the breeze by the river.

Brennan joined his friend there, sitting as they usually did, watching the final flickers of the sunset and the blue water turning to ink. Brennan cradled his side and tried to banish Jacque's tortured face from his mind, banish the touch of Rachel's hair against his face.

"At least it's not cold or storming," Levi commented after a while.

"Yeah." No, the storm churned inside the boy.

"And Miss Rachel's been feeding up the boy. Won't hurt him to go a night without supper."

Brennan nodded, his throat too tight for words.

"You move like you hurt yourself."

"Tripped. Might have cracked a rib."

Levi bowed his head. "I still don't know why Posey's grandmother won't let me talk to her."

Brennan shook his head. He had no answer for the man. He leaned against the wall and tried not to think of a little boy huddled against a tree in the forest. There were bears in those woods. He moved and then stifled a moan, rubbing his side slowly, cautiously.

Finally, the night wrapped around them, fireflies flickering green in the blackness, and Levi got up. "See you in the morning."

Rising painfully, Brennan reached over and touched the big man's shoulder, grateful for the company and understanding. Then he turned inside to climb the ladder to the empty loft.

Would the boy make it back? Had he failed the boy, too? Or had the final break with home come at last? If so, then he could leave Miss Rachel before he misled her. The thought clogged his throat. He wanted to stay; he must leave.

Rachel had remained dressed, sitting outside fanning away the few mosquitoes. The dry weather had reduced the numbers of the annoying little bloodsuckers, probably the only advantage of the drought. She listened to the encroaching night, filled with the sounds of frogs and crickets. She hoped to hear the boy's voice, tried to forget resting her head against Brennan's chest and hearing his heart pound.

Finally she gave up and went inside. Her hearth was cold but she'd left the outdoor oven burning very low, hoping the faint smoke could still be seen in the moonlight.

She had just let down her hair when she heard the tap on the door. She hurried to open it.

Jacque stood in the scant light with a grimy face and a torn sleeve.

She nearly cried out with relief. She controlled herself and didn't throw her arms around him. She had to remember who she was to him, just his father's employer. Since Brennan had stated he would be leaving and no doubt taking Jacque with him, she shouldn't let the child form an attachment to her. And now she should scold him but she couldn't do that. She focused on the practical. "Come in. Thee must be starved."

He stumbled inside.

"Sit down at the table," she said, heading toward her pie safe to fetch bread and cheese.

She turned to find the boy outside washing his hands. For some reason this brought moisture to her eyes.

He came in and slumped onto the bench, obviously exhausted and downhearted.

She set the plate down with a glass of water. She touched his head with her hand and for once— unable to completely hide her emotion—said grace, thanking God for bringing him home safely.

He devoured two plates of food before he paused to look at her.

She waited to hear what he said, but he said nothing, just looked at her. His eyes spoke pages and pages of pain, sorrow and distrust. She ached to fold him in her arms to comfort and reassure him. But she wasn't his blood. He belonged to Brennan. She hoped.

Finally she broke the silence. "I think thee will spend the night here." She rose and went to the linen chest and drew out her last pillow, just a small square, and a worn quilt her mother had made as a girl. She handed these to him.

Without a word, he lay down on the floor and rolled up into the quilt and went to sleep almost instantly.

She stood over him, both glad and worried. She wished she could let Mr. Merriday know he'd come home safe, but walking in the dark alone would not be wise or safe for her or Jacque. Bears roamed the area. And Mr. Merriday would come for breakfast. She would face him then and banish once and for all the pull he exerted over her.

In the dark, she dressed for bed and then slid between the sheets. The multitude of emotions she'd experienced today had left her depleted. But one part of the day refused to bow to sleep— Mr. Merriday pressed against her. He'd needed her comfort and had seized it.

No man but her father, and only when she was little, had held her like that. Just one day ago, she'd realized that she didn't want Mr. Merriday to leave and now she realized that she wanted him to hold her again—often. Oh, how could she hide these unsuitable feelings?

Rachel woke with Jacque standing over her.

"I don't want to have nothin' to do with that man."

Rachel sat up and considered the boy and his words. "He may be thy father."

"I don't care. I don't want nothin' to do with a Mississippi man who up and fought for the Union."

So it fell to her to soothe the troubled waters. She sighed silently. "Jacque, there is much I could say. But this is all I will tell thee. There are always two sides to everything. Mr. Merriday deserves to have his side of the story heard."

The boy stared at her, chewing his lip. "I don't want to have nothin' to do with that man," he repeated.

"That will be difficult. Where will thee stay?"

"Why can't I stay here? I'll work for you."

She tilted her head to one side. The boy was stubborn just like his father. She did not say this, not wishing to set a spark to straw, so to speak. "If thee stays here and works for me, thee will still be with Mr. Merriday."

He glared at her.

"Is that not true?"

He glared more narrowly.

"Staring at me will not change the facts."

He shrugged in obvious capitulation. "I ain't gotta talk to him."

Arguing would not solve this here and now. "Please go outside and wash up at the creek. I must get up and need my privacy."

He stomped outside, banging the door behind him.

What a pleasant day this was going to be. But thank heaven the boy had returned. Part of her wanted to race into town to let Mr. Merriday know. She knew, though, that like her, he expected that if the boy returned he'd come to her place. He would arrive soon enough to face the angry child.

So she brushed and bound her long hair, dressed and began her morning routine. Today she decided to make molasses cookies instead of candy as she'd planned. An easy drop dough and no standing over the stove inside. And who could refuse one of her dark, spicy cookies?

Before the first cookie sheets were in the oven, she heard through the open door Mr. Merriday approaching.

She stepped just outside.

Jacque was returning from his "swim" in the creek, damp and clean and very pointedly ignoring the man.

"You're here," Brennan said, folding his arms— to keep from reaching for the child? And Brennan looked as if he hadn't slept all night, worrying about Jacque.

Whatever Mr. Merriday said, he had affection for this child. She remained where she was and tried not to let her concern for the man show. "Thee might say good morning to Jacque," she prompted.

"Good mornin'," Brennan muttered. "Glad you found your way back."

Jacque looked away from Brennan and folded his arms over his scrawny chest—just like the man who might be his father.

"Jacque, when an elder speaks, thee will answer." She kept her voice pleasant and gentle and implacable.

Glancing over his shoulder, Jacque sent his father a scathing look. "I'm back. I'm staying here, not with you."

Brennan sent her a grim look in response, but did not scold the child.

She shrugged slightly. "We will all be civil to one another. Please come in. I have enough eggs left from yesterday to make breakfast before chores."

She turned inside and the two followed her. Soon she served up three plates and the trio ate breakfast in silence. She gazed at Brennan's hands, so tanned, strong, capable. She closed her eyes, dismissing her foolishness.

When Jacque finished, he rose. "Good eats. I'll

go gather more eggs." He carried his plate and mug outside and set them on the table by the basin. That left Rachel and Brennan facing each other. What was the man thinking?

Brennan looked at the lady, then as he recalled the way he'd overstepped the bounds of propriety yesterday, he lowered his gaze. He really did not want to talk about Jacque or anything.

"I suppose thee doesn't wish to discuss this?"

Glancing up, he frowned, confused once again by Miss Rachel's perception and no-nonsense approach to life. *She never flutters or gets flustered.*

She looked at the clock on the wall and turned, stood and headed toward her outdoor oven. "I must take my cookies out before they burn." She stopped and assessed him with a stern expression he didn't appreciate. "I told Jacque every man deserves to have his side of a story heard." With that pronouncement, she turned to leave.

Her cool attitude further disconcerted him. Any other woman would be jabbering, bending his ear about this. Miss Rachel was one unusual woman. "You're right."

Before she could reply, Brennan walked out and looked around. He didn't want to face Jacque, but he hadn't been given a choice. Posey Brown had seen to that.

He walked over to Jacque. "Come with me.

We'll go look for wild mustard for Miss Rachel."

"I'm not going anywhere with—"

Brennan stooped and stared into the boy's eyes. "It's time you and me talked and that's what we're going to do. A man has a right to be heard." That woman was getting into his head.

Jacque stared back and then nodded. He quickly gathered two more eggs and then set the basket inside. He came out with another empty basket and set off, walking north on the road away from town.

Still breathing with pain, Brennan caught up with him. At first they just walked, Brennan trying to come up with a way to tell the boy all that had happened in Mississippi before he'd been born. Jacque was just ten. Could he understand it?

From his own childhood, Brennan recalled a wrinkled, dried-up old farmer who'd lived nearby. He'd learned a lot from the man, who was nearly ninety and who'd come to Mississippi when the Choctaw still roamed there. Brennan remembered how the man taught him—with questions, letting him figure things out for himself.

"I want to ask you a question, boy." He waited.

Finally, Jacque cast him a resentful look.

"I was born 'n' raised along the Mississippi and lived there till I was over twenty. Everybody I knew said slavery was good, the way things should be. What would cause a man to go agin everybody he ever knew? What would cause a man to do something so bad that his wife left him and never even told him she was carrying his son?"

Jacque merely tossed him another more resentful look.

"You don't have to like me, but it's important you figure this out. In not too many years, you'll be a man and you'll be faced with choices. Will you just go the easy way, be like everybody else— even if you think different in your heart? Or will you stand up for what you believe is right?"

Each of the words jabbed Brennan painfully in his rib and in his heart. Life would have been so much easier if his pa hadn't taken him on that trip downriver to New Orleans.

Still Jacque said nothing. They walked in silence till they reached a meadow, a natural clearing in the forest. A doe and her fawns glimpsed them and then the three bolted for the trees.

He watched them flee, wishing he could, too. Pepin had been bad luck for him since the get-go. Then he thought of Miss Rachel and saw her lips curve into one of her smiles. Her smile made her shine so pretty.

Brennan barricaded his mind against Miss Rachel and bent to look for yellow wild mustard plants that Jacque said he could recognize. The meadow should have been thick with them. But it was dry and burned up. Just like he felt.

Bending hurt his side, so he sat down, futilely

200

moving his hand through the dry, lifeless grass searching for any green shoot. Time passed; the hot sun rose higher. They moved closer to the edge of the clearing where some green hid in the shade. They kept searching. Waves of heat wafted into the shade, nearly suffocating them.

"Why'd you do it? Go agin everybody?" the boy finally asked, not looking at him.

Brennan nearly drew in a deep breath but stopped himself. Instead he took several shallow breaths, minimizing the rib pain.

The words came easily, as if they had been waiting to be spoken. "When I was only a few years older than you, my pa and I went downriver to New Orleans. My pa had been savin' up and had enough money to buy a slave to work the land with him. I was real excited 'cause I'd never been all the way to New Orleans before. It was a big city with boats from the ocean." Brennan recalled that trip downriver, the last truly uncomplicated time of his life.

"Yeah," Jacque prompted.

"We went to the slave auction down by the docks. And that was what changed me." He recalled the gagging revulsion he'd instantly felt. "It was the worst place I'd ever been." He reached over and grasped Jacque's chin, turning his face to him. "It was the look in their eyes, the black slaves' eyes."

Jacque stared at him, looking confused.

"I'd been to horse sales. Pa acted like it was just like that. It wasn't. I never seen a horse being sold look that way. They were suffering. They were people and they were being treated like horses, worse than horses. No lady ever went to see the auctions. It was too . . ."

Words failed him. He couldn't speak what he'd seen that day even though the sights and sounds had been burned into his heart. He dropped the boy's chin and then stared at the dried, cracked ground.

The shadow of an eagle soaring on the hot winds passed over them. A cicada shrieked and shrieked again.

"That's why you wouldn't fight for the South?" the boy muttered finally, the heat gone out of his tone.

"Yes, I couldn't fight for slavery after that."

"Did your pa buy a slave?"

"No, the bidding went too high for him." *I was glad.*

Jacque kept running his hands through the dried grass though there was nothing green to pick.

Brennan had done his best to explain. But the boy had been turned against him since the day he was born. This hurt as much as the jab he felt with each breath.

"I want you to know one thing, though," Brennan continued, taking advantage of this rare, private time. "After the war, I came home even though I knew nobody wanted me back. I had to make sure your ma was all right."

Jacque's hands stilled.

"Even if she didn't want me no more, I was still her husband and I would have supported her till the day she died. But nobody told me anything except that she was dead. Nobody told me about you. I wouldn't have left you there with Jean Pierre if I'd known you had been born. But I couldn't stay to find out anything. They run me out of town at gunpoint—a second time." He hadn't meant to add that.

Jacque looked up then. "You didn't leave me on purpose?"

"No, I never knew you'd been born. Nobody told me."

Jacque only nodded in reply.

Brennan surveyed the cloudless blue sky overhead. "We might as well go home. Maybe there's some wild mustard near the creek."

Jacque rose and walked with him, but said nothing.

So much for honesty. And Brennan didn't like it at all when he realized that he was calling Miss Rachel's place "home."

When they arrived at Miss Rachel's clearing, he heard another familiar feminine voice. He didn't want to talk to anybody save Miss Rachel or Levi. Certainly not Posey Brown.

Jacque halted and looked up.

"Let's mosey down by the river," Brennan mumbled. "We'll try to catch Miss Rachel a few catfish for supper."

"Good idea." Jacque nodded and the two headed toward town.

Posey had come to Rachel's to apologize to Mr. Merriday for blurting out his private business in town. Listening, Rachel had just slid the last of her molasses cookies onto the racks to cool when the new school bell rang wildly. Now both of them looked toward the door.

"What? Why are they ringing the bell? School's out for the summer," Rachel asked.

Posey rushed to the open door. "Smoke! Toward town! We've got to go! They'll need us for the bucket brigade!"

"Here." Rachel thrust a spare bucket into Posey's hands.

The girl raced ahead of Rachel, who shut and latched the door behind her and snatched up her own water bucket as she ran.

The smell of smoke billowed, intensified, filling Rachel with gut-wrenching panic. The drought and the fear of wildfire had hung over them all. Had it come true?

The two of them burst through the forest onto the river flat of town. Orange flames danced with the wind like little wisps, dangerous wisps, catching every blade of dried grass on the dirt street and river flat, leaping onto anything dry.

"It's heading to the grass behind Ashford's!" Posey shrieked.

Rachel shuddered. The wind whipped the fire with every gust, driving it toward the trees. A forest in flame! Death and destruction. *God, help us! Now!*

Already a bucket brigade had formed across the main street from the river to the fire. The two of them joined the line, filling in wider gaps. Their toil began—passing heavy buckets forward and empty ones back.

Rachel saw Brennan run toward the front of the brigade.

"If it gets to the trees, we'll never stop it!" Brennan shouted in a strangled voice, pointing toward the forest. "Follow me, men! Grab shovels! Anything! We'll try to smother the flames as they leap toward the trees! The rest of you, keep the water comin'!"

These urgent orders from a man who never showed excitement and rarely talked magnified their effect. Men raced to join him. Frantic activity suspended every thought except—*fire, fire!* Rachel was aware only of the wet bucket handles passing through her hands. Terror raced through her like the wind, water splashing, worry mounting.

"We finished it!" Gunther Lang shouted in his distinctive voice. "It's out!"

Having trouble catching her breath, Rachel straightened to see for herself that he spoke the truth. Then the bucket brigade members staggered forward to view the effects of the fire.

The path of the fire was plain from the river's edge to patches of dry grass on Main Street, scorching the front of Ashford's store to the open clearing behind the stores.

"How did this happen?" Rachel asked.

"Merriday saw it first," the blacksmith said, panting, swiping his forehead with his sleeve. "Sparks from the riverboat smokestack caught dry grass on shore. The wind—you'd a-thought it would blow out the fire—instead it just spread it faster than Merriday and I could keep up with it."

Rachel's gaze sought out Brennan. He'd slipped to the rear with Jacque. He held his arm against his side. Her thoughts went immediately to his painful rib. *The poor man.*

"I saw . . . them trying to put out the fire," Gunther joined in, motioning toward the blacksmith and Brennan, "and ran to . . . the school to ring the bell." The young man spoke between gasps for air, leaning forward with his hands on his soaked knees. "Then I came back to help."

Everyone stared at the few feet separating the blackened grass from the surrounding forest. Rachel had a hard time believing they'd caught it in time. *Thank Thee, Father.*

"A close call," Mr. Ashford said, wiping his

sooty brow with a handkerchief. "What's bothering you, Merriday?"

Nearly doubled over, Brennan was holding his side.

Rachel went to him and gently probed, seeing if he'd done more harm to himself.

"I got so excited I forgot I was hurt," he murmured.

She realized then that everyone had stopped talking and was staring at her touching Brennan's chest in public. Heat suffused her face, which she kept lowered.

She dropped her hand and turned to face the town. "Mr. Merriday cracked or sprained a rib yesterday. I don't feel any further injury." Rachel wished her face would cool and return to normal.

"Well, looks like we need to thank you again, Merriday," Mr. Ashford said. "First you run off thieves and now this."

Everyone began to agree. Brennan's expression darkened and he edged farther away. "Just did what everybody else did."

His gruff tone warned everybody—not only her—away, the last thing she wanted him to do.

She decided to ease matters by deflecting attention. "Jacque, is thee all right? No burns?"

"I'm fine, Miss Rachel," the boy said, staying close to Brennan. "We couldn't find any wild mustard. Too dry."

"Indeed it is."

"We were gonna catch some catfish for supper," Jacque went on.

Rachel wondered what had caused the boy to be so chatty. He appeared to have lost the chip on his shoulder. Had Brennan's side of the story changed how Jacque felt? Or perhaps the excitement or exhilaration of fighting a fire and winning?

"That sounds like an excellent idea," Rachel said. "I have a taste for catfish."

Then a loud groan interrupted. Everyone looked over.

Posey's grandmother was clutching her chest, uttering short gasps. As Rachel watched, she crumpled to the ground.

"Grandmother!" Posey called and ran toward her.

Rachel and Brennan reached her first; both dropped to their knees, one on either side.

"What is it?" Rachel asked in a clear, firm voice.

The woman tried to answer but could not.

"Maybe her heart," Brennan muttered.

Rachel looked at him. Moments before he was backing away. But he'd come forward to help now as he had in the fire. What conflicted inside the man? He responded to any who needed help, but wanted no help or anything from anybody else.

"All the excitement," Mrs. Ashford said, sounding distracted, "must have brought on a spasm."

Or heart failure, Rachel said silently.

Rising also, Brennan met her eyes and she glimpsed that he too realized this was more than just a fainting spell.

"Will someone help Ned carry her upstairs?" Mrs. Ashford asked.

Soon the blacksmith and Gunther were carrying the plump woman on a makeshift stretcher. Mr. Ashford went ahead and held open the door.

Posey's eyes ran with tears. Rachel slipped an arm around her as they followed. Mrs. Ashford hurried past her husband to turn down the bed. "We'll take good care of her," Mrs. Ashford said over her shoulder to Posey. "Don't you worry."

The girl broke free of whatever held her in place and rushed toward the store.

Rachel wished the woman hadn't said those words, "Don't worry." They always seemed to ignite more anxiety.

At the sound of a strange voice, she glanced around.

A boatman who'd helped fight the fire was coming toward her. "Somebody say you are the lady, Miss Rachel, who sells sweets?"

Rachel looked at him and nodded, observing Brennan and Jacque heading toward the blacksmith shop. She saw them leave the shop with fishing gear.

"Do you have any sweets for sale?" the boatman asked.

"Molasses cookies." She began to hurry toward home, not willing to lose any business. "I'll be back in five minutes!"

"The captain say we wait!" he called after her. "We'll buy all you bring!"

And after she sold her cookies, she'd keep busy till Brennan brought catfish for supper.

She wanted to know what had transpired between Brennan and the boy. But would he tell her? Oh, the man was maddening. Admirable, but maddening.

Chapter Ten

In town selling her cookies, Rachel simmered with the frustration that stemmed from not knowing what had happened between Jacque and Brennan and more from the fact that she couldn't pursue the answer right now. She didn't see them at the riverside. How far downriver had they gone to fish?

After the cookies had been bought, she trundled home the cart, all the while wondering what had changed Jacque and Brennan's relationship. In the morning, they'd left with Jacque hostile to Brennan, whom the boy considered a turncoat to the South. And later they ended up going fishing together along the river—as if yesterday and Jacque's running away had never happened. Why? How?

The orange sun lowered and she kept herself busy with chores, churning butter for tomorrow's recipe and milking the cow in the late afternoon. Waiting to see the man and the boy bring home their catch, she paced in front of the door.

Restless, she baked a large cake of cornbread and with a pop, opened a jar of piccalilli Sunny had given her. And waited. What was keeping the two?

As the red melting sun finally dipped behind the treetops, the two males wandered up the trail. Brennan carried a stringer with three huge catfish on it, held out in front of him, the end hooked over his index finger.

Since she had nothing else ready to serve, Rachel was relieved to see the fish. Yet she noted that Brennan was holding the fish with the hand opposite his compromised rib and was walking slightly bent over. That meant he was still aching.

She hurried forward to relieve him of the catfish. "Well done!"

The shocked expressions on the two males' faces halted her in her tracks. "What's wrong?"

"You don't look in the mirror enough, Miss Rachel," Brennan drawled.

"You look funny," Jacque said, pointing at her face, grinning.

She whirled around and ran inside to the small

mirror on the wall. When she saw her reflection, she gasped. Smoke from the fire had blackened her face with grimy soot. "Oh, dear!"

She hung the fish stringer on a peg by the door and hurried outside to wash her face in the basin there.

When she was done, she looked up and Jacque handed her a linen towel. "How mortifying. I went into town and sold cookies looking like this!"

Brennan held his side as he tried not to laugh.

Jacque grinned at her. "We swam in the river to cool off and get rid of the smoke smell."

"And soot," Brennan added.

Rachel contemplated how good it would feel to be a girl again and go swimming in the nearby river. "I'm afraid I would scandalize the town if I did that."

"I'm glad I was born a boy," Jacque said, going inside.

"How is thy rib?" she asked, drying her hands.

Brennan rubbed his side. "Not much better."

"Putting out a fire probably aggravated everything. Thee must rest tomorrow. Just fish or nap in the shade."

"I can't do that."

"Why not? I'm thy employer and that's what I want thee to do." She looked at him more closely. "Where is the bandage I bound thee with?" she asked though she noted the bulge around his waist.

He tugged up the hem of his shirt and showed her that the bandage had slipped to his belt. "It got wet when we swam."

She swallowed a sigh of irritation. "Come. I need to bind that again." She waved him to the bench beside the door.

He shrugged out of his shirt and she bent to untie and then to rewrap the stout muslin around his chest. Again this brought her so close to him. Only a breath separated their cheeks as she worked wrapping and pulling the cloth tight.

For just a moment she was tempted to rest her cheek against his. The thought of this released such an explosion of feeling that she braced herself physically and mentally against it. She finished the last loop around him and then tied the bandage and stepped back. She turned away so he wouldn't note how her cheeks had warmed. This attraction to Mr. Merriday was so . . . lowering to her sense of self control. Where had her good sense gone?

Rachel hurried inside, running away from him. "I have to see to the fish."

Brennan followed her more slowly. Once inside he sank onto the rocking chair, leaning against its high back for support, and sighed with audible relief.

Ignoring him as best she could, Rachel quickly breaded the cleaned fish and laid one and then the next into a large cast-iron skillet to deep fry.

"We didn't find any wild mustard. It's too dry for anything to grow," Jacque reminded her, continuing his grumbling from the bench, elbows propped on the table.

Rachel sighed. "No doubt. And I was hoping for wild mustard and for wild berries to put up for next year. It is good that my business is taking, for it will be a long winter."

When she thought of the coming months, she wondered what winter all alone in this cabin would be like. An empty, hollow feeling tried to lower her spirits. Brushing this aside, she quickly eased the catfish onto its other side in the bubbling oil.

She looked over at Brennan, wondering if he would tell her what he'd done or said to cause this change in Jacque. She hesitated even to broach the subject for fear she would tip the delicate balance between the two of them and regret it.

"Hello the house!" a friendly voice called.

"Jacque," Brennan said, nodding toward the door, "welcome Levi in."

Though Rachel concentrated on the catfish sizzling in the pan, she too welcomed the blacksmith. Though why he had come? He never had before. "Just in time for supper," she said, smiling over her shoulder at him.

"I didn't come expecting to be fed, miss," he said, his hat in his hands.

"You loaned us your fishin' poles and hooks and stringer," Jacque said.

"We have plenty, Mr. Comstock." Rachel waved him toward the table and set another place there. She had an inkling what he'd come about and wished he hadn't.

Before long they were eating the golden catfish, buttery cornbread and spicy piccalilli. Then for dessert, Rachel set out the last dozen of her molasses cookies she'd saved and they vanished.

"Mighty good supper, miss." Levi looked at her shyly.

She noted that Brennan sent him a suspicious look and she wondered what that was about.

"Jacque, make sure the chickens are safe in their coop," Rachel said, feeling what Levi had come to say might be something Jacque didn't need to hear. She didn't want to hear it herself.

As soon as the boy moved outside of earshot, Levi appeared to gather himself. "Miss Rachel, I come to ask a favor."

She looked at him, unable to stop the flow of where this conversation was headed. "I see."

"I've taken a shine to Miss Posey Brown and I think she is not averse to me." The big man blushed.

"I had noticed," Rachel said without any encouragement. She noticed that Brennan Merriday had relaxed, now sitting at ease again in the rocking chair. *Odd.*

Levi looked everywhere but at her. "I was wondering if you could find out why Miss Posey's grandmother doesn't want me to court her."

This was what Rachel had expected, but was it her place to reveal Posey's confidences? "I don't know what I can do," she said in earnest.

"I don't either, but I don't have a sister or mother here to . . . to ask. I asked Mr. Ashford and he said it wasn't his business to say."

Rachel wanted to say the same. Even ill, Almeria would daunt anybody.

"I'm concerned for Miss Brown," Levi continued. "I mean, what if her grandmother doesn't recover from this spell? She'll be alone."

Rachel doubted the Ashfords would put Posey out on the street but understood Levi's awkward situation. After all, she had allowed herself to begin to care for a man with whom she had no possible future. This alone prompted her to say, "I'll see what I can find out, Mr. Comstock. But I have no influence over events here."

"I know that." Still the man looked relieved.

She wished she felt the same. The visit ended soon.

Jacque finished helping her wash and dry the supper dishes. Then he reminded her about her needing a bath. Rachel could have crawled under the cabin in embarrassment but when Brennan lifted her water bucket, she intervened. After the afternoon's exertion, Brennan couldn't haul water. Then over both Rachel's and Brennan's protestations, Levi insisted on helping Jacque fill a tub for her. Then the three males went off together, leaving her to wash away the lingering scent of smoke on her person.

Alone, she barred the door and prepared to bathe with her one indulgence, lilac-scented soap.

As she relaxed in the cool, refreshing water, she couldn't fight the flashes of Brennan's face—his sadness this morning, the flush from the urgency amidst fighting the fire, his evident fatigue and pain at supper. How did a person stop caring about someone?

The next day Rachel had her cinnamon rolls rising the second time before her two "hired hands" arrived for breakfast. She steeled herself to welcome Mr. Merriday without feeling anything beyond courtesy. She failed miserably.

As soon as she could after breakfast, she sent them outside. Brennan to rest and Jacque to gather fallen wood for winter. She needed the wood and she needed Brennan away from her.

As if on cue, just as she finished slathering buttercream frosting over the cinnamon rolls, a boat whistle summoned her. She peered outside and saw that Mr. Merriday was sleeping under his tree. A relief.

She reached town within minutes, rolling her

cart toward the boat. Passengers and boatmen clustered around her, buying cinnamon rolls, bagged or wrapped individually in wax paper. Levi stepped outside his forge and sent her a pointed look. She concentrated on business, trying to come up with a plan to help Levi.

The cook bought what remained on her tray. "You probably don't 'member me but I'm from that first boat you gave samples to of those fast-somethings."

"My fastnachts?"

"Yeah, that's it. We gone down to New Orleans and back twice since then. The captain tell all the other captains about you and how good your stuff is. You don't got any fastnachts today?"

"No, but when will you be back?"

"We gone on up to Minneapolis. Be back by in three days."

"Tell your captain I'll have a couple dozen ready for him."

The man beamed at her and nodded twice.

Flushed with pleasure, Rachel sighed and then turned to face the storefront. Her promise to Levi couldn't wait. She pushed her cart into the shade and went into the General Store.

Mr. Ashford was alone. When he saw her, he brightened. "I see you sold out again. Your business is doing well."

Rachel felt herself expand with his praise and chastised herself. God was blessing her, prospering her—no need for vain pride. "I came to see if I could visit Posey's grandmother. Is she receiving visitors?"

"Oh, please come up," Posey said from the rear staircase. "She is not well enough to get up yet, but . . ."

Rachel nodded, taking polite leave of Mr. Ashford, and headed toward the woebegone-looking young woman. "I understand. It is hard to be idle, especially in this late-summer heat." When she reached Posey, the girl leaned close and pressed a folded paper into her hands.

"This is the letter," Posey whispered, "where my father mentions Mr. Merriday. I want him to see it. But I didn't know . . ."

Rachel wondered how she had become everybody's confidant or go-between, roles she hadn't wished for. Yet what could she do but accept the letter? Nodding, she slipped it into her pocket and followed Posey upstairs.

She had gained access. Now all she had to do was come up with a way to introduce the topic of Levi Comstock to Mrs. Brown. A touchy subject, no doubt. No touchier, however, than the letter in her pocket for Mr. Merriday.

Mrs. Ashford greeted her with evident gratitude. "Oh, Miss Woolsey, would you sit with my cousin for a while? Amanda is helping Mrs. Whitmore today. Posey and I must get busy with laundry and we didn't want to leave Almeria alone."

"Of course, I have time. Perhaps I could read scripture to her?"

"An excellent idea." Mrs. Ashford handed Rachel the family Bible. "There is sweet iced coffee in the icebox. Help yourself." And the two of them disappeared down the rear staircase.

Before Rachel went into the guest room, she stopped in the kitchen to look over the Ashfords' icebox. She'd heard that in winter men cut ice from the frozen Mississippi. Mr. Ashford had built a commodious ice house and sold blocks of ice. She liked the new, metal-lined box with shelves and a thick door with a tight latch. She saw immediately that when she could afford it, she wanted one for herself.

Bidding farewell to enjoyment, she went down the short hall to the guest room. She halted at the doorway and looked in. "Good day, Mrs. Brown."

The older woman turned toward her. "Oh, it's the Quakeress."

Ignoring the listlessness of the welcome, Rachel responded, "Yes, it is. I have come to keep thee company. Would thee like me to read? Perhaps the Psalms?"

The woman shook her head. "Just talk to me. I'm afraid I'm not in good spirits."

Rachel thought secretly that hearing the Psalms would lift the woman's spirits more than anything Rachel could think to say, but she kept that to herself.

"I'm sorry thee isn't feeling well." Rachel thought about a topic that might interest the woman. "I just received a letter from my family. My stepmother is expecting another child later this year."

"You lost your mother?"

"Yes, when I was just about to finish eighth grade."

"I've lost everyone but my Posey." The woman blinked away sudden tears.

Rachel had attempted to begin a happy conversation and here they were talking about death. She tried again. "I think my father may hope for a son at last. He has just me and my four young stepsisters."

"Your mother only had one child?" Almeria asked.

"Yes, just me."

"What do you think of the blacksmith?" Almeria sent her a penetrating look.

This abrupt turn startled Rachel. "He seems honest and hardworking."

"Humph. Everyone says so. Katharine and Ned can't understand why I oppose him courting my granddaughter."

Should she feign ignorance? No, of course not. "Posey confided that thee preferred she marry a man with property."

"Exactly." The woman managed to add some starch to her voice. "I don't want her left with nothing again and when I may not be here to help guide her." The woman's face puckered but she kept control, brushing away a stray teardrop.

Rachel was moved. "I think the Ashfords would do their best for her."

"Yes, but they have a daughter of their own to marry off and grandchildren in other states. They've been very kind to us. But this town isn't filled with eligible young men as I had hoped."

Rachel considered the situation. And insight came. "If I may, I'd like to point out that there is no reason Mr. Comstock couldn't stake a homestead claim. Why can't a blacksmith own land, too?"

The older woman glanced at her sharply. "Would he have time to prove up? That man works sunup to sundown six days a week as it is."

Rachel considered. "I have staked a homestead claim and I could not do the work myself to prove up. Mr. Merriday has refurbished my cabin and built a small, snug barn and cleared some more land for me. My claim is nearly proved up."

Rachel experienced a hitch of pain in her breath. The boy had complicated matters but she had no doubt Brennan would go soon. "Perhaps Mr. Merriday would help Mr. Comstock, as well." *And stay longer in town?*

The woman looked Rachel full in the face. "An excellent suggestion. Do you think Mr. Comstock would stake a claim?"

"I think so." Rachel lowered her eyes. "He seems very taken with thy granddaughter and I have no doubt he would make an excellent husband to her. He's lived here several years and I've heard nothing but good of him."

And suddenly Rachel envied Posey Brown. She might be able to marry the man she had become attracted to. *I will not.*

The day went by with the usual chores but her tension over Brennan and Jacque mounted. Why didn't Mr. Merriday tell her what had happened between them? And when should she show him Posey's letter from her father?

Finally, the day neared its close. Jacque ran off to "swim" in the creek, leaving Rachel and Brennan sitting in the shade on the bench outside her door.

She decided directness was her only hope. "Jacque changed yesterday toward you. What did you say or do—"

"I don't want to talk about it."

She heard more than his words. She heard the lingering pain from the war. Twice now she'd tended to Mr. Merriday's physical injuries. How she longed to minister to his unseen wounds.

"I'm sorry," he said with regret. "I said that more sharp than I meant to."

She nodded, accepting his apology.

"And I should just go ahead and tell you,"

Brennan admitted. "I'm so used to hiding my past. But you deserve to know."

Rachel was afraid to even nod. *Lord, give me wisdom and understanding.*

"I told Jacque that going to a slave auction when I was near his age turned me against slavery."

"I heard an account of one from a runaway slave," she murmured solemnly. The account had horrified her.

"Then I don't got to spell it out for you. When Lincoln was elected and Mississippi seceded, all my neighbors formed a militia unit. I wouldn't join. I had kept my feelings to myself till then. But I told them I couldn't fight for slavery or for secession."

She heard more than the words; she heard the enormity of the day when he'd had to stand against his neighbors.

"The only thing that saved my life was jumping in the Mississippi and swimming away."

A simple sentence and so much more behind it.

"Thee has suffered much. Why did thee hide the truth from people here? From me?"

He shook his head as if warning away a deerfly. "I get back bad memories—sometimes nightmares and sometimes in daylight even. Talking about it stirs them up I think. Besides, it wasn't anybody's business."

She heard what each of these words cost him. So she'd been right. He did have spells like other soldiers she'd met. "Thank thee for telling me."

"I want to ask you a favor, Miss Rachel."

Not another one. It seemed like everyone wanted a favor from her. She waited, saying, encouraging nothing.

"I can't stay here. I'm getting restless again . . . like before I hurt my wrist. Jacque would be better off with you. I'm not fit to raise a boy."

Caught by surprise, she felt her spine tighten as if touched by ice. "Mr. Merriday—" she began.

And then the blacksmith walked into her clearing. "Good evening!"

Rachel leaned back against the log wall, disgruntled at the interruption. "Good evening, Mr. Comstock," she said with a sigh. "Why doesn't thee pull the rocking chair out here and be comfortable?"

The man evidently took this as a good sign because he beamed at her. Within moments, he had intimidated Brennan into taking the rocker for his rib's sake and was sitting beside her.

"I did speak to Posey's grandmother today," she said.

Turning sideways, Levi looked intently into her face.

"We discussed her objection to Posey marrying a blacksmith—"

"She doesn't like my trade?" Levi asked, looking startled. "Why?"

"She doesn't object to thy trade, merely that

225

thee doesn't own land. She does not want Posey in the future to be left with nothing but a forge—if anything would happen to thee."

The blacksmith seemed to take this as a blow. "That's why she won't let me court Posey?" He sounded mystified.

Rachel touched his sleeve. "Thee must take this in context."

"What do you mean?"

"Because of the war, Mrs. Brown has witnessed her granddaughter lose everything her father had worked to provide for the security of his family. She doesn't want Posey to find herself unprovided for again."

The big man chewed the inside of his cheek and pondered this.

"I made a suggestion to Mrs. Brown," Rachel continued. "I told her that thee could claim a homestead here if that's what she required."

Levi turned sharply to her. "What did she say?"

"She said that was a good idea. She said everyone vouches for thy sound character. It's just a matter of owning land."

"I intended to stake a claim," Levi said with audible relief, "just haven't gotten around to it. And I'd have five years to prove up."

"I suggested to Mrs. Brown that Brennan helped me prove up my claim." Realizing that she had used Brennan's given name, abashed, Rachel did not look in Brennan's direction. "And perhaps he might be persuaded to help thee raise a cabin before winter. And begin cutting winter wood."

She looked at him then.

Mr. Merriday glared at her.

Levi swung to him. "I know you're healing, but it wouldn't take us long to put up a snug cabin before fall even."

Brennan did not appreciate being put on the spot. But gazing into Levi's hopeful face, he knew he couldn't let down a friend. Friends were too rare in this hard world. "Sure. As soon as I can swing an ax again."

Levi leaped up. "Should I go tell Mrs. Brown that I'm going to stake a claim?"

"I think," Miss Rachel said, "thee should find a good claim nearby and stake it. Then go and show the paperwork to Mrs. Brown and Mr. Ashford and ask permission to court Posey."

Levi pulled Miss Rachel up and threw his arms around her, lifting her off her feet. "Thank you, Miss Rachel! You've made me so happy!"

Brennan fumed at the man's taking such liberties.

Miss Rachel looked startled, but chuckled. "I think thee should say these words to Miss Brown, not me!"

The big man laughed out loud.

"What's the blacksmith hugging Miss Rachel for?" Jacque asked, arriving in the clearing.

"Miss Rachel did me a favor." Putting her down, Levi looked like a different man as he thanked her again and started away.

"Jacque, you go along with Levi and get up to bed," Brennan said. "We probably got another busy day tomorrow."

Jacque looked as if he might object, but Levi scooped him up and tossed him onto his broad shoulder. "I'll give you a ride!"

Jacque objected but only a little as Levi began teasing him and asking him about fishing.

Brennan, still resting in her rocker, watched Miss Rachel sit again.

"Why did you volunteer me to work for Levi?" he asked, nearly snarling. "I just told you I'm restless."

She smiled at him in that way he didn't like. "Restless or not, thee must stay till the letter comes from Louisiana. And I'm sure Levi will pay thee and thee can use the money to set up in Canada. Isn't that right?"

He fumed. The woman always had an answer and she was usually right. He hated that.

"Mr. Merriday, I apologize."

Her gentle tone shamed him. She was so good, so kind, so special. He nearly leaned forward but his rib stabbed him. And he held back.

A few moments of silence passed. He brushed away a stray mosquito.

He looked at her then. He ached to tell her how

228

he thought of her. But his mouth wouldn't open.

The golden cast of twilight bathed her. She was such a pretty woman. A man didn't notice it right off because she . . . protected herself. Why was she so cautious? Didn't she think a man could love her? Count himself lucky to win her?

He shot up out of the seat, hurting his side. "I gotta git to bed."

She rose, too. "Thee must be very tired. Would thee like a cup of willow bark tea before—"

"No, thanks." He held up one hand. "See you in the morning."

"Stop." She drew a folded paper from her pocket. "Take this." She shoved it into his hand and moved out of reach. "Posey wants you to read it."

He tried to hand it back but she hurried into her cabin. "Good night," she called and shut the door.

Fuming at her managing ways, he shoved the letter into his pocket. Then he tried to walk as fast as he could without jarring his rib cage. He had indeed worsened his condition when fighting the fire. The toll of another day of pain hit him fully as he glimpsed the blacksmith shop.

He slipped inside and up to his loft where Jacque was already sleeping soundly. Brennan stifled a groan as he lay down. His mind spun with thoughts of the day, of Miss Rachel, but thankfully his fatigue was mightier. His last thought was *I must leave soon.*

• • •

Brennan woke hours before dawn and turned over. Pain and his persistent regret hit him simultaneously. His side ached worse than before the fire. Something felt odd in his pocket. The letter. The letter Posey's father had written that mentioned him.

A sudden curiosity sparked. He looked around. There was enough moonlight to see to go down the ladder. He didn't want to get up. Yet he couldn't stop himself.

Moonlight led him to the shelf near the door where the box of matches and candles sat. He felt around, removed a match, struck it, the sound loud against the night cries of frogs, toads and insects. He lit one fat candle, setting it on the corner of the shelf. He sat in the chair beside the open door to the river. He slid the letter out and opened it.

July 4, 1864
Dearest Wife and Daughter,
I write to you on this Independence Day wishing that we could be together to celebrate the birth of our nation. I cannot believe the war to preserve the Union has gone on this long. I thought we'd be home in Tennessee long before this. I do not wish to complain. I am in a band of brothers. Most of us are outcasts because of our love for our nation, our whole nation.

A welcome distraction comes. Brennan Merriday, the Mississippi man I've told you about previously, has managed to trap a few rabbits. And he is busily preparing them for the spit over our fire. Merriday's a good man, run out of his town because he wouldn't enlist in the local militia. He's a stalwart fellow who speaks little but I don't know anybody I'd want more at my back in a fight.

Brennan's eyes swam with sudden tears. He pressed his thumb and index finger to the bridge of his nose and willed away the outpouring. Now he remembered Posey's father. He began to hear in his mind Clyde Brown's voice speaking the words of this letter. The sorrow of lost comrades rolled over Brennan—names and faces of men who'd taken him in—let him be a part of them when he was an outcast.

Of course, Clyde had spoken the truth—they'd all been outcasts in some way. He'd told them of the day in '61 when he'd been attacked by his own outraged homefolk.

His fingers wet from his tears, Brennan pinched the candle flame, extinguishing it. If only he could extinguish the memories that kept him from peace, from putting it all behind him. He sat in the dark many more minutes, then rose and climbed the ladder.

Clyde Brown's letter had shifted something

inside him. He began to think of what he might do for a friend here and now. But was it the letter? Or was it the petite Quaker lady who had kept him here and who beckoned him even when he knew he could never be worthy of a woman like her?

Chapter Eleven

Brennan greeted Levi at another warm, sticky dawn and started to put into motion the half-formed plan that had come to him in the early hours of the morning. After all, he must do something while his rib healed. "I was thinking that I might look around for an unclaimed tract of land for you to stake."

Levi beamed. "I've been thinking about that, too. I was going to try to take off a few days, but . . ." The blacksmith raised both his hands.

"That's why I thought I could look for you. Miss Rachel just needs me to cut winter wood for her but with this rib, I can't do that." And he needed to keep away from Miss Rachel. He felt vulnerable to her in a new way he didn't understand and didn't want to examine.

Levi nodded eagerly. "There's some land near

Noah Whitmore's place. That's not too far from town and my wife . . ." The man blushed. "If I find one, my wife would be near some nice women, Mrs. Whitmore and Mrs. Steward. That's important to women. They need somebody to talk to."

Brennan felt his face break into a grin he couldn't hide. Younger than he, Levi had not been old enough to fight and Brennan was glad the war hadn't touched him. Levi would make Posey a good husband. A momentary twinge reminded him that he wouldn't make anybody a good husband, least of all . . .

Levi pointed out the trail near the Ashfords' toward the northeast where Noah lived.

Behind them Jacque splashed, wading out of the river, his face, bare feet and hands washed. "We going to breakfast?"

Brennan almost said no. He really didn't want to see Miss Rachel today, but not to show up for breakfast at her house would shout to the surrounding village that something had changed. And not going when expected would be impolite to the fine lady. So Brennan nodded, but he must give some thought to how things were now and might be in the future. What exactly had changed he didn't understand yet. But change had come, wanted or not.

Brennan walked beside Jacque into Miss Rachel's tidy clearing. She stood outside, singing to a little brown bird. The bird was singing back to her. He stopped, riveted, and laid a hand on Jacque's shoulder. The two waited and watched. Brennan half expected the bird to fly down and light on her hand like in a story. But the exchange lasted only a few more moments and then the bird flew away.

"You were singing to that bird!" Jacque exclaimed, running toward her flat out.

Miss Rachel smiled at him and the sun shone brighter. Brennan firmly took himself in hand. He must not let whatever had opened up inside him last night, when he was reading that letter, spill over on to Miss Rachel. He must not mislead the lady.

"It was a humble thrush, but they can sing so prettily," Miss Rachel said, leaning down and talking to Jacque in much the same way she'd sung to the bird.

"Can you teach me that? How to sing to birds?"

She looked to Brennan. "What does thee think, Mr. Merriday?"

"I think he could—easy."

The boy looked up at him shyly. "You think so?"

Brennan nodded, feeling a stirring around his heart.

"How do I learn to do it, Miss Rachel?"

"It is a skill that one must learn by himself. Thee must listen and then try to make the sounds.

The younger the better, if thee wants to sing to the birds." She chuckled. "My mother started me listening and trying to imitate the birds when I was much younger than thee."

Brennan patted the boy's shoulder while he tried to stop looking at her but it was like trying to ignore the sun. The place where iron gates had stood inside him was now melting. He stiffened himself.

She looked up then and caught him gazing at her. She lifted an eyebrow but smiled. "Come! Griddle cakes for breakfast! And I have some syrup my cousin Sunny gave me. She and Noah tapped sugar maple trees this March."

His mouth watered. Griddle cakes with syrup. *What a woman.* And for so much more than just her delicious meals . . .

Later Rachel watched Brennan and Jacque head off to scout land for Levi. She had packed them a lunch in case they couldn't get back to her at noon. Something had changed about him, but she couldn't put her finger on it.

Did this have to do with Posey's letter from her father? She had hoped he would talk about the letter, but no, not a word. *That man.*

She turned back to her day's work. Before long, she heard a boat whistle. She had made more caramels and sponge candy earlier and headed to town to sell several trays of it.

"Miss Rachel!" Levi hailed her from his doorway.

She waved and then had a thought. "Mr. Comstock, when Mr. Merriday returns, please accompany him and Jacque to my place for the evening meal."

He looked surprised and pleased. "Thank you, miss! I'll do that."

She hurried on with only a nod in reply.

People from two boats vied for her candy, some pushing forward like children. A tall man in a suit bought a bag and one individual portion and then stood in the shade, eating it and observing her. His attention caused her to be wary. Why was he watching her so intently?

She sold out and then began to turn.

"Miss Rachel?" The man who'd been looking at her moved closer.

She sized him up. Dressed in a neat, dark suit with a stiff white collar and a gold pocket watch, she guessed from the elaborate fob, he didn't incite anything beyond polite interest. "My full name is Rachel Woolsey."

"Is there somewhere we could discuss a matter of business?"

This stopped her in her tracks. "Business?"

"Yes," he said, smiling.

After a few moments of surprised indecision, she led him to the wide front porch of the Ashfords' store and invited him to sit beside her on the long bench there. No one could make anything of that.

The man drew a small ivory calling card from a gold case in his inner pocket. "I'm the owner of several concerns in Dubuque, Iowa. I am interested in adding an exclusive candy counter to my food emporium. Have you ever considered selling in bulk?"

She stared at him and then read the card. "James Benson, proprietor and owner of the Benson Food Emporium. Office Second Street, Dubuque, Iowa."

"I must confess that I am surprised at this question," she murmured at last. *And that a man will talk to a woman about business.*

"The news of your fine candies has traveled down the river. A friend brought me a few not long ago and, Miss Woolsey, I have never tasted a better caramel. And your sponge candy—" he held up a piece "—is excellent, too. I always like to meet the person I do business with if I can. So I decided to come up and see if you'd like to supply my stores with your caramels and perhaps sponge candy."

She blushed at his praise. "I never thought of selling in bulk," she admitted. "I work alone."

"Then perhaps it's time to expand your operation," he replied, smiling. "I hope you will write to me soon and let me know if you could supply me with several dozen caramels a week—until the river freezes. I have an open account with certain riverboat lines to convey products to my warehouse. I would of course expect exclusivity in your distribution to Iowa."

"I will . . . I'll think about it," she stammered.

"We will need to discuss pricing and my percentage of each sale, but we can do that by mail after you've had time to consider my suggestion."

She managed to nod.

He rose. "Thank you. I look forward to hearing from you, Miss Woolsey."

She shook his hand and he strode away toward the boat landing. Her mind whirled with this news. The man had spoken to her as one businessperson to another, a revelation.

Mrs. Ashford whipped outside, her skirts snapping with her haste. "Miss Rachel, Ned told me you were talking to a man on our porch."

The woman's nosiness acted on Rachel like a spring tonic. She rose and held out his card. No use sparking speculation by withholding the facts. "He wants to order my candies in bulk."

Mrs. Ashford snatched the card and read it. "Benson Food Emporiums. Oh, my. That is a large concern. How did he hear of you?"

Rachel recounted what she could recall of the interesting yet surprising encounter with Mr. Benson.

"Well!" Mrs. Ashford exclaimed. "Well!"

Rachel couldn't decide whether the woman was

happy for her or disgruntled or just surprised. "I must be getting back to my place. I have a lot to do today." *And a lot to think and pray about.*

As she hurried homeward, rolling her cart through town, she felt Mrs. Ashford's curiosity-filled gaze burn into her back. When she reached her place, she rolled the cart into the shade and then sat down on the bench near her door. *Sell in bulk? What an idea.*

She wished suddenly that Mr. Merriday were here. She'd become accustomed to his being available . . . but perhaps that wouldn't last much longer. He still wanted to go to Canada.

She'd have time to observe him again at supper. Maybe then she could figure out what had changed. And what that change might mean.

Rachel took pains to look her best, sweeping her hair up, changing into a fresh white apron and splashing cool water on her face. She told herself it was because Mr. Comstock was to be her guest, but she knew better. She wanted to look her best for Mr. Merriday.

The sweltering day had been a long and lonely one. She'd tried to ignore the lonely part, singing to the birds that hopped on the nearby tree branches and even chatting away to the huddle of chickens in the yard. But now she could share her news with Mr. Merriday. What would he have to say?

Finally she heard male voices and forced herself to remain inside until the last moment. She didn't want to betray how eager she was for their company, for his company. So she opened the door to find Brennan and Jacque washing their hands by her door.

Levi waved from behind them. "I washed up at home."

She grinned at this. "I'm glad to have thee join us tonight. This is a sort of celebration. I'm anticipating that Mr. Merriday will have news about thy property and I . . ." she paused for effect ". . . have news of my own today."

"What happened to you?" Jacque asked, drying his hands on the hucksack towel.

"All in good time," she teased. "Come in."

She'd prepared fried chicken. Mrs. Brawley, a neighbor, had decided to thin her chickens and had delivered birds already plucked. Since Rachel expected company for supper, she had purchased three.

"Wow! Fried chicken!" Jacque exclaimed and Levi joined in, too.

Soon the four of them sat at her table. She bowed her head for grace and then looked up. "Mr. Comstock, please help yourself."

The blacksmith grinned and took a piece from the platter of crisp, golden chicken. By the time it reached Jacque, only a drumstick remained. She rose and filled the platter again to vocal approval.

"Now, Mr. Merriday, did thee find some land for Mr. Comstock?" she asked as she began to slice her chicken breast.

Brennan chewed and swallowed. "Good chicken, Miss Rachel, and yes, I found two tracts that are near the Whitmores."

"Great," Levi said and then bit into a crispy wing.

"Which one does thee think is best?" she asked.

"The one with its own spring," Brennan said between bites. "In a drought year like this one, springs flow while wells may dry up."

For a moment all four were silent as they contemplated the dry weather and the recent grass wildfire.

"What else?" Levi asked.

"Got a good stand of trees a-course. Creek runs near it, too, and a small meadow where we could build your cabin."

Rachel's heart lifted against her will at this news. She shouldn't care that this sounded as if Brennan would be staying longer, but she couldn't lie to herself.

"Sounds great." Levi continued eating his chicken and cornbread with a smile on his face. "I'll apply for the claim on that land tomorrow."

"Sight unseen?" Brennan asked.

"You were a farmer, weren't you? You know more about land than I do. I was raised in town to be a blacksmith like my dad."

"Is it hard to learn to blacksmith?" Jacque asked.

All three adults turned to the boy.

" 'Course you could," Brennan said.

"I think it would be interesting," Jacque said with a shrug. He tried not to look pleased. Then he looked to her. "What's your news, Miss Rachel?"

From her pocket, she retrieved the business card and handed it to Brennan.

He read it aloud and looked at her questioningly.

"Mr. Benson wants to buy my caramels and sponge candy in bulk."

All three males stared at her. Openmouthed.

"Well, what does thee think of that?" she asked.

"What does in bulk mean?" Jacque asked.

"That means they want her to make large batches and they'll sell her candy in their stores in Dubuque," Levi replied. "That's big."

Rachel felt herself turn rosy with pleasure. "I don't know if I can handle that. I mean soon Mr. Merriday plans on moving on—"

"What?" Jacque turned to Brennan. "What? Where we goin'?"

Brennan sent her a dark look. "Nowhere—yet. I had thought of Canada, but I'm not going nowhere anytime soon. It's just I been helping Miss Rachel prove up her homestead and now I'm going to help Levi. No time to get my own land."

Rachel frowned at him. Giving only part of the

truth ranked as bad as an outright lie. And getting his own land—that was downright misleading. What about Canada? Had that changed? She wouldn't let herself hope.

He sent her a stern look, forbidding her to contradict him. And he squeezed the boy's shoulder. "Don't be worryin'."

Jacque looked down.

She drew in a deep breath. "Whether or not to sell in bulk is a big decision for me. But a welcome problem."

The meal passed then with the three males talking little and eating every last piece of chicken. She wished Levi were married and Posey had come with him so she would have had someone to chat with, someone to distract her from staring at Mr. Merriday.

Afterward Levi sat with Brennan outside near where Jacque and she washed and dried the dishes. Then Levi thanked her again for a wonderful meal and at Brennan's request let Jacque walk with him toward town.

Rachel guessed why Brennan remained behind and why he didn't want Jacque present. She put the dishes away and came outside. The setting sun was fiery red, predicting another hot day on the morrow. She sat down next to Mr. Merriday. "Thee is planning on scolding me?"

"Why'd you say I was leaving?"

At his unfair question, she starched up.

"Because thee has been saying that since the day thee was able to begin 'talking in June. Thee didn't tell me not to mention it in front of Jacque."

He grumbled, "I know."

He'd poked her and she felt like goading him in return. "If thee plans on reaching Canada before winter, that will interfere with thy plans to help Levi."

"Don't you think I know that?" he snapped and then grimaced. "Sorry, that was not polite."

"Matters have not gone as thee had foreseen," she allowed. *And I'm glad.* Of course she couldn't voice that sentiment.

"I wish that letter would come from Louisiana."

She turned and looked him full in the face. "Does thee really think thee will be able to leave Jacque behind, even if he isn't thy son?"

He glared at her, his brows drawn together almost fiercely. "He's a great little kid. He's had it rough but my keeping him won't do him any favors—whether he's my blood or not."

His statement shocked her. "Whatever does thee mean? Thee is a fine man, Brennan Merriday. Thee has proved that over and over. I'm sorry thy homefolk cast thee out, but the fault did not lie with thee, but with their wicked, hard hearts."

"I don't know why I say things that I know will just fire you up. And I guess after drifting so long and people looking down on me, I just—"

"Then stop thinking that way. Thee is a fine man, Brennan Merriday. No one told me to think that. I know it from thy own actions since thee came to town."

He didn't reply and she let the silence grow between them.

"I read the letter from Posey's father. He understood how it felt when everybody he'd ever known turned against him." The sadness in his voice caught her breath.

She swallowed to clear her throat. "I think thee still believes that the people in thy hometown had a right to turn against thee. They didn't. They were wrong. Thee was right."

He rose, looking as if he were struggling to digest what she'd said. "I thank you for another good meal, Miss Rachel. And I bid you good night."

He walked away with a wave of his hand, leaving her dissatisfied. The man was impossible. Why couldn't he see that he'd done nothing wrong? Why couldn't he let go of the past and live in the present—here in Pepin? Was she foolish to hope in the end he might stay?

On Sunday morning next, Brennan appeared at the door, his hair damp from the river and with Jacque beside him. Brennan was wearing his newer clothing from the Ashfords instead of his work clothes. "We ready to head to church?"

Rachel hid her surprise behind a bland nod. Brennan had never attended church with her or been a part of anything in the community. What did this change mean?

Was this due to his son's presence or Posey's letter? Brennan clearly had not healed from whatever had separated him from his wife and started him wandering. Rachel began praying that God would take control of this morning—more than in general. *God, why does he want to go to church with me and the boy?*

Brennan watched her turn and pick up her Bible from the bedside table and then snag her bonnet from the peg. Brennan accepted her Bible while she tied the pale ribbons under her chin, a pleasant sight.

Brennan tried not to back out now. He'd decided to go sit in the schoolhouse church. But his reasons tangled in the back of his mind. The one that had prompted him clearly was Jacque, what was best for him—whether he turned out to be his blood or not. If the boy had a future here, Brennan didn't want to do anything to harm that. Wanted the boy to fit in. Besides, church was good for a boy—would teach him right from wrong.

As the three of them walked through town, Levi joined them in his Sunday best, too. Levi's happiness over staking a claim and the subsequent granting of permission to court Miss Posey worried Brennan. The grandmother had given her permission, but she seemed an unreasonable kind of woman.

Soon the four of them joined the wagons and people on foot, converging on the log school-house. Noah stood at the door, greeting his congregation. Here was one man Brennan respected. When Noah offered him a hand, Brennan shook it, smiling.

"I'm glad to see you, Mr. Merriday," the preacher said without any reproachful tone in his words.

"Thanks, preacher," Brennan replied.

Inside the door, an older man Brennan had seen around town in a wheelchair held out his hand. "I'm Old Saul, Mr. Merriday. I'm glad to meet you."

Brennan shook the man's gnarled hand, hoping he wouldn't hear any scolding about why he hadn't come sooner.

"I've met your son here before." Old Saul reached over and shook Jacque's hand and Levi's. "We're glad to have you with us this Sunday and in our town."

Brennan doubted that but he mumbled something polite.

The older man appeared frail but he had a look that could pierce a man. Brennan nodded and moved ahead to let others greet Old Saul. He glanced at Rachel.

"I usually sit with my cousin's wife," Miss Rachel murmured.

"Yes, miss," Brennan replied. "I think we'll sit with Levi today."

She nodded and moved forward to the front to sit beside Noah's pretty wife, Sunny.

Then Levi led the two of them to a few pews behind the Ashfords. "This is where I usually sit," the blacksmith murmured. The men sat with the boy between them. "Old Saul used to be the preacher before Noah," Levi said quietly. "He's a good man, always a kind word to everybody."

Nodding, Brennan noted but didn't acknowledge any of the interest his attending church elicited. He didn't want to fit in here. He'd just come because he wanted the boy accepted—that was all.

One tall, elegant lady approached him. "Good day, Mr. Merriday. I am Mrs. Lang, Johann's aunt."

Brennan, Levi and Jacque rose politely.

"I am going to continue as teacher here at least for a few months," she said. "The school board has a teacher coming but the man has met with an accident and so has been delayed. I hope you will be sending your son."

"Of course," Brennan replied without hesitation. "Schooling is good."

Jacque looked undecided about this.

"Johann, I know, is looking forward to the start

of school," the woman said, smiling at Jacque and touching his shoulder.

This brightened the boy's face. Mrs. Lang bid them good day and moved to sit with her husband, their baby, Johann and Gunther.

The wall clock read ten and the service started with a hymn, "Just As I Am, Without One Plea," led by an older couple at the front. Brennan stood but didn't sing a note. He was surprised to hear Levi sing with a strong tenor and Jacque piping a boyish soprano.

Levi must have sung louder than usual because people turned to look at him. And then Brennan saw Posey glance behind at Levi and smile. Brennan figured it out. Singing louder was like a bullfrog croaking to attract feminine attention. Brennan wished he could preserve the flash of amusement this brought him.

But soon everyone sat and the singing was done and the preaching began. He wondered what kind of preacher Noah Whitmore would turn out to be. He didn't expect fire and brimstone and pounding the pulpit and he was right. Then Noah read Matthew 10:

Think not that I am come to send peace on earth: I came not to send peace, but a sword.

For I am come to set a man at variance against his father.

And a man's foes shall be they of his own household.

Each word struck Brennan like a hammer blow. The terrible sinking feeling began in the pit of his stomach. He gripped the bench underneath him and willed away images of that dreadful day, the day the state of Mississippi had seceded, the day he'd made his decision known.

He fought free and looked at Levi to see if he'd exposed any of his inner turmoil. Levi wasn't looking at him. He was gazing at the back of Posey's bonnet. Surreptitiously Brennan surveyed the people around him who were blessedly ignoring him also.

He blocked out the rest of Noah's words, forcing himself to stare at the wood floor and go over in his mind what he had to do at Levi's newly staked homestead now that his rib had healed. Surely before fall had passed, he'd receive the letter and have Levi's work done.

At the end of the sermon, Brennan rose with everyone and listened to Noah's benediction. "The Lord bless thee, and keep thee. The Lord make his face shine upon thee, and be gracious unto thee. The Lord lift up his countenance upon thee, and give thee peace."

Brennan felt a touch of that peace. *Must be due to Noah Whitmore, one lucky man.* The three of them turned to find Miss Rachel waiting for them at the rear of the church with—of all people—Mrs. Ashford.

Brennan didn't want to talk to the woman but he had brought Posey's letter. He had meant to slip it to Posey when no one was looking, but when would that be?

"We want to invite the four of you to Sunday dinner," the storekeeper's wife said brightly.

Brennan tried not to look surprised or distressed, as he was both.

"That is a kind invitation," Miss Rachel said, looking to him as if asking him to come up with a good excuse.

His mind was a blank slate.

And that's how they ended upstairs, sitting around the Ashfords' table. Posey's grandmother had not been well enough to walk to church but she sat at the table. Brennan almost felt sorry for her. She had obviously lost flesh everywhere but in her swollen abdomen, another sign it might be heart trouble.

Mr. Ashford said a long and flowery grace and then the meal began—roast beef, mashed potatoes and fresh green beans with bacon. *Almost as good as Miss Rachel's meals.*

Brennan had made up his mind. He would eat and say nothing except thank-you at the end.

Mrs. Ashford started the conversation. "Mr. Merriday, you have certainly improved your situation since coming to Pepin." He swallowed not only his mouthful of food, but also the sharp reply that came to mind. *He didn't want to be judged. Nobody did.*

"You've become quite respectable," the woman continued.

Miss Rachel gasped audibly.

Saying that Mrs. Ashford lacked tact was like saying the Mississippi flowed south to New Orleans. Brennan stared at the woman without a word to say.

"Mr. Merriday was a friend, a comrade in arms with my father," Posey said with quiet dignity. "Mr. Merriday may have come to town sick and in a bad situation, but he has always been respectable."

Levi beamed at her.

"Indeed," Miss Rachel murmured.

"Mr. Comstock," Almeria said, filling the uncomfortable silence, "tell us about your claim."

Brennan was taken aback. He'd never expected this woman to come to his aid.

Chapter Twelve

Levi stepped into the fray, another buffer between Mrs. Ashford and Brennan's temper. "Well, Brennan went out to look at land for me—I've been so busy with work at the forge. And he's a farmer so I thought he'd know how to assess land better than I would."

Grateful to Levi, Rachel felt her tension ease a fraction.

"You didn't go yourself?" the older woman asked sharply.

"I trust Brennan," Levi replied. "And after staking my claim, I went to the land and he chose the right tract. I saw that right away. Has a spring and a creek running near it. We'll not want for water—no matter whether rain comes or not."

The older woman appeared appeased.

Rachel relaxed. Now if Mrs. Ashford would concentrate on Levi, not Brennan—

"Why don't you stake a claim for yourself, Mr. Merriday?" Mrs. Ashford asked.

Steadily chewing his food, Brennan stared at the woman.

Rachel spoke up. "Mr. Merriday never planned

to settle here." Was the woman completely oblivious to the effect of her questions? "He's only here because he was left by that boat captain when he was ill. And he graciously agreed to help me prove up my homestead."

"But why move?" Mrs. Ashford said. "There's land and work for you, Mr. Merriday. Why not settle here?"

Rachel wondered where Mrs. Ashford's change of attitude was coming from.

Brennan continued eating, looking more and more as if he would let loose with something rude at any moment.

Rachel nearly stopped eating but forced herself to go on.

"I'm going to write my parents," Levi said, again diverting attention, "that I'm courting a young lady. I'd like them to come up and meet Posey before—" the man blushed "—before . . . winter."

Rachel was certain he meant to say *before we become formally engaged* and her heart softened. "I'd like to meet thy family, Mr. Comstock."

"Are you two really gonna get married?" Jacque asked.

The boy's question, which so obviously revealed his opinion that girls were to be devoutly avoided, lightened the mood around the table.

Rachel chuckled.

"Yes, we are," Posey said, smiling at Jacque.

"Children should be seen and not heard," Mrs. Ashford said stringently.

"Sometimes," Brennan began, "adults should be—"

"I've decided to write that Mr. Benson in Dubuque," Rachel interrupted, fearing Mr. Merriday was about to insult their hostess. "I may need to find some local help. Producing in bulk and then shipping the candy while still fresh might force me to find someone to work with me."

"I'd love to help you," Posey said.

"Me, too!" Amanda joined in.

Their responses did not surprise Rachel yet she saw Mrs. Ashford look a bit irritated.

"I will need to discuss terms with Mr. Benson first," Rachel said, "to see if doing business with him would profit me enough that I could compensate anyone."

"Very wise," Mr. Ashford said. "So far, Miss Rachel, you have made very sound business decisions for a woman. Please feel free to discuss Mr. Benson's terms with me."

In spite of the "for a woman" slur, Miss Rachel smiled at him. He had been helpful in ordering her new oven and she liked the man. He and his wife, especially his wife, wanted to be thought important, but they were honest, good people. She tried to catch Brennan's eye to encourage him to show some grace.

He merely sent her a brief scowl.

As soon as he finished his meal, he rose. "I thank you for the good meal, ma'am." And with that he left.

Mrs. Ashford looked surprised. "Well," she said, "well."

Mr. Ashford gazed at her pointedly. "Katharine, Mr. Merriday went through the war and like your sister lost everything because of it. We can afford to be charitable."

While these words appeared to calm the lady of the house, they stirred up a storm in Jacque's eyes.

Everyone but Rachel seemed to have forgotten this boy came from Mississippi.

"The news from the South is disturbing," Posey said. "It's like people still want to fight the war. Hasn't there been enough suffering?" The young woman's tone radiated despair.

"You Yankees took everything!" Jacque stood up, red-faced. He barged from the room and they heard his footsteps thunder down the back staircase.

"Well!" Mrs. Ashford exclaimed once more.

Rachel rested a hand on the lady's. "I think Jacque suffered greatly in the war, too. He lost everyone except his father and I'm sure he witnessed fighting and . . . killing."

"But we—" Mrs. Ashford began.

"She's right," Almeria spoke up. "You didn't

suffer as we did. Your son was in California, a long way from the war and you didn't lose anything to a marauding army or suffer for your support of the Union. There's an old spiritual that starts, 'Nobody knows the trouble I've seen. . . .' " The older woman shook her head and laid down her fork. "I'm tired, Posey. Please help me to my room."

Levi stood up. "I'll help you, ma'am. If you'll permit me."

Rachel had never seen the older woman smile.

Almeria did now. "Yes, please."

Levi helped her out of her chair, offered her his arm and let her lean against him as he walked her down the short hallway to her room. Posey trailed behind the two.

When Rachel turned, she found Mrs. Ashford dabbing her eyes with a hankie. "I don't know," the woman whispered in a choked voice, "how long we'll have her with us."

Rachel had thought the two strong-minded women would grate on each other's nerves. Yet Mrs. Ashford's sadness appeared completely genuine. Rachel tilted her head and murmured a sympathetic phrase. Mrs. Ashford was a mixture of the maddening and the benign. *Well, aren't we all? Even Brennan Merriday.*

Rachel found Jacque sitting in the shade of her shed where a bit of coolness could be found.

Once again she must pour balm upon this young, wounded heart. Where was Brennan? She'd fretted over him all day. But right now dealing with Jacque was all she could handle.

"I ain't gonna apologize to that Yankee," he said, firing up.

"Jacque, I am a Yankee, too, remember?"

He wouldn't let her catch his eye.

She reached down and claimed his hand. "Thee missed a really good apple pie."

He let her take his hand and lead him to the cabin but still kept his eyes lowered.

Inside, she nudged him to sit on the bench at the table and brought out a cookie and handed it to him. "Thee must give up the war, Jacque. The Union was preserved. Slavery is abolished forever. And it's time to let go."

He sent her a disgusted look.

The boy had much to learn and school started tomorrow. She couldn't let him go to a school full of Yankees and continue hating them. The truth would set him free, so she would give him truth. "I'm a Quaker. Thee knows that many Quakers were abolitionists?"

He chewed the cookie slowly, ignoring her.

"Jacque, I understand the war injured thee in many ways, but that does not mean I will tolerate impoliteness. I asked thee a question, please answer it."

"Yeah, I heard of abolitionists and Quakers."

"And the Underground Railroad?"

He looked up at this. "You didn't do that, did you?"

She nodded. "My family hid runaway slaves twice when I was a child."

Jacque looked at her as if she'd just said that a wanted outlaw and she were best friends.

"Slavery was wrong." She sat down across from him.

He folded his arms across his narrow chest and glared at the tabletop.

Her heart ached not only for this boy but for all the suffering slavery had unleashed upon them. God was not mocked. Whatever a man or a nation sowed, that it would reap. "Would thee have wanted to be a slave?"

He glared up at her then. "It's not the same."

"Because thee was born with white skin? Take a moment and think of life if thee had black skin." She fell silent. "Thy mother died, but how would it have felt to have been sold away from thy mother?"

The silence grew and the outdoor noises, the clicking of insects and singing of birds, grew louder.

"My pa . . ." Jacque corrected himself. "I mean, Mr. Merriday says he went to a slave auction and it was awful." The boy's tone said that he had given this a lot of thought.

"I'm sure it was."

Jacque looked at her then. "He said he saw that they were people. But everybody told me slavery was best for black people. That they weren't smart enough to look after themselves."

The old lie. Rachel rose and lifted one of her books down. "This book was written by a man named Frederick Douglass." She forced Jacque to take the book from her. "He was born a slave, ran away and became an educated man. He is certainly able to look after himself. It is titled *Narrative of the Life of Frederick Douglass, An American Slave.*"

Jacque looked at the book as if it were a snake about to strike.

"Tomorrow thee will begin school and will learn how to read and write better. And as soon as thee is able, we will read this, Mr. Douglass's story, together. He knows what it was like to be a slave. After we finish the book, we will discuss slavery."

She realized that she'd just given a promise she might not be able to keep. What if Brennan left, taking this boy with him? Or just left her? Her heart felt crushed by a dreadful weight.

Jacque stared at the book a long while. Then he glanced up. His face had lost its stubborn rebelliousness. "I want to hear what that man's book has to say. You've treated me better than anybody ever has. You feed me good food. You make me new clothes. You talk nice to me."

"Mr. Merriday has done good by you too," she prompted.

He grimaced. "He's okay . . . for a Yankee."

She let it go at that. They were making some progress here.

He ran his hand up the spine of the book and then handed it back to her. "You think school will be good?"

Rejoicing silently, she accepted the book, returned it to the shelf over her bed and turned to him. "I liked school. That boy, Clayton, will be there but Mrs. Lang will keep him in line at least till the new teacher comes. Make sure thee obeys the teacher and all will work out well."

Jacque nodded. "How come you're so nice to me?"

Rachel let herself stroke the boy's hair and cup his cheek. "I was raised to treat others as I would want to be treated. I suggest thee lives that way, too."

"Even to Clayton?"

She laughed out loud and ruffled his hair. Suddenly it was so hot and she longed to do something she'd done as a child. "Let's go wading in the creek and cool off."

"Miss Rachel! Really?"

Grinning, soon Rachel walked beside Jacque toward the creek, looking forward to taking off her shoes and wading in the cool water. But where had Mr. Merriday gone?

And what would she do when he finished helping to build Mr. Comstock's cabin and left for Canada? Or would he stay? When would that letter from Louisiana come and did she really want it to come? Would this truth set them free or just set them at odds?

After a day of wandering near the river and keeping out of sight, Brennan finally gave in and headed for Miss Rachel's cabin. He didn't want to need her, but he couldn't stay away.

He paused to look through the trees into her clearing. Everything was as usual—neat and tidy, well ordered. Jacque was sitting on the bench by the door, whittling a stick with a small knife. A striped black-and-white stray cat had come from somewhere and was lying at the boy's feet.

Mrs. Ashford's voice came back. *Mr. Merriday, you have certainly improved your situation since coming to Pepin.* Brennan gritted his teeth. That obnoxious woman's words had repeated in his mind all day—no matter what he did. She might be right and he didn't like it. Resisting again, he started to turn away.

Then he glimpsed Miss Rachel come to the open doorway. She scanned the edges of the clearing. Was she looking for him? He didn't like the way his heart lifted at this thought. But it was just a false twinge. He had no heart left. It had been beaten out of him long ago.

Still, he went into the clearing and tried to ignore how her welcoming smile captured him.

"Where you been all day?" the boy demanded.

"That your cat?" Brennan responded, ignoring the question.

"I don't know. She just come this afternoon when we were wading in the creek." Jacque leaned down and the cat let him rub her head with his knuckles.

"You know it's a she?"

"Miss Rachel says she's gonna have kittens soon."

"Yes," the lady spoke up. "I'm hoping she's come to stay. One can always use a good mouser. But, Jacque, remember I said she might have decided merely to visit us. We'll just have to see."

Brennan stared at her. This woman was always taking in strays—this cat, Jacque, him. He stalked to the basin and washed his hands. "I'll go milk the cow."

"I already did that," Jacque said.

Mrs. Ashford intruded again—*You've become quite respectable.*

Brennan's jaw tightened. If only he could have told off the storekeeper's nosey wife, she wouldn't still be digging her spurs into him.

"Come in to supper." Miss Rachel waved him forward. "We're having cornbread and milk."

"And the last of the cookies?" Jacque asked hopefully.

Brennan couldn't help himself. He laughed out loud.

Miss Rachel beamed at him.

He followed her, the boy and the cat inside. Yesterday Miss Rachel had baked a double batch of buttery cornbread, which now disappeared, eaten from bowls of milk drizzled with maple syrup. He savored the salty and sweet and the rich flavors of cornmeal and maple.

The quiet of the cabin and Miss Rachel's good food worked on him, soothing him. Here he felt at home, an unwelcome thought.

Why don't you stake a claim for yourself, Mr. Merriday? Mrs. Ashford had asked.

He put down his spoon and rubbed his forehead. The awful restlessness he'd experienced that evening down by the river goaded him again. He wished he could bid Pepin farewell. He would never feel easy till he put the war behind him and that was impossible here. But some part of him reached for Miss Rachel as if she might make everything right.

"Jacque will be going to school tomorrow," Miss Rachel said. "I will walk with him and thee."

Brennan stared at her. He knew why she said this. She was insisting he act as father to this boy. He nodded, looking her full in the face and then away as her sweetness broke over him afresh. "No trouble. We'll walk over after breakfast and then

I'm headin' out to Levi's place. Your cousin is going to help me do some more logging out the clearing. And plowing up rocks for the foundation."

She nodded. "I'm glad to hear that Noah is helping."

"Yeah, the sooner I get Levi set up, the sooner I can head north."

Jacque looked up quickly. "We still gonna leave?"

Brennan didn't like the strain in the boy's voice. And it prompted him to be honest. "I've always planned on going north to Canada."

"But it's terrible cold up there," the boy whined.

Brennan shrugged and Miss Rachel pressed her lips together.

They finished the meal in silence and then Jacque went outside to play with the cat and a bit of string.

Miss Rachel didn't mince words, as usual, but spoke in an undertone. "I don't understand why thee fights settling down and being a father. Why isn't thee happy having a son and friends here? What's stopping thee from staking a homestead claim here?"

He rubbed the back of his neck. "I just can't be free till I leave this country."

"If thee believes that, thee is fooling thyself. Thee will take the war with thee wherever thee tries to settle. The past is a part of us, not a coat one can shed."

He rose abruptly. Words of denial jammed in his throat. "Thanks for the meal," he managed to say. "I'll see you in the morning."

He walked out and told the boy to come to the forge when he finished the dishes for Miss Rachel.

Jacque pouted and Brennan walked away. But with every step, he felt the pull, the unseen bond connecting him and the lady who stood in her doorway watching him leave. She was right, of course, about the past, and that made it all worse.

The first Monday of September the two of them walked Jacque to the schoolyard and Mr. Merriday enrolled him in school. Though the boy was ten, he would work with the first graders but be allowed to sit beside his friend, Johann. Rachel was intensely grateful to Mrs. Lang for her understanding.

Rachel and Mr. Merriday barely reached the main street and he was off, heading toward Levi's homestead. She watched him go. Not for the first time, she wished she could get inside his mind. Or maybe his heart. He'd suffered so and insisted on carrying it forward into the present. Why?

Christ had said, *Let the dead bury their dead.* Why couldn't Brennan bury the past, not let it control him? Slavery had been a bondage to everyone it touched.

But who was she to think she could solve this

problem or any other? Shaking her head at her own pride and praying for Brennan, she walked home to set her cinnamon rolls in the oven to bake. She expected boats today and was not disappointed.

Later, as she sold the last of her wares, she watched Mr. Ashford accept the mailbag. For some reason she slowed her steps homeward.

"Miss Rachel!" the storekeeper-postmaster called out. "There is a letter for Mr. Merriday. From Louisiana!"

Suddenly finding it difficult to breathe, Rachel turned and accepted the letter, then slipped it into her pocket. "I'll make sure he gets it. He's working on Levi's homestead today."

Mr. Ashford nodded, but she could tell he was curious about the letter from Louisiana, too.

She trundled the cart homeward, intensely aware of the letter in her pocket. Now she must wait hours for Mr. Merriday to come and open it. She would have to keep very busy so she didn't rip it open herself.

Brennan tried to keep the pace of the work steady enough to reduce the chance for talk. Brennan respected Noah and still owed him for saving his life, but he didn't want any advice. And couldn't preachers always be counted on to give advice?

Noah had brought his horse and plow to turn over the ground where the cabin would be and where a future garden would sit. They turned up a fresh crop of Wisconsin rocks. Brennan had never seen soil like this. Every furrow was clogged with stones.

Noah had brought over a wheelbarrow the night before. After they had dug out and piled up all the rocks from the cabin site, the two men filled the wheelbarrow with them. Then they rolled the rocks with strenuous effort to where the two-room cabin would stand.

Then Mrs. Whitmore brought over a fresh pot of steaming coffee and lunch. She left them with a friendly wave.

"I'm a lucky man," Noah said when the two of them were alone again.

Brennan nodded.

"I know you plan on leaving, but have you considered staying at all?"

Brennan concentrated on chewing the sandwich and damped down his ire at the meddling. "I just want to get away from the war, from anybody who fought in it."

"I understand. I came to Wisconsin for just that reason."

Brennan looked up. "Then you understand."

"I came to Wisconsin to live but to keep myself separate from the folk here. Sort of live like a hermit."

The idea appealed to Brennan.

"But 'no man is an island,' " Noah quoted. "I

found myself sucked into the community and couldn't keep apart. I'm glad now because I've been healing. I used to have nightmares and spells where I'd be back to that awful waiting time just before a battle. You know what I mean." Noah shook his head.

Brennan looked at him then. Noah had nightmares, too? And that dreaded feeling of being dragged back into the living nightmare of waiting to charge into battle? "I've had a few spells myself," Brennan admitted, not meeting Noah's gaze. "You still have 'em?"

"Not often anymore. Having my wife and children and living in this fresh new place, I got a new start. And letting God in, not holding Him off. All that is healing me."

Brennan didn't know what to say to this. He and God were not on speaking terms. Noah understood, but he hadn't lost everything, everyone in the war. Noah was a lucky man, luckier than he was.

"I'll say no more." Noah sipped his coffee. "But you could do worse than settle here. You've made friends and . . . there's Rachel."

Noah's mention of his cousin in connection with Brennan came completely unexpectedly. He ignored it, merely nodded once curtly to acknowledge that he'd heard Noah. But no matter what anybody said, he wasn't settling in Pepin. Miss Rachel would be better off without him.

Dry-mouthed, Brennan stared at the letter on Miss Rachel's mantel. Earlier she'd told him it had come at last, but quietly so that the boy wouldn't hear. Jacque didn't know about the letter and what it might mean for him. Supper had ended and now Jacque played outside with the striped cat, leaving the two of them alone in the cabin.

Brennan reached for the letter. Part of him strained to head out and read it alone. But Miss Rachel had written his letter and he could imagine how much self-control she'd used to keep from tearing it open this morning.

She handed him a clean butter knife and he slit open the envelope.

Saint Joseph's Church
Parish of Alexandria
Alexandria, Louisiana

August 16, 1871
Dear Mr. Merriday,
I write to inform you that Jacque Louis Charpentier Merriday was born on November 13, 1861, son of Lorena Charpentier Merriday and was baptized. You are listed as the father. Lorena's death is recorded on December 24, 1864, and she is buried in the churchyard.
May God bless you and young Jacque.
The Right Reverend August Joseph Martin

Brennan read the brief letter twice and then handed it to Miss Rachel.

"So we have the answer to the question," she murmured. "Jacque is thy son."

He couldn't speak. His face felt frozen.

"What now?"

He stared at her. Finally, he said, "I don't know."

"Jacque must be told."

He rose and shook his head. "Not yet."

She gazed at him a long time. "Soon."

The woman was relentless. "All right."

He left then, memories of his few years with Lorena spinning through his mind. He waved to the boy and the two walked through the dying light to Levi's.

This boy is my son. He repeated the words silently. Some part of him had known that Jacque belonged to him, but he'd resisted it. And it had nothing to do with the boy.

The evening before, Rachel had watched Brennan walk out of her clearing and then she'd barely slept all night. Now she tried to go through her morning routine, mixing batter for muffins to sell today and waiting for Brennan and Jacque to arrive for breakfast. Had Brennan told Jacque? That didn't seem possible. But he must.

Finally Jacque arrived—alone. "Mornin', Miss Rachel!" The boy stopped and washed his hands outside.

"Where is Mr. Merriday?" she asked, hiding her sharp reaction to his absence.

"He went straight out to Levi's place. I asked him, didn't he want breakfast, and he said Mrs. Whitmore would give him something."

Rachel held in all the aggravation and disappointment and words that wanted to be released. Did the man think avoiding her would let him avoid the truth?

Soon Jacque had eaten and he set off for school. She watched him go and finished her baking. A boat whistled and she hurried into town to sell her muffins.

Then she parked her cart in the shade near the schoolyard and headed up the road. She could not wait till this evening to hear what Mr. Merriday was going to do now.

It was just like him to pull back instead of talking matters over. The man nearly drove her insane and yet she dreaded the day he might act upon what he'd said since the beginning. *I can't bear to have him leave.*

The miles under the relentless sun passed quickly and she was drawn by the sound of someone cutting down a tree. She turned toward the sound and saw Mr. Merriday ahead, working alone. That bothered her, too. A man should never cut tall trees by himself. It was too dangerous.

She waited till the tree trembled and then fell, bouncing and rolling to a halt against the surrounding trees. "Brennan!" she called and then halted abruptly. Why had she called him by his given name?

He turned to her and scowled. "Is something wrong?"

She shook her head at him, disappointed, exasperated. "Surely thee can guess why I have come?"

He motioned for her to come closer while he mopped his forehead with a kerchief. He waved her to sit on a stump and he sat down on one across from her. "The letter."

"Yes, the letter. What does thee plan to do about the fact that Jacque is thy son?"

He covered his face with the kerchief for a moment and then lowered it. "I've decided to ask you to marry me."

His words were so unexpected that she thought she'd imagined them. "What?"

He repeated the proposal or something that might be deemed a proposal. A sorry one.

"Marry? Me?" She stared at him, her heart suddenly bounding with hope. "Has thee fallen in love with me?"

He wrinkled his face. "Love? What's that got to do with us?"

She drew in air so sharply she nearly choked. "Indeed." Her word could have frozen water.

"You're not one of those foolish women," he said with disdain. "You're a good woman and you have good sense." He said the words fiercely, as if someone were arguing with him.

Rachel was not complimented. Her heart began beating in a sluggish kind of funeral rhythm. "And that's why thee wants to marry me?" She mocked him with her words.

He didn't hear her sarcasm or ignored it. "No, of course not. It's the boy. He needs a home and family. And you're right. If I want to shed the past, going to Canada won't help. I'll have to find a way not to remember the war, root it out of my memory —though how that's possible, I don't know."

Being valued for only the services she could provide, not because she was worthy of love. It was happening to her again. "I see."

"It makes sense for you and me to wed. Jacque likes you. You're a good cook and a good woman. I'd do my part. We could be content."

She had told Brennan in all honesty about the previous proposal she had received. Obviously he had forgotten or ignored her. "Content?" she asked icily.

He eyed her. "You're not going to get all fluttery and feminine on me, are you? It could be strictly a business arrangement. If you don't want me to touch you, I won't."

The final insult was too much. She rose—ice gone—molten lava rolling through her. "Brennan Merriday, as a *spinster,* I have been insulted many times in my life. But I don't think anyone—not even the man who needed a mother for his six young children and who asked me to marry him a week after he buried his wife—insulted me quite as thoroughly as thee has done today. Do not darken my door again."

She turned on her heel, ignoring his protestations.

Noah was coming up the trail toward them. She nodded at her cousin and went on without looking back.

Strictly business—the words twisted inside her like red-hot iron. And she knew the hurt was not Brennan's fault. She'd allowed her heart to overrule her head. She'd let herself have feelings for a man, incapable or unwilling to admit he could love or that she was a woman worthy of love.

She would marry no man for *sensible* reasons. Or for *his* convenience. Or to be *content.* Not even Brennan Merriday, the man she loved with all her heart.

Chapter Thirteen

Brennan's stomach growled as he notched a log, preparing to set it in place when Noah arrived at Levi's claim. He'd started a day's work with only a cup of Levi's bad coffee and a scorched egg for breakfast. Levi hadn't questioned why he'd sent Jacque alone again to Miss Rachel's this morning. But he would soon.

Feeling mauled inside, Brennan couldn't face Miss Rachel. He'd clean forgotten she'd already turned down one marriage proposed by a man who wanted only a mother for his children. Of all the people in Pepin he hadn't wanted to hurt, it was Miss Rachel. But the words could not be unspoken.

A phrase from her response to his proposal of marriage repeated over and over in his mind—*Brennan Merriday, I have been insulted many times in my life.*

I should have known better, done better.

Whistling, Noah walked up the trail and hailed him with the smile of a contented man. Soon the two were wrestling a log into the notches Brennan had carved. Brennan concentrated on the work, wishing he and Noah could work faster because as soon as this cabin was up, he would leave Pepin and take Jacque with him. He couldn't stay after what he'd said to Miss Rachel. He'd ruined everything by thinking of himself, not her. And now Jacque would have to leave the place where he'd just begun to feel at home. It looked like the stray cat had more sense than Brennan did.

It was past time to go. He blocked out Miss Rachel's sweet smile and gentle gray eyes and how they'd revealed the hurt he'd caused her. His leaving was for the best or that's what he tried to make himself believe.

From her doorway, Rachel waved Jacque off to school as naturally as she could. She had never ached so in her life. At the edge of her clearing, Jacque turned back, looking troubled. She tried to smile for him, her lips quivering.

Then he disappeared around the bend and she looked down at herself. Why did she look the same? Feeling this mangled and clawed within, she should have been covered with bruises and bloodstains.

She went inside and sank into her rocker. She must not just sit here, but she could not move. She'd told Brennan not to darken her door again and he hadn't. Jacque had looked confused and troubled at coming alone for breakfast. What had Brennan told him? Jacque had not mentioned the letter so Brennan must not have told him yet.

She pressed a hand to her heart and rubbed at the sharp and insistent pain there. She hadn't been completely aware that Brennan had won a place in her heart—an understatement. But she could have given him no different reply.

The hurt she now felt was beyond anything she had experienced for a very long time, nearly as great as losing her mother when a child.

Rachel realized now that when she'd lost her mother, she felt she'd lost the only person who loved her for herself, not for what she could do. She'd told Brennan about the proposal she'd received and rejected in Pennsylvania. *I thought better of him.* "Oh, Father in heaven, why has this happened?" she whispered, pressing her hand to her throbbing forehead.

"Why did Brennan Merriday come into my life and so misunderstand me that he would say those words?" The offer not to touch her . . . "I know I'm not pretty," she whispered, tears budding in her eyes, "but . . ."

She rocked and wept into her hand, wishing she could forget the hurt that offer caused.

"Hello the house!"

Rachel groaned. Company, and it sounded like Amanda Ashford. Rachel's door stood open and she couldn't hide. She rose swiftly, wiping away her tears. She splashed cool water on her face and stood very still for a moment, as if regaining her balance, before walking to the door. This might prove to be the longest day of her life.

"Hello, Amanda. And Posey." She cleared her thick throat. "What can I do for thee?"

"We thought we'd come to help you today," Amanda said cautiously. "Thought you might want to show us how to work with you in case you decide to make a business arrangement with that Mr. Benson."

278

"A good idea." Rachel couldn't bring up any enthusiasm for work, but having someone with her would be better than sitting alone and crying all day, wouldn't it? "Come in."

Both girls eyed her as if they sensed her distress but thankfully neither asked what had upset her. Soon Rachel was showing the girls the ingredients for cinnamon rolls.

"But my handful is smaller than your handful," Amanda pointed out.

Rachel considered this, trying to gather her wits. "Let's use a teacup to see the difference." All three of them filled one palm full of flour and then poured it into a tea cup. Indeed the girls' cups were not as full as hers or each other's.

Rachel didn't really have the patience to deal with this, but she worked her way through the problem, showing the girls how the batter was to look and then letting them experiment with how many handfuls it took to make their batter take on the same consistency as hers.

By the time this had been accomplished, she understood the phrase, fit to be tied. She couldn't erase the awful words Brennan Merriday had spoken to her.

Brennan would leave now, taking Jacque with him, and she would live alone here in this cabin and make a living selling her baked goods and sweets. She would be a success and she would be miserable.

Evening came. Jacque arrived for supper but Brennan did not. Jacque looked worried. "What's wrong, Miss Rachel?"

She forced back the tears that had hovered all day. "Did Mr. Merriday read thee the letter from Louisiana?"

"What letter?"

She pressed her lips tightly together to keep from saying something uncomplimentary about the boy's father. "Come in. We will cat our supper and I will make up a plate for thy father. After he eats, thee must ask him to read the letter."

Then Jacque did something he had never done before. He threw his arms around her waist and clung to her. "I don't want to leave you. I want to stay here. I like school and I got my first real friend and you treat me good. Don't let him take me away."

Rachel bent over and hugged the boy to her. Tears fell yet she stifled her sobs for the boy's sake. Finally she commanded herself again and straightened up and wiped her face with her fingertips. "Jacque, I care about thee a great deal and would love to have thee stay here. But that is not my decision, it is Mr. Merriday's."

"Why do I always gotta do what other people say I gotta do? When I'm bigger, I'll do whatever I want."

She brushed his curly black hair back from his

forehead. "I am bigger and I don't get to do whatever I want, Jacque." She leaned down and kissed the place between his eyebrows. "I will always be thy friend, Jacque. No matter where thee goes, thee can always come back. My door will always be open for thee. And I hope thee will learn to write and send me letters so I know where thee is."

Jacque nodded, but did not look comforted.

They tried to eat their supper. Then Rachel fixed up a plate for Jacque to take to Mr. Merriday. Downcast, he carried it, covered with a clean dishcloth, out of her clearing.

The stray striped cat wandered into view and walked over to Rachel and then rubbed her ankles, mewing softly.

Rachel bent down and petted the cat. "Hello, Mrs. Cat. Has thee come for scraps? Please come in."

The cat followed her inside and ate the plate of food Rachel had no appetite for now. When Rachel sat outside on her bench, the cat lay at her feet, purring loudly. Rachel was comforted and she could bear the pain—not forget it, but bear it. Could God use a stray cat as a blessing? Why not?

Brennan saw Jacque coming, bearing a covered plate. The sight brought Miss Rachel to mind and her image grabbed him in its clutches. His whole body tightened with the anguish of hurting her.

He'd regretted much in his life but this was the worst.

Jacque handed him the plate with a resentful look. "Miss Rachel says to read me the letter."

Brennan held the plate but didn't move.

"What does a letter got to do with me? I know you're fixin' to leave, but I've decided I ain't goin' with you. You're not my pa. I want to stay with Miss Rachel."

Brennan set down his plate and reached in his back pocket and withdrew the creased letter. He opened it and read it to the boy.

Jacque stared at him; Brennan returned the stare.

"That means you're really my pa?"

Brennan nodded, dry-mouthed.

"Why don't you go to Miss Rachel's anymore?"

"I have finished working for her," Brennan said, concealing all the important information. "I'm going to build Levi a house and then we're heading out."

"I don't want to leave!"

I don't either. How could he tell the boy he'd ruined everything? "Now we know you're my son and that means you'll go where I go. And I got to go where I can get more work. I hear they want men for logging and building a railroad east of here. We'll go there."

"I thought you wanted to go to Canada," Jacque pointed out.

"Maybe we will. Maybe we won't. We need

money to get established with a place to live. Both of us will need warm clothes for the winter. You'll need boots and I need new ones. That all costs money."

"Why can't we stay here? You could marry Miss Rachel and we could be a family."

Brennan drew in air. The boy's words pierced him like daggers of ice. "Marrying is a delicate matter. Just because Miss Rachel is nice does not mean she wants to marry someone like me."

Jacque stared at him. "You're not good enough for her?"

"That's right. I'm not good enough for her."

"I know she likes you. She looks at you when you're not looking."

More ice plunged into his heart. If that was so, he'd hurt Miss Rachel even more deeply. He was an idiot lout and no doubt about it. "Go to bed."

Jacque glared at him and turned away, muttering to himself. "I don't want to go . . ."

Brennan didn't blame the boy. He hated himself for what he'd done. If only the past didn't hang on to him so tightly, if only he hadn't failed Miss Rachel, if only he hadn't insulted her as bad as a man could insult a woman . . .

Saturday had come and Levi had shut down his forge so he could work on his cabin. In addition to Brennan and Noah, Gordy Osbourne, Kurt Lang and Martin Steward, all near neighbors, had come to help raise Levi's roof and shingle it today. Then the cabin would be ready to furnish.

Brennan didn't like all the company but it would finish the job and his obligation to this friend quicker. Jacque was with Johann playing at the nearby creek. The September sun rose high yet the day felt as hot as July. The men paused to drink cold water from the spring and mopped their brows.

A wagon creaked into the clearing. Mr. and Mrs. Ashford, with Posey's grandmother between them, sat on the wagon bench. In the rear wagon bed, Amanda, Posey and Miss Rachel clung to the sides as the wagon rocked over the ruts.

Levi hurried forward, beaming. "Miss Posey! Everyone! Welcome."

Brennan hung back toward the rear. Why had Miss Rachel come? He'd avoided her ever since he'd been fool enough to propose to her. But with all these people present they wouldn't have to speak.

Mr. Ashford tied up the reins and helped his wife and Posey's grandmother down. The older woman was breathing with the effort but she smiled. "I wanted . . . to see . . . where Posey would be living."

"You'll be living here, too, Grandmother," Posey said and Levi nodded in agreement.

Almeria merely smiled and took a few steps, leaning on Levi's arm. "A good-sized cabin."

"Two rooms with a loft and root cellar," Levi said. "Thanks to Brennan and Noah and everyone else who has helped, it should almost be done today."

Almeria nodded to the men, thanking them breathlessly. "Walk me inside . . . please, Levi."

Rachel did not like how the woman sounded or looked. She had tried to persuade Almeria to wait to see Levi's place but the grandmother had insisted she view the cabin today. So the Ashfords had left Gunther in charge of the store and set out. Rachel wished there were some medicine to help the woman, but there was so little a doctor could do. And the stress of a trip down to Illinois or to upriver Minneapolis might kill the woman.

Posey had insisted Rachel come, too. Of course the whole town was aware of the breach between Mr. Merriday and herself. Did Posey hope to bring them close enough to begin speaking again? But he'd said nothing and neither had she. She saw how Brennan avoided her. They would just be polite to each other and not incite further gossip.

Inside the cabin, Posey's grandmother looked around, wiping her eyes with a hanky. Rachel moved farther into the cabin and looked out through a square hole where a window would soon be.

"I need to sit down," the grandmother said, holding on to Levi's arm tightly.

Noah hurried outside and he and Mr. Ashford brought in a bench the men had used. Soon Almeria sat on the bench leaning against the wall. The men moved outside and the women gathered around Almeria.

Rachel began to worry. This short jaunt might have taxed the older woman too severely. She was gasping for air and her face was beet-red.

"Perhaps we should take you home now, cousin," Mrs. Ashford said.

"I . . . am going . . . to die . . . today."

"No!" Posey exclaimed. "Grandmother, don't say that."

Rachel looked through the window at the men gathered there. "Someone please fetch the lady some cold water."

Martin leaped to obey. Brennan and Gordy stood at the window; Noah and Levi remained, hovering close to the door.

"Levi," the older woman gasped, "come here."

He ducked inside, doffing his hat.

"I am glad . . . you have . . . provided Posey with . . . land. I wanted . . . to see . . . it . . . before . . ."

Martin Steward came in and handed the mug of water to Posey.

Posey held it for her grandmother, who sipped slowly, feebly.

When she'd drunk enough, she said, "I . . . wish . . . I could . . . live to see . . . you wed."

Levi looked to Posey who was weeping, clutching the cup. "Ma'am, I love Posey with all my heart. I'd marry her today if I could."

Posey nodded her agreement.

Sadness swept through Rachel. Posey's grandmother shouldn't be denied the joy of witnessing Posey's wedding. "You can," Rachel said, an idea coming swiftly to her. "Noah, could you help these two? Can't they recite their vows here in their home for her grandmother's sake?"

Noah stepped over the threshold. "I can see no objection. Both are free to marry and of honest character. I could perform the ceremony here before these witnesses."

"But we're sewing her wedding dress," Mrs. Ashford objected.

"There's no reason they couldn't have a formal ceremony later," Rachel said.

"Yes," Almeria gasped. "I . . ." The woman couldn't go on.

Mrs. Ashford sat beside her on the bench and put her arm around her, trying not to weep.

Noah cleared his throat. "Levi, Posey, do you wish this?"

Posey looked at Levi. Each asked the other this question without words. In reply they joined hands in front of Almeria.

Rachel shifted and saw through the open window Brennan outside, also frozen and watching.

Noah bowed his head and prayed for God's

blessing. Then he began the ceremony. "Will you, Levi, have this woman as your wedded wife, to love her, comfort her, honor and keep her in sickness and in health and, forsaking all others, keep ye only unto her, so long as you both shall live?"

Levi cleared his throat and answered, "I will."

Rachel could not tear her gaze from Brennan's. The two of them were riveted by these words.

"Will you, Posey . . ." Noah continued.

Rachel felt almost as if she were taking the same vow as the young woman holding Levi's big hand—to Brennan who stared back at her.

"I will," Posey whispered, her voice muffled by tears.

Then Noah led the two through their vows.

"I, Posey, take you, Levi, to be my wedded husband, to have and to hold, from this day forward, for better, for worse, for richer, for poorer, in sickness and in health . . ."

Rachel felt her heart wrung. How she longed to make the same promises to Brennan. But he wanted her only as a mother to Jacque. Or that was all he would admit.

Noah finished, "Those whom God hath joined together, let no man put asunder."

Rachel realized she was weeping and wiped her face with her handkerchief. When she looked up, Brennan had vanished from the window. Of course he had.

Posey knelt in front of her grandmother, as did Levi.

"Now . . . I can . . . be easy," the older woman managed to say. "Take care . . . of . . . my girl."

"I will, ma'am. I'll make sure Posey never has reason to regret this day," Levi said with an evident frog in his throat.

The older woman patted his hand and then Levi carried her out to the wagon and set her on the bench. Mrs. Ashford clambered up beside her and Almeria leaned heavily against her. Mrs. Ashford was openly weeping.

Rachel glanced once more around the clearing for Brennan but he had vanished. She climbed onto the rear of the wagon and watched Levi kiss Posey goodbye till the evening.

"We'll finish up the roof, dearest," Levi said. "I'll come as soon as I wash up tonight."

"Yes," Mr. Ashford turned to say. "You're family now, Levi. You'll eat meals with us till you two move into your cabin." Then he urged the team to make a wide circle and head back to town. Rachel wrapped an arm around Posey's waist and held the girl close, letting her weep on her shoulder—while Rachel wept unseen for the vows she would never say.

Brennan rose early the next morning and roused the boy. Levi had paid him last night and now made him a breakfast by the river.

"I wish you wouldn't go," Levi said again. "You could work steady here."

"We're going," Brennan said with as much force as he could.

Jacque said nothing, just looked dejected.

Soon they finished the eggs Levi had scorched for them and drank the bad coffee and set out, heading eastward. The day was a windy one. Brennan traveled at a spanking pace, wanting to be away from the settlement before people began streaming toward the school for Sunday worship.

The plan worked. Soon they were far east down an Indian trail and then onto an old military road that would take them toward Green Bay. Birds flew high overhead in large groups. Brennan and the boy had days of walking ahead. His heart weighed as heavy as lead and his feet did not want to carry him away from this place, from Miss Rachel.

But he'd wounded a fine woman. He'd carry this latest guilt the rest of his life. He'd been run out of his own town by his own people like Cain in the Bible. And he would wander like Cain the rest of his life.

All that day Brennan and Jacque walked east away from the lowering sun on the old military road—really a track of wagon wheels through the forest—to Green Bay.

Something was making Brennan uneasy. The

farther they walked eastward, the more he glimpsed glimmers of fire far away in the trees. Once in a while smoke lifted above the forest.

Everything was tinder dry and each footstep sent up a plume of dust around their feet. Jacque did not speak and neither did Brennan, but he kept watch on the flickers of fire far back in the trees.

Ahead was a clearing and a small cabin. The owner must have heard them coming because he was standing at the end of the trail to his home. "Hello. Where you come from and where you going?"

Brennan still did not feel like talking but he took pity on the man who so obviously wanted some news from outside the forest. "Hey. We're from Pepin on our way to Green Bay area. I hear there's work there for loggers."

"You got a ways to go then."

Brennan nodded and decided to ask the question that had been bothering him. "I've been wondering about the flame I see sometimes back in the trees—just a flicker here and there."

"Oh, hunters leave campfires burning when they set out in the morning. Some Indian. Some whites. It's been so dry they should throw some dirt on them, but . . ." The man shrugged.

The hunters' carelessness troubled Brennan but he let the subject drop.

"This your boy?" the man asked affably.

Brennan had to swallow down the sudden

thickness in his throat. "Yes, this is my boy." *My blood, my only kin.*

"I got a good spring here. Need water or anything?"

"Yes, thank you." Brennan smiled at the man. After drinking deeply at the spring, they started walking.

"Good luck!" the man called after them and within moments he was no longer in sight when Brennan glanced over his shoulder.

The two trudged onward, Brennan surveying the thick forest on both sides of the faint old road. Rachel's face kept coming to mind. He kept pushing it away. The solitude of the trail was not what he wanted or needed right now.

He picked up his pace, trying to think ahead for him and the boy. He hoped he'd find some school in Green Bay for Jacque but his mind didn't seem to be able to concentrate. He would deal with that when he got there. Working with a group of loggers would keep his mind busy and tire him out so that he'd sleep better than he had since he'd insulted a lady who didn't deserve such.

Rachel had wanted to stay home and lick her wounds, but she'd forced herself to go to worship at the school and had accepted Noah's invitation to spend Sunday at his house. Now she sat beside him on the Whitmores' wagon. He was taking her home.

"I'm sorry Mr. Merriday left," Noah said.

"I am, too." Each word was torn from Rachel.

"I know you had feelings for him."

She nodded, not bothering to deny the obvious, still aching with such suffering. It was beyond words.

"It's too bad he didn't let God begin healing him from the war. I'd hoped being around you, Levi and then his son would begin to help."

"Sometimes the pain becomes part of a person and he can't let it go."

Noah exhaled in a sign of dejection. "Rachel, I know you say you never intend to marry, but I hope you know that any man would be fortunate to win you."

She turned to look at him, her mouth open.

"You and I lost our mothers too young. That hurt runs deep. But you are worthy of love, Rachel Woolsey."

Rachel remained speechless. What had caused her cousin to say such things?

They rounded the bend into town. Many people had gathered on the porch of Ashford's General Store. Noah pulled back on the reins, stopping the pony.

"Glad you're here, preacher," a man Rachel didn't know said. "Mrs. Ashford's mother is dying."

Noah turned to her. "I'll drive you home and come back."

"No, I'll stay. I might be of help." *And I might as well be miserable here among the mourning instead of miserable alone.* Rachel shook off this self-pity. These were her neighbors and they needed her as much as she needed them.

Chapter Fourteen

When Jacque nearly stumbled, Brennan realized the hour had come to set up camp for the night. He'd been distracted, watching the gleamings of fire that still appeared, scattered in the distance. He'd also been aware of a large stream nearby, hearing it run over the rocks. He wanted, needed to be near water.

Gripping the boy's shoulder, he stopped to listen for the subtle sound. "This way, son," he said, leading the boy through the thick evergreens and scarlet maples.

About a quarter of a mile from the military road, Brennan and Jacque arrived at the creek. Its creekbed was unusually deep, but after the dry summer the water ran low. While Jacque gathered dried twigs and branches, Brennan quickly gathered rocks, lining a small hollow for their campfire.

Soon Brennan had started a small fire and was brewing coffee in his battered kettle. With a knife, he opened two cans of beans and set them to warm on rocks edging the fire.

"How much farther we got to walk?" Jacque complained.

"I don't know. I guess we'll get there when we get there," Brennan said, still scanning the surrounding forest, fear simmering in the pit of his stomach. "Why don't we cool off in the creek while the beans warm?"

Jacque sent the two cans of beans a sour look.

Brennan didn't blame him. Both of them had become accustomed to Miss Rachel's fine fare. At the thought of leaving her, Brennan's heart squeezed so tightly, he almost gasped. "Into the creek, boy. We'll wash the day's dust off."

The dip in the creek did refresh them and they sat down and ate their beans and coffee. Then Jacque dug into his knapsack and pulled out a wax paper bag. He opened it and offered it to Brennan. "Want one?"

The sweet fragrance of caramel hit Brennan full in the heart. Miss Rachel's caramels. The scent caused his mouth to water and his knees to soften. Why had he hurt her? "No, thanks." He looked down.

"I'm going to make them last," the boy confided. He unrolled just one from wax paper and popped it into his mouth, then he sat, not chewing, just letting the caramel melt on his tongue.

Brennan didn't blame the boy. Miss Rachel's caramels should be savored. He banished her face from his mind. Or attempted to.

The wind began to blow harder. Brennan glanced up, watching the tops of the trees sway. He stacked more rocks on the windward side of the campfire to keep it from being spread or blown out.

He didn't have to tell the boy to go to bed. Jacque rolled himself into his blanket and fell sound asleep within minutes.

Brennan sipped the last of his bitter coffee, feeling the rushing wind strong on his face. He'd walked all day; he would sleep tonight. He added wood to the fire, then rolled into his blanket and closed his eyes.

Sleep came, but also dreams. He woke with a start. "Rachel . . ." The darkness was relieved by scant moonlight. He heard the trees around him swaying with the wind. He rolled onto his back and stared at the blackness, listening to the trees creaking, and felt leaves falling onto his face, covering his eyes wet with regret. *Rachel . . .*

Dawn had come. Rachel tried to eat breakfast and ended up giving it to the cat. She then punched down the dough that had risen overnight in her cool root cellar. She rolled out the dough and formed the cinnamon rolls and set them to rise a second time. When she went out to preheat her oven, the wind stirred up swirls of dry leaves, whispering around her ankles.

She looked up. The birds were having trouble flying. The wind drove at them and they beat their wings, fighting to keep from being blown away. Her robin managed to get back into her nest in the deep crook on the leeward side of the wide oak trunk. Rachel hadn't felt strong wind like this here in Wisconsin. A sense of foreboding tried to wrap itself around her. She resisted it and went on with her tasks.

The ache over losing Brennan and Jacque had not lifted. As she headed back to her kitchen, sudden tears splashed down her cheeks. She pressed a hand over her mouth, suppressing a sob. How long would this wrenching loss torment her? A week, a month, a year, the rest of her life?

Brennan rose with the sun. All around the wind gusted and birds squawked and flew in bunches like waves overhead. He set coffee to brew and stared at the fire, listening to the bubbling, boiling water. The sound mimicked his inner unease.

Dreams of Rachel had interrupted his sleep over and over last night, rendering him less able to face what the day might bring. He rubbed his eyes and watched the boy still sleeping.

The fir trees around them shuddered with the

force of the wind. The flames under the kettle danced with the stiff draft in spite of the ledge of rocks he'd stacked to protect it. Brennan tried to keep his balance mentally, not let fear get a toehold. Everything within him shouted, *Go back!* But he couldn't. He couldn't face her.

He shook Jacque awake and they ate a breakfast of hardtack and hot coffee. Jacque's dislike of the hard, tasteless bread and unsugared coffee blazed on his face. He looked at Brennan with accusation in his eyes. Or was Brennan just imagining it since he felt so guilty for obliging them to leave Miss Rachel?

The wind bumped up another notch and then another. The trees around them swayed lower. Squirrels and chipmunks and other small creatures raced past as if fleeing the wind.

After finishing the coffee, Brennan scooped up wet sand from the creek bank and threw it onto the fire. The flames sizzled and died. He caved the rocks into the fire site. He looked around. In vain he wished this hard wind would blow out the flames in the forest he'd seen yesterday.

Rachel heard no boat whistle but when the cinnamon rolls had baked, cooled and been frosted, she started to roll her cart toward town. If she couldn't sell them, she'd give them away. Food must never go to waste.

The wind gusted against her, trying to lift the

hem of her skirt immodestly high. She turned back and found a length of string and tied it loosely but securely just below her knees to keep her skirt from flying. Then she gripped the cart handles and headed for town, walking like a hobbled horse.

The birds that often flew with her and chattered to her must have all taken cover. *An ominous sign.* She glanced high and saw how the treetops of the high pines swayed above her. When she reached town, she did hear a boat whistle.

But before she reached the dock, the boat was already pulling away. The one passenger that had been let off held on to his hat and bent into the wind. He paused to pull his hat brim politely to her and then headed toward the land agent's office.

Rachel realized as she watched why the boat had left so quickly. It fought against the west wind as it wended its way out into the current away from the shore. Did the captain fear it might have been battered against the eastern shore?

A gust hit Rachel and nearly knocked her from her feet. She saved herself by holding on to the cart handles. She rolled the cart toward the Ashfords' store and parked it in back. Dust swirled up into her face and she shut her eyes and mouth till it passed.

Then Rachel lifted the first of two trays of rolls from the cart and carried them up the back stairs to the Ashfords' living quarters. The wind wanted to grab the tray from her and fling it into the trees. She hurried up the last few steps and kicked the door hard, asking for entrance.

Posey opened the door.

Rachel handed her the tray and stepped inside, grabbing the door as it tried to bang against the side of the building. She dragged it back and secured it. "The wind is wild today."

Posey looked crestfallen.

Rachel suddenly hoped she hadn't blundered into a scene of mourning. "Thy grandmother?"

"She lingers, sleeping but restless," Posey said.

Rachel reclaimed the tray from her and carried it to the large dining room table and set it down. "I'm so sorry. Is there anything I can do?"

Posey shook her head tearfully.

Mrs. Ashford stepped into the hall and saw her. "Miss Rachel."

"I brought rolls," Rachel said lamely.

Mrs. Ashford hurried forward and grasped both Rachel's hands. "Thank you for your thoughtfulness. I'm so distracted I don't think I did more than make coffee this morning."

"I have another tray I'm going to give Mr. Ashford. I'll take them to him now."

"Then please come back," Posey implored.

Rachel did not want to come back to this house that no doubt would soon be plunged into mourning, but staying alone would be worse.

"I'll put on some tea," Mrs. Ashford invited.

"I'll be right back." Rachel hurried to deliver the rolls to Mr. Ashford, telling him to give them away to anyone who wanted them. Then she gripped the railing outside and climbed back up to the Ashfords' door. She heard a bump. Looking down, she saw that her cart had been blown over and it hit the side of the log store.

She ducked inside. She began to think of her root cellar at home. She would stay for a while and then go home and prepare for whatever this storm brought. Her fear billowed like the wind. Where were Brennan and Jacque? Had they found shelter?

The wind knocked Jacque off his feet. The orange sun had risen higher and the gusts had become harder to resist. Brennan stopped and helped the boy up. Jacque clung to him, his arms around Brennan's waist. The boy looked up, fear plain on his face. Far in the sky high above the treetops, an eerie red glow flickered.

"We'd better . . ." Brennan said, the wind snatching at his words, "find a low spot . . . and wait this storm out." He gripped the boy's hand and led him back into the woods toward the creek they had been near all day.

In a sudden gust, the trees bent nearly double. Brennan dropped to his knees, shoving the boy under him. He resisted the wind, huddling to the ground. When the gust ended, he hurried the boy between the swaying trees and flying twigs and branches.

They found the creek again and Brennan, bent protectively over the boy, guided him to an area of rock, carved out by higher water, a shallow cave. He pushed the boy back under the ledge. Just a few feet from them, even the creek's low water leaped in whitecaps.

"What's happening? A tornado?" Jacque cried out.

In the din, Brennan crawled under the ledge and pulled the boy near, speaking into his ear, "I don't think so. There's no rain. Just a windstorm." Turning his back to the wind, he wrapped his arms around the boy, grateful for the narrow outcropping and its protection. What was coming? Had this hit Pepin? Was Rachel safe or hurt?

Unable to maneuver it in the wind, Rachel left her cart wedged between the Ashfords' store and their shed. The wind tore away the string and whipped up her skirts. Holding them down, she stumbled, head bent, to her cabin. When she arrived, she found Mrs. Cat huddled by her door, mewing. She let the cat in.

And then she hurried around her place, moving her cow and shooing her frantic chickens into the small barn—the coop seemed a dangerous shelter for them in the high wind. After carrying water and feed to the barn, she shut the door and tested the latch and found it secure. The water bucket banged against her side so she carried it into her cabin with her.

As the wind tried to snatch them from her, she shut and latched her shutters. Then she bolted the door after herself and said a prayer for the safety of her animals, her birds. Mrs. Cat rubbed against her ankles. In the dim light, Rachel scanned the stout, full-log walls around her. Would they stand against this storm?

"Don't worry, Mrs. Cat. We'll be safe inside." Her heart thumped at the perilous wind, loudly buffeting the walls around her. But what of Brennan and Jacque? Had they found shelter? Or were they on the open road without stout log walls and a root cellar for protection? *Oh, Father, protect them in this storm.*

The wind gusted harder, harder, and then flames blew past them. Brennan had been looking east but now he saw another burning branch fly by. He gasped and pulled Jacque more tightly to him. The wind wasn't extinguishing the fire that had shimmered in the distance; it was fanning it to leap higher. Higher into the trees, into a vast forest as dry as tinder.

A thought occurred to him. He tried to let go of Jacque, but the boy clung to him.

He put his mouth next to the boy's ear. "I need to wet a blanket to put over us. There's fire in the air." He'd seen this in the war, in the midst of cannon barrages in battle.

"Fire?" Jacque tore from him and tried to bolt.

Brennan gripped him. "Don't run! We're safe here by the water! Under cover!" *As safe as we can be.* The wind kept snatching away his words. "I'm going to soak a blanket in the water."

Jacque looked wild-eyed, but he nodded.

"Stay in the cave, son." Brennan shoved the boy as far back as he could into the shallow protection. Then he tore a blanket from his backpack and waded into the creek, pushing the blanket under the water. The wind knocked him to his knees. He was able to grab a protruding rock with one hand, fighting against the wind and current.

The howling and whistling of the wind deafened him. He crawled out of the creek, dragging the wet blanket behind him. He saw Jacque's mouth open as if he were crying out, but the word was carried away.

He slid close to the boy and wrapped the blanket around them loosely. But the wind dragged at it—even heavy with water—and he found he had to sit on the edge of it and tuck it around Jacque.

More burning branches, many large enough to knock a man out, blew past them. The shallow cave below ground level wasn't much but it was enough to keep them from the worst. He hoped. A noise assaulted his ears and he realized it was the crackling of the fire.

It surged into a roaring. He craned his neck and in the distance saw the fire begin to devour the forest—flames leaping from treetop to treetop, racing toward them. Yanking the sopping blanket overhead, he wrapped himself around the boy. *Dear God, help. Save us. Rachel.*

The wind buffeted the cabin without cease. Rachel rocked in her chair. She'd been forced to move away from the chimney because strong gusts of air blasted down it and into the room, flaring ash and bringing the smell of soot. To escape, she had moved to the far wall near the end of her bed.

Mrs. Cat had—for the first time—leaped up onto her lap and sat huddled there. Rachel was grateful for the cat's company. She stroked the soft fur and murmured comforting words that soothed the cat and herself. Her pulse raced with the wind.

She prayed silently. She imagined everyone at worship in the town school and went through the rows, naming those she knew and praying for those she didn't by description. But the faces of Brennan and Jacque lay like a transparent photograph over all the other faces. The thought of them out in this . . . She blanched and prayed more fervently. *Save them, God—even if I never see them again. Save them.*

Something large slammed the side of the cabin. She cried out and the cat jumped and raced under the bed. Rachel sat, shaking, hearing something like a locomotive outside. She reached under the bed, grabbed the cat by her scruff and was down in the root cellar within moments.

She clung to the cat who yodeled with fear. Her heart pounded. "Oh, Lord, do not forget thy servant here! And keep Jacque and Brennan safe and oh, Lord, bring them back—alive!"

"Rachel! Rachel!"

She roused in her bed and rolled out and blinked in the sunshine seeping in around the shuttered windows. She had not undressed the night before, fearing her cabin might break under the wind's assault and she would be forced to flee. Early in the morning when the wind had finally ebbed, she'd crawled out of the cramped, hard-dirt root cellar and fallen into bed.

"Rachel!"

For a moment her mind tried to transform it into Brennan's voice. But it was Noah's.

She ran to the door and unbolted it. "Cousin!" She ran and threw her arms around him, gratitude flooding her.

He held her close. "Thank God. You're safe. I couldn't come until the wind died and the sun came out."

Then Sunny ran over, carrying their little son. "Rachel! Oh, thank God!"

The three of them drew together with little

Dawn squeezing in their midst, clinging to their knees. The embrace released Rachel's tears. She couldn't hold back her fear. "I'm so worried about Brennan and Jacque."

Noah and Sunny stepped back. "We are, too." Noah claimed her hand. "But there is no way of knowing where they are."

"We'll just have to trust God," Sunny said, jiggling her son on her hip, but looking somber.

Dear Sunny. Dear Noah. Rachel gazed at them, knowing there was no other recourse. Then she scanned her familiar clearing. Leaves, pinecones and downed branches littered her yard. Part of a tree had slammed her west wall. "What was it? A tornado?"

"We never got any rain," Noah said. "It was some terrible cyclone is all I can figure."

"Did you look outside last night?" Sunny asked.

"No, why?"

"The sky to the far east was red," Noah said grimly.

"Fire?" she whispered.

Noah nodded, looking sickened. "I'm afraid so. The forest was so dry . . ."

To the east—the direction Brennan and Jacque had gone. Fire vast enough to turn the sky red. Her throat constricted. She turned to look east, but saw only the fresh dawn.

"I'm driving around, checking on my flock,"

Noah said. "So far no one has been seriously hurt. But many will need repairs to their roofs."

"Rachel, if you're up to it," Sunny said, "Posey wanted you to come to town. Her grandmother passed away last night."

Rachel felt a twinge of sadness, then gratitude that God had provided Levi for Posey. But where was Brennan? Would she ever hear from him? Know what had happened to him? To Jacque? *Please.*

"Has thee had breakfast?" Rachel asked.

The cow bellowed from the barn, reminding her she'd not been milked last night. The sound prompted her stomach to growl with hunger.

"Yes, we've eaten and we need to get going. We have many more settlers up this road to check on," Noah said, shepherding his wife and daughter toward the wagon. "When we're done, we'll stop at the Ashfords' before we go home."

"I'll do my chores and go there as soon as I can," Rachel said, yet remained outside and waving to them until they disappeared around the bend.

Mrs. Cat sat at her feet, licking her paws. Then she mewed plaintively as if saying breakfast was an excellent idea.

A robin warbled from above.

Rachel looked up with joy. "Her" robin had made it through the storm. She answered the bird who then flew away to find her breakfast also.

Rachel's mind brought up the words from

Matthew: *Are not two sparrows sold for a farthing? And one of them shall not fall on the ground without your Father.* Brennan and Jacque were precious not only to her but also to God. Tears trembled from her eyes. "I will trust thee, Father."

She walked to the barn, allowing tears of sorrow and thanksgiving to fall freely. She milked the cow then let it and the chickens out and then went in to make herself and Mrs. Cat breakfast.

She would take time to bake a cake for the Ashfords. People would be coming and a cake would be welcome. She would not give in to despair. God's eye was on Brennan and Jacque. But how she wanted to see them for herself.

Chapter Fifteen

Four days had passed since the storm. Each day added another millstone around Rachel's neck. Images of Brennan and Jacque in a fiery forest streamed through her mind—memories by day and dreams at night, horrible dreams that burned with bright orange flames.

She moved through her days trying to appear normal. She was failing, of course. Even Mrs.

Ashford spoke in a gentler voice to her. Did everyone guess that she walked around feeling half dead? And why?

In spite of her unrelenting anguish, Rachel had baked all morning. The town was holding two memorial services today. Almeria and Old Saul had expired hunkered down during the terrible storm, perhaps their hearts could not survive the stress, no one knew for sure. Noah had asked everyone to attend to honor and bid farewell to the dead and to give thanks that no one nearby had been injured or killed by the terrible storm that had raged over them. After the funeral would be a meal to spend time together, sharing memories and comforting the mourning.

Boats had brought the news of a terrible fire in Chicago that had killed thousands and destroyed much of that city. And then came the news yesterday that in eastern Wisconsin near Green Bay two villages, Peshtigo and Sugar Bush, had been destroyed—literally. The combination of the forest fires and the cyclonic winds had whipped many small wildfires into a deadly maelstrom. Over a thousand had died and vast acres of forest had been reduced to ash.

Rachel felt sick every time she thought of it. She'd turned away when the boatmen began sharing tales of whole families being caught by the flames in their cabins and dying. She'd been taught as a child that she lived in a fallen, cursed world but she had never felt anything this disastrous so close to her, not even the war.

Feeling as if she were a windup toy, now she loaded her wagon with the cakes she'd baked. Before leaving she returned to her cabin to make sure everything was as it should be and checked on her animals to make sure she hadn't forgotten their care. Yesterday she'd burned rolls. Only their smoke roused her to the fact that she had been lost in thought, sitting on the bench, awake but in a daze.

Her robin called to her and she looked up, but she couldn't reply to it. Her voice had become rusty. She smiled feebly and then gripped the handles of her cart and started for town, leaving Mrs. Cat sleeping in the shade of the barn.

Father, I need to know. Please let me know whether they are alive or dead. The word *dead* shook her to her core. Despair wrapped itself around her lungs, but she pressed on.

She was glad of the people milling about the schoolhouse. Posey hurried up to her and hugged her. Posey tried to speak but her tears clogged her throat. Rachel hugged her close.

Levi stood behind his bride, his hat in his hand. Rachel read his concern for Brennan and the boy. When he looked at her, his expression of general sadness deepened. She held out her hand and he gripped it. "Miss Rachel," he murmured.

He then nudged her from the cart and rolled

it toward the tables of food under the shade trees. He returned. "Let me escort you both into the schoolhouse." He offered her and Posey each an arm.

Rachel was touched by the tender and gallant gesture of kindness. She tried to smile at him but her lips trembled too much. "Thank thee," she whispered.

Inside the church, Levi led her to Sunny and then he and Posey moved to sit with the Ashfords. Sunny kissed Rachel's cheek and held her hand. Their little boy slept on Sunny's lap and Dawn sat beside her. Noah already stood at the front of the schoolhouse. A few more people entered.

And then Noah cleared his throat. "Heavenly Father, our small village has suffered little compared to many. We thank you for your protection and ask you to comfort those who mourn and those who have suffered this week."

Noah's words were honey to her heart, but the deep ache remained.

"This week we lost one who was our shepherd . . ." Noah audibly struggled with his own grief. "And we lost a dear sister in Christ whom we had just started to know. We know they are with you, Father. In Christ's name. Amen."

Everyone looked up.

Then Noah's expression startled Rachel. He looked as if he were staring at a ghost.

She swung around to find out what had shocked him so.

At the rear a disheveled and grimy man and boy stood in the open doorway. Rachel cried out, "Brennan! Jacque!" She leaped up and raced to them, heedless of everyone else.

When she reached him, Brennan stopped her from embracing him by grabbing both her hands together. "Rachel," he said in a raspy voice. "You're safe."

She burst into tears. These were the words she had almost uttered.

Rachel looked more beautiful than Brennan had remembered. And she shone with her special joy and even better—appeared happy to see him.

She looked down. "Jacque, thee is safe."

Heedless of his grime, Jacque wrapped his arms around her waist. "We come home, Miss Rachel, for good."

She burst into tears.

The sound wrenched Brennan's heart and he dropped to one knee. "Yes, we've come home, Miss Rachel. If you'll have us. I was a fool. But now I see it doesn't matter if I'm not worthy of you. I love you. Will you be my wife?"

Rachel heard "I love you." And then she heard applause around her. The sound startled her back to herself. She glanced around and mortification seized her. She broke free and ran outside.

Brennan raced after her and caught her just as she entered the cover of the trees. "Rachel, stop!" Then he coughed and couldn't speak for a moment.

She halted. "What's wrong? Is thee ill?"

He bent over, gasping, and then managed to say, "I did breathe in some smoke. It makes me cough some."

She grasped his shoulders. "Thee was in the fire?"

"Not the worst of it, but bad enough. God kept us safe. We're a little singed and smoky but alive." His expression turned grim. "Many died."

"God kept you safe?" she repeated. "When has thee ever spoke of God?"

He claimed her hands. "I don't want to talk about that now. I just want to know if you'll marry me or not."

She gaped at him. "Thee is in earnest? Thee loves me?"

"Miss Rachel, I was a fool, but God opened my eyes. You're the best thing that ever came into my life. I love you with all of my sorry heart. Will you marry me and make me the happiest man on earth?"

She couldn't help it. After all the strain, she laughed, feeling the fear that had bound her release. And then she threw her arms around him. "Of course I will marry thee, Brennan Merriday. Thee is the only man I have ever loved and will ever love."

And then Brennan did what he'd longed to do for the past five days—and longer if the truth be told—he drew her into a full embrace and bent his head. He claimed her sweet lips and kissed her as if he didn't, he'd die.

And Rachel kissed him back with all the love she'd saved for one special man, this man, her brave Brennan.

"You two gettin' married then?" Jacque's hopeful voice came from behind her. "And I don't ever got to leave Miss Rachel and Pepin ever again?"

She laughed again and turned, but did not step out of Brennan's embrace. "Yes, Jacque, we are getting married and thee will be my son and we will stay here together."

Jacque ran to them and they included him in their embrace, their joy.

Finally, Jacque pulled free. "I'm hungry. There's food on those tables."

Again Rachel chuckled with a joy she could not hide. "Come, I have brought two cakes and several dozen cookies. Thee can eat some cookies."

She recalled then today's solemn occasion and her joy receded and she became serious then. "We must go into the schoolhouse quietly. Old Saul and Posey's grandmother have passed. Noah is holding their memorial services."

Both Brennan and Jacque accepted a handful

of cookies to nibble and drank from the school pump, then the three of them entered the school as quietly as they could.

Noah finished his sentence about Posey's grandmother witnessing the small wedding in Levi's barely finished cabin and then looked toward the three of them. "Brennan, I take it from your singed clothing that you were in the fire."

"Not the worst. The boy and me were fortunate to just be on the far edge of it. God protected us."

Noah waved them forward. "Please come and tell us what you experienced. We've heard there was a great conflagration and many died."

While Rachel and Jacque sat down beside Sunny, Brennan walked forward. Noah shook his hand and sat with his wife, too.

Brennan turned to face the people he thought he'd never live to see again and his heart softened toward them. They weren't perfect and they had misjudged him, but he'd kept his truth hidden so it wasn't their fault.

"My son and me walked down the Indian trail to the old military road to go to Green Bay. I could see fires in the forest. It made me wary. Then that wind come up. God provided a creek beside a sort of cave. It was just a ledge of rock and a crevice where the water, when it was higher, had carved out a place. We hid in there and fire broke over us."

Not a sound was heard inside the schoolhouse.

"I wet a blanket and threw it over us. The fire raged around us, but I kept wetting the blanket. That and the cave preserved our lives."

A murmuring flew through the congregation.

Brennan decided now was the time to let it all out. "I've been mad at God a long time. Too much bad. Too much loss. Too many years. It made me a bitter man." Brennan shook his head, pausing to cough. "But that was all the war and that was due to men's wickedness and hate. This fire was bigger, greater than anything man can do."

He paused to swallow. "I had forgotten how big God is, how powerful." He looked up. "A lot of people died and I grieve for them. But God's ways are higher than I can understand. Who am I to judge God? I'm just a mortal and I'll live my life as best I can, do what I can for others."

He steadied himself against his fatigue. "That's all I got to say." He felt a smile break over his face. "Except that Miss Rachel has accepted my proposal and will be my wife."

"Oh! Wonderful!" Mrs. Ashford exclaimed, leaping to her feet. "Oh, I'm so happy."

Brennan laughed. Today even Mrs. Ashford blessed him.

Noah went to the front. "How close did you get to the big fire?"

"Jacque and I walked toward it to see if we could help, but the desolation was so great that we turned back and headed home." Brennan

317

paused to look at Rachel. *Rachel, you are my home.*

"We couldn't do much," Brennan went on. "But on the way here, a courier passed us and he said he was spreading the word that our governor's wife has called for Wisconsin people to send whatever they can to the Peshtigo and Sugar Bush survivors. They are sending boxcars of supplies from Madison—"

"Couldn't we get a wagonload and drive it to Madison to be sent on?" Levi had risen and now looked embarrassed to have spoken up in the meeting.

Noah nodded. "I think that's an excellent idea."

"I would be glad to drive the wagon," Brennan offered. "I wanted to do more but the suffering was heavier than I could help. I had nothing but a knapsack."

Noah requested contributions of charity and within minutes the relief effort had been organized. On the morrow people would bring what they could spare—food, clothing, medicine—and Brennan would drive the wagon down to Madison.

Noah urged Brennan to take his seat. He held up his hands and everyone turned to him. "This has been a momentous day. We have honored Almeria Brown and Old Saul, one a newcomer and the other known well and much beloved by us all. We've announced the marriage of Levi and Posey Comstock and witnessed the return of two we thought we might have lost forever. And—" Noah

318

grinned "—saw Brennan get smart enough to propose to my cousin."

General amusement greeted this statement. "Let us rise and thank God for His mercy. Our village could have been devastated by this fire. We were spared but we will stretch out our hands to those who were not. We cannot understand why this happened.

"As Isaiah the prophet said, 'For my thoughts are not your thoughts, neither are your ways my ways, saith the Lord. For as the heavens are higher than the earth, so are my ways higher than your ways, and my thoughts than your thoughts.' We will accept God's will in this and do what we can."

Then Noah blessed the food for the meal. And everyone went out into the quiet sunshine.

Brennan held Rachel's hand and would not let it go. He and Rachel sat with Levi and Posey at one of the tables. No one appeared to fault them for not helping set up the potluck picnic. Indeed everyone smiled and teased them.

Rachel felt as if a great weight had been lifted from everyone. She leaned her head against Brennan's shoulder. She smelled the smoke in his clothing and shuddered to think of him and Jacque under a wet blanket in a shallow cave, while flames raged around them. Without any self-consciousness she leaned over and kissed him. He kissed her back.

Johann Lang came over. "Can Jacque come and play?"

Rachel beamed at him. "Of course."

"I'm glad you and Brennan will marry," Johann said. "It is good to marry."

Brennan listened to the boy's words and his own laughter bubbled up. "Remember that when you get older."

"I will!" Johann shouted and then he and Jacque were running to the other children gathered around the swings.

"I'm so happy," Posey said, though wiping her tears with her hanky. "I was so afraid you wouldn't return and Miss Rachel's heart might never heal."

"I'll admit it," Brennan said ruefully. "I was a fool. Levi was the smart one." Brennan winked at his friend. "He had enough sense to find a girl and stick to her."

Mrs. Ashford bustled over. "Ned and I planned on having a party to celebrate Posey's wedding a week from next Sunday. So why don't we add your wedding to the party? I talked to Sunny about it, Rachel, and she said you get your dress ready and we'll do the rest. I love weddings!"

Rachel smiled and nodded. "Yes, Mrs. Ashford."

The stranger who'd come to town the day of the storm and who'd been staying at the land agent's office came up behind Mrs. Ashford. "I thought I wouldn't be seeing you. I was going to leave tomorrow. Remember me? I'm Jake Summers, I sit in the state legislature."

Brennan looked at the man. "You talked to me . . . earlier this year." Brennan decided to leave out the fact that they'd talked in the saloon.

"Yes, I came back to ask you once again to run for county sheriff. I have just enough time to get your name on the ballot."

"I'm not leaving Pepin," Brennan began.

"You don't need to. If you win, you just need to make regular rounds after you meet the mayors of the towns and villages. We don't have much crime. And your reputation from running off those river rats this June has spread. You can win in November."

Brennan began to shake his head.

"I think thee should let him put thy name on the ballot," Rachel spoke up. "If thee is to be sheriff, then the people will vote for thee. If not, then we will accept that. Thee would make an excellent sheriff."

Brennan stared at her, then chuckled. "You heard the lady who is going to be my wife. Go ahead then. We'll let the people decide."

"Oh!" Mrs. Ashford exclaimed. "The county sheriff from our own town!"

Brennan watched the storekeeper's wife hurry off to spread the news.

The state legislator shook Brennan's hand and

said he'd ride with him on the wagon to Madison so they could talk more.

Rachel leaned her head on Brennan's shoulder again, sighing with obvious contentment.

The sound ignited such joy within Brennan, he felt fairly lifted off his seat. *Thank you, God, for this precious woman and her love. And my son. And now perhaps a new career. I have more than I ever expected.*

Epilogue

Rachel had not thought it necessary to have a special dress for her wedding, but Mrs. Ashford had insisted. Rachel was not marrying just anybody. She might be marrying the next county sheriff!

Rachel had allowed herself to be outvoted. Posey had brought out a royal-blue dress her late mother had saved for good occasions and with some alterations and new embellishments, Rachel's wedding dress had been prepared.

When Brennan returned, he found that a ready-made black suit had been presented to him by the town. After all, if he won the election, he'd need a good suit to wear to his swearing in.

Brennan was inclined to refuse but when he

looked at the Ashfords' happy, expectant faces, he relented. The old anger that had simmered just under the surface had drained out of him. He was a happy man.

Now he stood between Noah and Levi, his best man, at the front of the schoolhouse. He looked over all the smiling faces.

Within a few months, he'd changed from an abandoned tramp, a reviled Reb, to a man with a son and a groom who was marrying the sweetest woman in town. If his chest expanded any farther, his buttons might go flying off around the room. Jacque sat in new clothing beside Sunny, beaming.

The door at the rear opened. Posey, Rachel's matron of honor, stepped inside, carrying a bouquet of fall flowers, rich in gold and deep red. Then he saw Rachel in the doorway. Sunshine glowed around her as if God's light came from her. Well, it did. If others couldn't see it, he could.

Everyone rose for the bride as Posey led Rachel down the aisle to his side.

Brennan found his mouth had gone dry. Rachel's subtle beauty was radiant today in the rich blue that reminded him of a clear, untroubled sky.

Noah began, "It is odd for me to ask, Who gives this woman to marry this man? because of course, as her cousin standing in for her father who couldn't be here, I do. And I must say that I am very happy to see that Rachel has found a man who truly values her. I give Rachel to Brennan unreservedly."

Noah continued the wedding ceremony. Rachel handed her bouquet to Posey and took Brennan's hand.

She smiled at her groom, her lips trembling with tears of joy. She had come to Wisconsin to begin a new life and God had given her a rich one. The emptiness in her heart had been filled with love. She'd always had God's love but now she'd been gifted with a good man's love. It was a treasure more dear because she had thought it would never be.

"Brennan, you may kiss your bride," Noah said finally, beaming at them.

Brennan bent and she rose up on her toes and their lips met—briefly but completely.

Then they turned, hand in hand.

Noah lifted their clasped hands. "Ladies and gentlemen, I give you our newest couple, Mr. and Mrs. Brennan Merriday."

The congregation rose and applauded.

Brennan pulled Rachel under his arm. He'd been driven out of his hometown once and here he was applauded and welcomed. He had found home, family and love at last. *Praise God from whom all blessings flow.*

Dear Reader,

I hope you've enjoyed the three books in my Wilderness Brides miniseries as much as I have enjoyed writing them. Three very different couples allowed God to turn their sadness into joy.

I know that many of you have never heard of the Peshtigo Fire that took place on October 8, 1871, the same day as the Great Chicago Fire. The Peshtigo fire is often overlooked—was over-shadowed—even at the time.

The Wisconsin governor's wife, Mrs. Lucius Fairchild, heard of the Chicago fire first while her husband was away. She sent supplies to Chicago and then heard of the disaster in her own state. She quickly led an effort to send supplies to the devastated area in Wisconsin, as well.

It's hard for us in the information age to realize how spotty communication was in 1871. Tele-graph lines connected only the largest cities, so though Madison could get news from Chicago, it couldn't from unconnected Peshtigo. And at that time, Wisconsin—now mostly farmland—was a vast forest. If you'd like to read more about the Peshtigo Fire, check out the Wisconsin Historical Society website at: www.wisconsinhistory.org/highlights/archives/2012/11/peshtigo_fire.asp.

Lyn Cote

Questions for Discussion

∽✑∾

1. Why did Rachel refuse to marry for convenience sake? Why did Brennan think he was unworthy of love?

2. Brennan was misjudged by people in Pepin. Why?

3. What challenges did Rachel face as a business-woman in 1871?

4. In 1871, women had very little in the way of rights. In most states, a woman's wages belonged to her husband. Why do you think that was?

5. Have you ever visited a Civil War battlefield or monument? Which one and what did you learn?

6. When Brennan was taken to a slave auction as a boy, his life was changed. Have you ever experienced something like that? If so, what, and how did it change your life?

7. Why was Brennan able to see that the slaves were people but the others ignored this? What blinded them?

8. Rachel believed that when she lost her mother, in a way she lost her father, too. Do you think that was true or not? Why?

9. Brennan and Jacque went through a life-threatening experience. Have you or anyone you know faced something similar? Did this change you or them? How?

10. I misspelled Jacque's name so my readers would pronounce it the way it should be. Jacque is not French for Jack and it's correctly spelled with an s at the end. What is the English counterpart of Jacques? Hint: it's a biblical name.

11. Do you have a favorite family cake or sweet handed down through generations? Why is it your favorite? Fifteen Love Inspired Historical authors contributed some of these to a booklet titled "Old Family Recipes." If you would like a copy, email me at l.cote@juno.com and I'll email a pdf copy to you.

Also I referred to old-fashioned sponge candy many times because it is one of my favorites. It's also called seafoam candy. Here's the link to one recipe for this delicious sweet treat! allrecipes.com/Recipe/Old-Fashioned-Sea-Foam-Candy/Detail.aspx?prop24=RD_RelatedRecipes

Center Point Large Print
600 Brooks Road / PO Box 1
Thorndike ME 04986-0001 USA

(207) 568-3717

US & Canada:
1 800 929-9108
www.centerpointlargeprint.com